"WHAT HAPPENS NEXT?" DENNIS ASKED UNEASILY

President Snelling leaned back, his eyes fixed on Dennis.

"We beef up the Gulf," he said. "Go about our business helping protect our friends and wait for one more jamming incident."

"Then?"

"Ron, tell the doctor what the ultimatum means. I'm not getting it across."

Pryor looked at Dennis, then at Snelling, as if to see whether the President was serious. He turned back to Dennis and spoke calmly. "The ultimatum encircles Riga for knockout. Detonation will come from a jamming signal detected here or in Israel. If they do it again, we fire."

STEVE LOWE

A GOLD EAGLE BOOK FROM
WORLDWIDE®

TORONTO · NEW YORK · LONDON · PARIS
AMSTERDAM · STOCKHOLM · HAMBURG
ATHENS · MILAN · TOKYO · SYDNEY

Dedicated to Shirley, my wife, who translates:

"Perhaps someday recalling even this will be a pleasure."

AURORA

A Gold Eagle Book/December 1987

The epigraph on page 5 is excerpted from
The Comet Is Coming! by Nigel Calder, copyright
© 1980 by Nigel Calder. Reprinted by permission
of Viking Penguin, Inc.

First published by Dodd, Mead & Company, Inc.

ISBN 0-373-62113-2

Forsan et haec olim meminisse iuvabit.
—*Virgil,* AENEID

*In a world where the nuclear weapons
are ready on the instant to defend us
against one another by blowing us all up,
to fret about cosmic impacts is like
worrying about being struck by lightning
during the battle of the Somme.*
—Nigel Calder

Chapter One

A mixture of snow squalls and chilling rain churned its way from the sharp peaks of the Canadian Rockies and whirled southward to Evergreen, Colorado. Institute director Dennis Covino watched the storm, seeking solace in the September swirl of gray and white. Darts of rain pecked at the wall-size window, making him edgy yet grateful; at least it gave him an excuse to turn his attention away from his animated guest. He palmed the desktop, turning toward the fat man, William Hendley of Hendley International Industries, who waved home another point, grabbing at the air above his bald head like a magician preparing a finale. Let it be the finale, the director thought. Wind it up. Please God, wind it up.

"Make no mistake, Doctor," Hendley continued. "The other side is still years—I might say light years—ahead of us in celestial research, and you know it. This project will send chills down their spines. Like the moon landing. We get there first. It'll freeze them in their tracks. We are needed, both of us, to keep the other side honest."

Covino nodded. "The other side," he thought. Never "the Reds" or "the Russians," just "the other side." Devils versus angels.

Hendley pointed a chubby finger at the red folder on the desk between them.

"Take it, Doctor. Take it. Hendley Industries can have a mock-up delivered to you in three, two, days. The Pentagon is set to sign on this one. We've checked. But of course they won't move without your say-so.''

The director acknowledged the compliment with a tight smile. ''How did you learn about a comet the Soviets claim to have discovered?'' he asked.

''Your assistant asked me that same question.'' Hendley smiled broadly. ''All I can say, as I told him, is that Hendley Industries is a multinational company with many reliable contacts.''

''Aren't you afraid it might be just a rumor, for you a costly rumor? Your report doesn't even mention where we should look for a comet.''

''Qui ne risque rien, n'a rien,'' Hendley said, winking.

''Is French a clue, Mr. Hendley?''

''I'd rather say no more. These are uneasy times, I think you'll agree.''

Uneasy? The day's first understatement. An incumbent president running for reelection, threatening weekly to push the button on the Soviet Union, and now a crazy plan to fire a weapon on an alleged comet only the Soviets have detected. What the world needs now, Covino thought. Another light in the sky.

''Uneasy. Yes,'' Covino said. ''But I can't help wondering. What sources would lead you to invest forty million dollars searching for a comet no one here knows anything about? Comets scare people. A comet the Soviets choose to keep secret from everyone but you scares me.'' Covino tapped the thick red folder at his fingertips. ''A presidential order bans the intelligence you've included here. Don't you think our side should prove a comet exists before we go after it?''

Hendley smiled. ''Ever the scientist.''

Covino countered, ''Ever the salesman.''

Hendley leveled his glance on the director. "Dr. Covino, six years ago, in '85, you squashed a Halley project of ours. We bit the bullet, as did our competitors. Halley's shook up a lot of people, and you sat here calmly telling the world there was nothing to fear. You were decorated by the President, while we missed the chance to get into the head of a comet. Now, I grant you, the circumstances were different—"

Covino raised his hand, cutting him off. "Halley's has a known path," he said. "I'd say that's different. This new search you propose has us relying on Soviet data for an object that our instruments haven't even detected. Do you really think the President would go along with anything they chose to share?"

"I'm not a politician."

"Nor am I. But I have an institute's reputation to protect." Covino grabbed the red folder and thumbed the pages. "Perturbations detected near Jupiter: no confirmation here. A possible anomaly six hundred million kilometers away: no confirmation here. Halley's came within sixty-five million kilometers, and only the best instruments could see it. For all the comet fever, most people went away disappointed."

"Halley's was once out near Jupiter," Hendley said.

"Yes, it was. And we knew when and where to look. Where it was headed and where it was going. This comet, if it is a comet, is a flicker on someone else's console. You know we're under orders to ignore Soviet intelligence. You're just ready to turn forty million into a hundred and forty million. At Pentagon expense."

"There is profit, of course," Hendley admitted.

"And little else. You're cashing in on a rumor, hoping the military will act quick enough to shake funds from Congress. Comet or no comet, you prosper."

Hendley shook his head. "Dr. Covino, probes like this are where the market is headed. In a big way. I think Colorado should lead the charge, don't you?"

"The charge?" Covino echoed. "Who is your contact at the Pentagon, General Simpson?"

"Wainwright."

The director squinted at a name he didn't recognize.

"Special Technologies," Hendley said. "Sector Seven. He's a clear-sighted, innovative man. I'd be pleased to introduce you."

Covino declined the peace pipe with a wave of his hand. "He believes in comets, does he?"

"You're the comet expert. But he does believe in keeping up with the state of the art."

Covino tossed the red folder onto the desk and focused on the contractor. "Mr. Hendley, the Evergreen Institute will not approve this project."

Hendley inhaled deeply, then placed both hands on his knees. "I was told you were a reasonable man, Dr. Covino. Your Institute is well regarded in Washington."

"Thank you."

"You are a good friend of this administration. In fact, I understand you'll be going to Washington to sit at the President's right hand before long."

Covino turned his head away at the sound of a fresh barrage of rain against the window. *Vindictive bastard! He's going to do it again. Scare me with a new team of Pentagon brass all lined up to second-guess my decision to save Uncle Sam from another bloated Hendley invoice. And this time for an unknown comet.*

Hendley shifted to the edge of his chair.

"Let me remind you my comet probe has top security clearance at the desk of Air Force Secretary Holmes. Top dollar is involved here," he added, tilting his head slightly, in a way Covino took as a signal—the kind boys share in the secrecy of a treehouse. "And there's plenty to go around."

Enough.

"Mr. Hendley, with all due respect, your project is space junk. Overpriced, arcade-style, orbiting shit, of value only to right-wing Pentagon freaks and to Hendley's board of directors."

Hendley's face reddened with each word. Before he could speak, Covino raised a palm. "Let me finish. You've persuaded some tough people to help you impress the Russians. Our technology can beat theirs to a new comet. We'll be the first to blow one up. But the only advantage I see is huge profits for you. The Evergreen Institute will not march in this parade. The Pentagon no more needs this show than you need another tax shelter. The answer is no."

Hendley launched himself from the chair. "Who in hell are you to decide what's best for the country?"

"Fortunately, your equal. What's best for the military is decided in Washington. Not here at Evergreen, or in your board room. I won't allow this light show to embarrass us."

"You self-righteous bastard. You think your Washington friends make you the doorkeeper of national defense? That your okay is the last word?"

"Of course you're free to peddle your wares wherever you want," Covino began.

"Damn right I am!"

"When you have a project of scientific worth, I'll be happy to present it. Unconfirmed perturbations near Jupiter are not in our current catalog."

Hendley inhaled once more, making a loud wintry sound that could have come from outdoors. "The whole world knows you had us sit out Halley's. The first chance to study a comet from orbit, to advance our standing, and you said no.''

Covino deflected the remark with a shrug. As true as it was, time had closed that wound. It had been six years since all his scientific instincts had led him to close the Institute's eyes on space probes aimed at the head of Halley's comet. He remembered the wild schemes, Hendley's and all the others. They came rushing toward him like frenzied ghosts, shaken from slumber behind the same fearful door. McDonnell-Douglas's design to intercept the comet, TRW's complicated model that would land a spacecraft within the fiery coma, Gregory's mad, eighty-four-million-dollar plan to blow it up and retrieve the fragments for international study. Buttons, lights, shining simulators flashed in his head until even the least outrageous scheme seemed as crazy as Mattel's project to ride Halley's until both returned in another seventy-six years.

To each frantic engineering team, he had said no. He knew he had made the right decision in turning them down. And for the right reason. "Use earthbound instruments," his report had urged the new President. "On-line equipment will tell us all we can hope to learn from this once-in-a-lifetime apparition. Present technology has the required sixty-five-million-kilometer reach. Bottom line: Space probes are unwarranted for close-pass comet study." He had been right. After six years, the exact wording came back to him, as he shot a satisfying glance at the framed presidential certificate of appreciation on his far wall.

Covino rose and moved to the door. Gripping its large silver handle, he opened the door wide. Hendley followed, huffing close behind.

"You were wrong on Halley's."

"Perhaps I'm wrong again," the director said. "Good day."

Hendley curled his lips. "How many wrong decisions is this lofty think tank allowed?" he snarled in a voice loud enough to make Covino's secretary look up from her word processor.

"When we find a comet, we'll give you a call."

"Don't bother."

Hendley tore a tent-size raincoat from a crowded rack, ignoring the secretary who rose to help him on with it. With a go-to-hell stare, Hendley slammed the door behind him.

Covino raised his eyebrows at the startled secretary in mock offense. "Marge, cross that man's name off the Christmas card list."

She smiled her relief, then returned to the humming machine on her desk.

"Marge, send for Dr. Lee, would you?"

He returned to the inner office to await his chief assistant. The outside chaos attacking the window bothered him now. He searched through the rain and fog for the familiar peak whose company he normally enjoyed. Not a chance. Not today. The early morning office lights conspired with the powerful change of season to make viewing futile.

The timing couldn't be worse, he confided to the storm. A "Soviet" comet approved by the country's next-top scientist. Wouldn't the President love that combination! Staff zeal, like the weather, was unsettling and just as unwelcome. His assistant, Norton Lee, must have given Hendley the Institute's provisional okay for the comet probe. It must have been Lee. He should have known better than to encourage a rumor now. The call from

Washington could come any day, and the Institute's approval on a new light in the sky would certainly send the President's search team elsewhere.

Dr. Covino, the noted astronomer-administrator from Colorado, was one of three finalists for the post of science adviser to President James Snelling, who, under pressure from a vocal academic community, had pledged to announce his choice before making his reelection statement. Yet after three months of red and green lights from Washington, Covino was tiring of the game. Had he not valued the prize so much, he would have long since erased his name from the exclusive list. Armand Robinson from MIT waved two Nobel prizes in Snelling's direction, but hadn't he also spoken out once too often on nuclear disarmament? On the other coast, Bruce Switzler, more of a diplomat, was midwifing another generation of silicon chips at Cal Tech and had let colleagues know he was too busy making money to fight with a politician, especially one who saw science as the military's stepchild.

Dennis Covino held no such reservations. He had made all the right moves. A wall full of commendations proved it. Director of the prestigious Evergreen Institute, a working partner of those who pushed important buttons in Washington, a respected ally of contractors and the military, who relied on the industry's stunning technology and on his institute's judgment, he was ready for the move. So ready that he had decided what would go where in his new office. His platinum medal from the Swedish Academy of Science deserved a new case, one with a light. Five moon rocks from NASA Commander Crippen would go on the mantel above the fireplace. An office needs a fireplace, even one that doesn't work. And the sealed letter from Niels Bohr addressed to Father Covino—the last personal letter the Nobel atomic physicist wrote before his death in 1962—would capture a visitor's attention better at the center of its own wall. A beige wall, he decided. No more stark white.

Not a bad setting for a rather average astronomer, an almost-Jesuit with a gentle disdain for authority, the author of simplified textbooks for kids: kids like a precocious pharmacist's son from the Bronx whose unbounded curiosity for the dark skies above the dusty tenement roof had propelled him through four universities and as many degrees. Not bad. From the dirty streets of a crowded city neighborhood to the pinstriped elbow of the forty-first President of the United States. By way of the stars.

The desk buzzer sounded, announcing Lee's arrival in the outer office. Covino pulled the drapes closed with a loud snap of the cord and moved toward his desk. The sight of the red folder brought a tightness to his lips. He picked it up and tossed it onto a table between two silver-framed blue chairs. Never in his fourteen years as head of the mountaintop Institute had he overruled his excellent staff. Is it the hovering advisership that let this one get by me? he wondered. No. It's the right decision. For the right reasons.

A tall bearded man dressed in dark slacks and loafers appeared at the door. He pushed frameless glasses higher up on his slim nose, then brushed the breast of his white sports shirt as if to hide the initials NLJ. He looked a full decade younger than his forty years, more like an intern than the Institute's second in command.

Covino motioned to a nearby chair and took a seat behind his desk.

"I've dumped the Hendley probe," the director announced.

"Marge told me. Sounds like you dumped him along with it."

"Norton, what did you tell that screwball?"

"That it's feasible."

"Recommended?"

"No. That's your department."

"What else?"

Lee kneaded his thumb and first finger over the chair's arm. "That his probe looked like the Halley Watch, and maybe now the time was right."

"The time is not right!"

"Hey, Dennis. Who cares if a right-wing industrialist wants to track a comet? He can afford it."

"What comet?"

Lee pointed to the red folder on the table without saying a word.

"That one?" Covino said. "Did you read the report?"

Lee nodded.

"And then you contacted the Smithsonian in Cambridge? Dr. Lyle?"

"No."

"Kitt Peak?"

"No."

"Where's the verification?" Covino snapped. "One redneck's opinion about some anomaly six hundred million kilometers away, and you tell him we are set to tell the Pentagon to go ahead and fund a rumor!"

"What's the harm?"

Covino shot up from his desk, then pressed his arms across his chest. "Thinking like that will turn this place into another damn condominium and send us both lecturing at a state college."

Lee fingered a silver Cross pen in the pocket of his shirt and looked up. The young physicist didn't need a lecture any more than Covino was in the mood to deliver one. For all his impulsiveness, Lee was a thorough scientist. Covino had carefully chosen the word "gifted" as the operative word in his June staff evaluation.

Taking advantage of the momentary remorse, Covino continued. "You know Evergreen's reputation goes out with every project. You really see no harm in chasing a red star because some fatcat is on the prowl for more profits?"

"What are you objecting to?" Lee asked. "His motives or the chances for a comet?"

"I have no quarrel with the chances, Norton."

"He says this one could be close. A spectacular."

"He says that's what the Soviets say. You can bet he's negotiating right now with his Pentagon pals on TV rights."

"One of these days we'll land on one of those jaywalkers, and turn it into a lab."

"In the meantime, Hendley wants to claim this one for the red, white, and blue, then blow it up in their faces the Fourth of July. You're saying we should let him?"

"Of course not," Lee said, scraping his loafers on the thick carpet. "I'm saying it's feasible."

"On their say-so?" Covino shook his head. "The Institute reports on scientific fact. We do not approve projects to one-up the Soviet Union. And we do consider nuclear accident a constant possibility."

"But not a new comet?"

"From that distance? And kept secret from everyone but Wild Bill Hendley? Come on."

Lee drew in a breath. "Our comet watchers are all amateurs. Apparitions come by accident. The Russians could have found something, something Hendley's probe could uncover."

"He wants to feed from the military's trough, that's all."

"Who doesn't?" Lee smiled.

"We have a place at that same trough, Norton. But we pay for our meal ticket with our credibility. If we send madness on to the Pentagon with our seal of approval, we'll be shut off." Covino paused. "You might make a note of that when I'm gone."

"You'll be going to Washington, then?"

"Whenever the President's staff gets around to that file, yes," Covino replied, grabbing the thick red folder. "Nowhere in this report is there verification of a comet. Perturbations out near Jupiter. 'A detectable pull somewhere between Leda and Callisto,' 'an anomalous glow,' 'a faint stream of light.' And the numbers. No way to confirm any of them on our computers. For all we know, Hendley is being sucked into a hoax. Anyway, he can't lose, but we can."

"You mean you can."

Covino sighed as he fixed his eyes on the assistant director. "I will not jeopardize a Presidential appointment on a comet rumor."

"Dennis, no one wants you installed as science adviser more than I do. You've earned it. But when I opened that report, I saw a feasible project. Expensive, but feasible. I wasn't looking for motives. It sounds to me like you're making a political decision before the call from Washington comes in."

"You can call it what you like," Covino said. "I see this as an invitation to another Halley fiasco. Farmers are still blaming last summer's heat wave on the comet. And I'm sure you've heard that airline crash last month over Morocco was caused by a meteor shower. God help us all if an Air Force plane goes down in the Persian Gulf while a comet passes by."

"You're talking about your future boss."

"I'm talking about comet fever," Covino shot back. "Can you imagine how fast we and the Soviets would race to the button if either country decided to explode a comet over our heads?"

"You give him too much credit, Dennis. Snelling doesn't need that much of an excuse to fire any missiles."

Covino tried to ignore the sarcastic grin mounting from the corners of the young man's mouth. He drew back to end this conversation. "The Institute cannot be associated with spending public money for a possible comet," he said.

"In an election year."

"Any time."

Lee shook his head, unwilling to give ground on a subject they had both locked horns on before. "The Soviets could grow wheat from seaweed, and we'd be the last to know," he said, staring at his hands. "If our friends at Palomar had found a comet instead of the Russians, you can bet Snelling would find a way to use it."

"How do you use a comet?"

"Only he would know. Remember the *Kennedy*?"

Lee's cynical reply took the director by surprise, even though he was used to Lee and his young colleagues wearing their hostility for the President like a badge of honor. Yes, he remembered the *Kennedy*. A nuclear near miss off Georges Bank. Snelling's ticket to the White House.

While Senator Snelling was counting voters in the Midwest three years ago, the U.S. Trident submarine *Kennedy* surfaced to launch. Eighteen seconds from firing, the false order was detected. But not before a Soviet "trawler" had fired on the *Kennedy*. By the time the captured *Vanya* had given up its launch code secrets, the candidate had appeared on TV, showing charts and photos to a stunned national audience. In televised hearings, Snelling threw back official Navy department testimony that the nuclear fleet was unjammable. The candidate tore into the incumbent as too lax on defense, too trusting of experts, too soft on scientific assurances. An agitated electorate agreed.

The nerve-jolting mistake of firing on the *Kennedy* had put a new man behind the nuclear button in 1988. As if to reward his mandate, the new President quickly brushed the dust off a campaign pledge and announced Executive Order 047. From that winter day forward, all scientific intelligence was mobilized under Pentagon control. Research of any kind became a matter of national security. The "defense blanket" was down, covering independent inquiry. Then, the day after President Snelling's glittering inaugural ball, five Soviet divisions rolled tanks into Baghdad to assure stability in the newly combined kingdom of Iran-Iraq. Immediately, all international scientific exchanges were canceled or interrupted. Disgruntled scientists—Lee included—landed at airports as dispirited as the American athletes pulled away from the 1980 Moscow Olympic Games.

Lee was too young to remember the Institute's struggles before 047. He knew only the prosperity that came from smooth relations with Washington, a prosperity Covino guarded with silence on any criticism of Executive Order 047.

Any talk of this past history was bound to turn off his assistant the way a rich son scoffs at a father's reference to coming up the hard way. This thought and the sudden feeling of being as old-fashioned as the wire-handed stationmaster's clock on his wall, the one that ticked in mockery of the digital age, made the director brush off his colleague's remark on the *Kennedy*. Yes, he could agree, it was a hassle to check with the Defense Department for clearance on authorized intelligence, but 047 had never proved a serious obstacle to his scientists. A symbolic thorn in their sides, but easy to work around. An inconvenience, no more. Not an enforceable ban, and certainly not a hurdle for William Hendley.

Covino broke the long silence.

"You think I'm protecting the President," he said. "Sparing him the inconvenience of coping with a new comet scare."

Lee stood up to leave. "I think you're already working for him."

"Then you tell Hendley to reapply when you're director," Covino said, turning his back.

"So that's it," Lee said.

"That's my decision."

Another half-grin spread across Lee's face as he turned at the door. "If only Hendley knew," he said.

"Knew what?"

"If he'd been smart enough to say his source for a new comet was Canada, he'd have his probe." He left, closing the door behind him with a solid thud.

Just then, a light flashed on Covino's phone desk. "Doctor, it's the White House. Line one."

He punched the first button.

"Hello, Doctor." He recognized the clipped voice of Presidential Chief of Staff Ron Pryor. "The President would like to know the status of the Hendley project. Any recommendation?"

Covino gripped the paperweight and marveled at the man's timing. "Yes," he said. "Yes. Our staff says it's a loser."

"No?"

"That's correct."

The voice from Washington paused for a second, then Pryor asked, "Can you tell us why?"

Covino hesitated, then answered, "First, there is no comet. And second, the proposal is for useless hardware. If you guys are looking for election-year dramatics, a comet probe should not be on your list."

"I see." Pryor's voice lowered. "Any chance we might be in the way of any new comet?"

"No. None," Covino said, concealing his irritation at the question and at his own quick reply.

"Okay. We just need to know."

"Now when can I expect a call from you?"

"On the adviser thing?"

"Yes, dammit."

"Soon, Doctor," came the reply. "The President says he plans to decide at Camp David this weekend, if nothing else comes up."

Covino closed his eyes and shook his head to throw off the disappointment. "I need to know on this end too," he said. "One way or the other. My staff is on pins and needles."

"I can understand that. You'll hear from us early next week."

"That'll be fine," Covino said. "Then we can all get back to work."

"Yeah. Thank you, Doctor."

"Mr. Pryor, can you tell me why the President is interested in the Hendley project?"

"No, I can't."

The line clicked dead.

Chapter Two

On his way home, he wasn't sure which bothered him more, Pryor's hanging up the way he did or Lee's blunt assessment: "I think you're already working for him." He's the President, for chrissake, he wanted to say.

Driving his rust-rimmed white Volvo onto the highway toward Desmond Hills, he couldn't remember now what his reply had been. He's the President. And I'll be his adviser. Who cares if James Snelling is a tight-assed Redbaiter? And so what if "when the President gets angry, the country 'sees red'?" So what if the pompous Dr. S. T. Mott had turned down the advisership, calling it a gesture, a joke. Let him spin in his new cyclotron at the Reisinger Institute till his mind snaps, if it hasn't already.

James Snelling is the President. Order 047 or no Order 047, he has a vacancy and a proven need for advice. Critics pointed that out daily in the newspapers. The President was about to send millions to Israel to keep a keener eye on the Persian Gulf. He had given NASA the nod to go ahead with another space station and, even though he had managed to turn the country against them, didn't he owe his first term to scientists? While he seemed to spend more time with generals than with diplomats, James Snelling had also curbed the AIDS epidemic with massive funding. He had established a humane form of national catastrophic health insurance for transplant recipients. And he had started the much-heralded task of

repairing every bridge and overpass on the never-ending
interstate highway system.

The steering wheel shook beneath Covino's hand, another message from a weary front end. Where was Colorado on that repair list? He passed the regional landfill,
turned left at the only stoplight between the Institute and
home, and wound downhill on Parkland Drive. The Volvo
lights picked up the match-head reflection of each snow
stake as he slalomed his way onto Cross Street. That time
of the year already. In a month this storm would mean a
foot of snow to shovel. Another winter. Washington would
be kinder.

His thoughts turned back to the impending appointment. Surely the President recognized the need for a
science adviser. It might not keep him up nights, but the
vacancy made his administration incomplete, untidy, so
close to an election year. If nothing else, the appointment
would mean one more civilian, one less general in Washington. That would be a plus. He stiffened slightly, still
thinking about Lee's remark, ''working for him already.'' Maybe it was true, but the President was no more
than a media personality to him. An energetic man approaching a vigorous sixty, aging gently, the way Covino's own father had. He recalled recent pictures of
Snelling smiling with that rough, rounded profile remi-
niscent—intentionally?—of Harry Truman; that no-
nonsense bearing that had swept the country and could
still hush the harshest critics whenever he swaggered to
the microphones. He had never thought of Snelling as a
boss, as a man who might even be amused to learn that
Covino hadn't voted for him. And this time? His vote was
certain. Snelling was taking on the youthful governor of
Covino's adopted state, handsome David Henderson,
about whom he knew next to nothing. Local affairs take

care of themselves. Like snow stakes that appear after Labor Day and seem to melt away in time for April's school vacation.

If Snelling doesn't win next year, it might be better to rent in Washington rather than to buy, as Sandi had suggested. We'll see. The call hasn't come. Not yet.

In the gray driveway at 32 Corona Drive, he shut off the ignition. The car sputtered as if in pain, and a nagging thought returned. He withdrew the square-headed key to an insistent suspicion that the White House had no plans to name a science adviser until that comet probe had been settled. Now it was settled, but he faced another weekend of waiting, "if nothing else comes up." Why had Pryor cut him off short? And why the interest in a comet probe stillborn in Soviet secrecy?

He showered these questions away, luxuriating in the frothy soap Sandi had bought him for his birthday, special soap, cue-ball size and with the number fifty eroded now to smooth, faint canals. He gripped its slippery blue surface and smiled at the thought of staying in with Sandi, expected home at any minute.

Sandi, his "roomie"—she called him hers—also worked at Evergreen, as staff assistant to Professor Lagrange, the botanist. Sandi had walked into his life three years before. Literally.

Lagrange, with typical flair, had arrived at Covino's office one Monday morning accompanied by a serious-looking graduate student from "back east." She was wearing a shiny red blouse that reminded Covino of holiday gift-wrapping. Her straight blond hair fell onto slight, sloping shoulders, to line up perfectly with the stripes on her blouse.

Lagrange promptly ordered the director to "hire her"— his exact words. No interview, no résumé, just the two words. The professor left the office, obviously taking Covino's surprised nod for official consent. Sandi stayed to answer off-the-cuff social questions from the startled director. How did she know Lagrange? From graduate school, where she had excelled as a botanist. What had brought her to Colorado? Further study, and the state university's doctoral program.

She answered each question confidently and with disarming self-assurance. Covino was impressed with her poise and easy grace, rare in an aspiring scientist, and unknown to a man whose own academic background excluded women. She told him her ambition was to teach at the university level, not in one of those spoiled suburban high schools filled with kids named Bobsie, Kiki, and Maura. She spoke softly. A wisp of a gold ankle bracelet caught the room's light. He winced when she mentioned she was "Ohio State, Class of '87." He had been a professor the decade before, and so this young woman would have been a prom queen when he was teaching at the University of Chicago. Worse, a quick calculation put her in the first grade the year he had discovered his comet in 1971. And in diapers when he had published his first paper on apollo objects at McArdle Observatory on the grounds of the Arizona seminary.

Within twenty minutes Covino had learned that Sandra Whitman was twenty-three, from a suburb of Cleveland, sharp of wit, and even more attractive when she allowed herself a smile. Perfect teeth flashed behind her full lips. Her cornflower-blue eyes caught his attention, making him eager to elicit another warm smile. He commented that working with Lagrange would call on all her reserves of flexibility. That word did the trick. She smiled, but her nod made him feel suddenly preachy in an unsatisfactory, big-brother way. Then a second smile came to his rescue. Fatherly advice was one thing she didn't need and would not accept.

They dined and dated regularly, soon enjoying what his church used to condemn as recreational sex. She got a lover to match her ambition, and he had found a love that rolled back years of self-denial. On winter weekends they headed for the nearby Kandahar Ski Lodge, where, hating the cold, they avoided the slopes in favor of the warmer pleasures of wine, fireplace, and each other. Summers, they sipped gin and tonics on the sundeck he had designed to capture the sun's direct rays. "You might have the right solar angle," she had teased, "but the landscaping is early lunar." He replied with a slap to the bottom of her sunsuit and a blank check made out to a local nursery. Two weeks later, the job was done. His roughwood deck jutted from a hillside covered with a rainbow of plants and shrubs.

"This romance has certainly blossomed," he could still recall saying the night he asked this mature, independent woman nearly half his age to join his private life as a full-time partner. They lived together in Desmond Hills, a planned community younger than Sandi, in the small ranch house where, neighbors boasted, flowers seemed to bloom all year round.

Covino rinsed himself now in the bathroom fog. He moved to the oak-paneled bedroom and stood before the mirror on his closet door, something he did more often these days whenever Sandi wasn't around. Five decades, after all. He was still proud of his slight build, his firm stomach that defied middle-aged expansion. Although he rarely exercised, his shape and weight had held steady since college days. Straight hair, black and full, covered a forehead that had yet to show the first permanent wrinkle. What he saw made him content and a little vain, as his mind flashed to an image of what the others must look like, the older kids who used to make fun of his under-nourished look.

He returned to the bathroom to shave.

"Sandi," he called to a sound he thought he heard over the running water. "Sandi?"

"Hello," came a cheery voice from the hallway. "How'd it go? Did you get your call?"

"Washington called, all right," he said to her in the mirror. "Wanted to check on a space probe."

"And?"

"Pryor hung up on me."

"Hung up!"

"Yup. No news yet. Snelling might get to it this week-end."

Sandi slumped against the doorjamb and crossed her arms. Covino turned and, placing a quick kiss on her forehead, moved to the bedroom. He snapped on blue briefs, his back to her.

"Maybe we'll be lucky if they don't call back," he said.

Sandi sat on the bed while he dressed.

"You don't mean that. You want to go to Washington more than I do."

"Maybe, maybe not."

"What are you saying?" she asked.

"Norton Lee says I've made a political decision. Thinks I've lost my scientific objectivity."

"Have you?"

"I turned down a lamebrained comet probe. He thinks I did it as a convenience to the President, some kind of favor before I get the appointment."

"But you didn't?"

"I'm not sure," he sighed. "Sandi, maybe I've been sucked up in the President's paranoia. I saw Soviet data in the proposal and I closed it. Like a good American. I may be called on to plug political holes as science adviser. Nothing more."

"There was White House pressure?"

"No, but this job could be window dressing in an election year. It's been vacant for months, and Snelling has a whole team of top scientists telling him what he wants to hear."

"Army scientists," she said. "He needs at least one civilian."

"Pryor cut me off. He called just for the comet," Covino said, disclosing the fact like a tardy revelation.

Sandi stretched out on the bed. "I don't see how what Pryor did has to do with Lee."

"I may be seeing too much. Snelling's office puts me off, dangling the advisership, and Lee breezily recommends a comet probe that'll embarrass the Institute. It doesn't make sense." He sat down at her side, his arm reaching for her waist. "Maybe I'm not fit to be a Washington bureaucrat and a scientist." His eyes searched hers for a response that might lighten his mood.

"You are a bureaucrat and a scientist," she said. "Besides, there are other candidates: Robinson, Brickman, Switzler."

"Brickman dropped out."

"Dennis, why worry? If it bothers you, say no to the President." Her tone was serious now, helpful.

"I'm getting good at that," he said. "I overruled the staff's recommendation. For the first time."

"Good for you. The bureaucrat triumphs."

"In this case, I think it was the scientist. But I can't get over the feeling that Pryor wanted a 'no' on the comet for me to get a 'yes' on the advisership."

"Like he was testing you?"

"Could be." He frowned. "Even the possibility of going to Washington has me caught between men I respect and men I don't even know. And why hang up on me. What's that say, huh?"

Sandi stood up, inviting him to follow. "That you need a drink," she said. Moving to the kitchen, she called to him.

"A Washington appointment is automatically and ipso facto political."

"Ipso facto?" he called back with a laugh.

"You choose sides when you join an army, you know. Anyway, what do you think of Jim Snelling?"

"He's the President," he replied, buttoning a fresh shirt.

"Do you like Snelling the candidate, I mean?"

He remembered a recent letter from a colleague in Wisconsin who feared the President's intention to send nuclear arms to Israel before the year's end. The letter had urged him to reject the appointment, with some off-the-wall warning like selling his soul to the devil. The bottom line remained the same: Snelling is the President. A sure bet in the election year to come, against Henderson, the long shot.

He entered the tiny kitchen with two martini glasses. Sandi took down a frosted bottle of gin.

"He's dedicated to making believe the Russians don't exist," she said, mixing the drinks. "Can you live without them too?"

"Of course."

She struck a comic pose. "Do you have the makings of a Dr. Strangelove?"

He shook his head at the unexpected reference.

"All the bombs are built," she said. "Would you ever advise him to push the button?"

He made a shrug his reply.

"So why let it bother you? He's on top of the world, surrounded by an electronic fortress you've helped him build. He just wants to share the view." She paused, then asked, "You haven't been approached by Governor Henderson, have you?"

"No, but thanks for the compliment."

He sipped his drink, taking in its pleasant juniper tang. The pair moved to the living room's spacious couch.

"Sandi, who needs it? Let's just stay here."

"'The Folks Who Live on the Hill'?" she said sarcastically. "You're looking a gift horse in the—"

"A Trojan horse."

"I see the job as a reward, and who deserves the laurel more than you? If you refuse it, you'll regret it."

"And you?" he asked.

"Dennis, if I wanted Washington, I'd go to Washington. I don't need anyone to take me, but I'd love to go with you." She kissed him. "After I get my degree. We'll be a two-doctor household soon. Ransom says he'll finish correcting the second draft of my dissertation by Thanksgiving."

"Hallelujah!" He raised his glass in a toast. "Two doctors in the house. Before I know it, you'll be director of the Institute."

"Better me than Norton Lee?"

"You can have the job for the asking. But no Washington."

"Do you feel threatened?" she asked.

"Threatened? Why?"

"Most men would. A roomie of equal academic standing."

"Hold on a minute," he said. "Drape those pretty shoulders in academic robes and you become an equal, huh? You don't have a comet named after you."

"Only because I'm not a famous astronomer."

Sandi pouted in the way he found so sexy; first the offended lower lip, then the disarming smile. "When I discover a new fern I might apply for your job," she teased.

"By then there's sure to be an opening. Let's have supper."

"Okay. You cook. You have no equal there."

Over his specialty of veal and white wine, they chatted about a rainy autumn and the incongruity of Lagrange's current work on plant resistance to drought. Dennis pretended to show interest, knowing the full report would soon reach his desk. At the same time he wondered if he or Lee would be the one to read it. As he listened to Sandi, Dennis could tell why he loved her so much: her enthusiasm, her joy in sharing the smallest detail of her work. If she displayed such fervor for the lab, what would she be like in the classroom? Sandi would make an outstanding professor. He listened, envying her passion for botany and wondering how he could help her keep that spark alive. From a spot deep inside, he knew his own spark for astronomy was flickering in the cold breath of routine.

SATURDAY WAS A WORK DAY. Sandi, as was her habit, spent the morning at the University's Denver campus library lost in yellowed pages of flora. Dennis cleared the breakfast dishes and worked at home on notes for his latest book—a high school science text. This would be his third in a series that over ten years had become a staple in Colorado's public school curriculum. As much therapy as another career milestone, this work afforded him the pleasure of simplifying advanced concepts for the uninitiated, of demystifying points large and small. On more than one occasion he had addressed colleagues on the "Covino Credo": the scientist who could not explain the complex in simple terms was of limited value.

At the kitchen table he rewrote captions for his illustrator. Then he rechecked the scale of relative distance against *Margrave's Star Atlas*. Despite his attempts to fight it, his mind turned to the previous day's conversation with his Evergreen assistant. Feasible, Lee had said. Like the Halley Watch. Feasible. But what wasn't, today, when orbiters routinely beamed back to the earth graphics of neutron stars, pulsars, and accretion disks, when everything had been accounted for in this waiting game called astronomy?

Only one Big Bang remnant still evaded accurate prediction, as it had for the ancients a mere two thousand years ago—the comet. While even these celestial snowballs had long been classified, a new one, an uncharted one, was always a possibility, however remote. Like a nova explosion, a new comet could appear in ten thousand years or tomorrow at sunset. Illuminated by the sun, attracted to its inevitable death by solar gravity, a new comet could appear in Earth's sky at any time.

With a light touch, he sketched the course of his own comet, Covino 1971-e, on the map. Was it ego that blocked acceptance of what he was telling youngsters happened with frequency? Is no one else allowed to find what accident had placed in front of his telescope? Of course not. Comets come and go as they please. Man has better things to do than go out and reach for them, blow them up, and admire the power of his technology.

He erased the thin line of his comet, but the question of Hendley's source did not erase so easily. A comet 650 million kilometers from the earth would be invisible. No instrument could probe space that deep for an object that faint. Nowhere in the West, at least. If Soviet scientists had detected a mysterious perturbation near Jupiter, why hadn't American scientists discovered the same effect? Feasible or not, it was no time to beat the Russians to a comet that only they recognized and chose to keep secret. Not while Dr. Dennis Covino's name remained on Institute stationery.

The clock sounded noon.

He had come far since 1965, when he had traded his black cassock for a polyester suit and tie and an eminent place in the scientific establishment. Now this brotherhood's top place was about to be his, and nothing would prevent it: not Hendley, not the exuberant Lee, not the impulsive Ronald Pryor, and certainly not a perturbation near Jupiter.

He cleared the table, stuffing his papers into a folder marked "Perspectives." When he returned to the kitchen, he saw Sandi had come in and was already preparing lunch. Her smile released a familiar cue.

"Gentiana calycosa," she said. Reluctantly he joined in the game.

"Ah, Pacific bloodroot," he guessed.

"No."

"A weed from the goldenrod family?"

"No. One more chance."

"An exiled Persian princess."

"Strike three. Ranier pleated gentian, blue and white."

"Pretty, and I wasn't even close."

"Round two?" she said invitingly.

"Pass." His voice was joyless, distant.

Now it was Sandi's turn to guess. "Dennis, is your book stalled?"

"No. It's right on schedule," he said, taking a seat at the table.

"Did you get much work done?"

Dennis paused, then said, "I can't get one thing off my mind. The President's interest in Hendley's comet. Pryor called me specifically to see if we were going to recommend that probe. Something about the comet has them shaky."

"The comet that may not exist?"

"It's the Soviet connection that has them worried. I'm sure of it."

Sandi turned. "Dennis, you're the one who stopped it, correct?"

"Yes."

"Lamebrained, you called it."

"That's right."

Sandi set sandwiches and salad on the table between them. "It's too late for second thoughts," she said.

"I have no second thoughts," he said, playing with the fork at his fingertips. He cleared his throat to add, "My decision is all the White House wanted from me. I've been useful."

"How do you know that?"

"A hunch, that's all," he said. "It would explain Pryor's cutting me off."

"I think he's just naturally rude," she said. "It's all very simple to me."

Dennis looked at her, readier now to accept another explanation. "Oh, it's simple, Dr. Whitman."

"Yes. It came to me in the library," she said. "He wants to deny you Pryor knowledge."

THE CALL FROM WASHINGTON came Monday afternoon. Dr. Dennis Covino was named to replace former presidential science adviser Seymour White. Dennis jotted notes furiously as Ron Pryor recited a checklist of things to come: final security clearance, White House reception, press conference. After arranging a White House briefing for Wednesday and adding a perfunctory congratulations to the one-sided conversation, Pryor signed off.

Before Dennis had settled the receiver into its cradle, his secretary burst into the office to smother him with hugs and kisses. He kissed her and then sent her off, teary-eyed, to make the travel arrangements for Wednesday.

"Shall I get Dr. Lyle at the Smithsonian Observatory?" Marge asked at the door.

"Please," he replied, suddenly remembering the order he had preprogrammed for this occasion. "I'll speak to him right away."

The usual frenzy in Lagrange's department made an announcement to Sandi by telephone futile, but he suspected she would hear of the appointment by five o'clock. He'd take her to dinner to celebrate, to Mario's and their favorite corner table. He pulled the third draft of a resignation letter from a top drawer and reread it, then added a stronger sentence to the one recommending Dr. Norton Lee as his successor.

The phone buzzed.

"Dr. Lyle is not in," Marge announced. "So I left a message."

"Call back, Marge. It's very important."

As science adviser to the President of the United States, he now had more than a request for the head of Cometsville at Harvard. He had an order.

"Have them page him," he told Marge. "Tell him I want a complete sky sweep by the end of the week."

"A sky sweep?" she repeated.

"He'll know what I mean. He's a Navy man. Say, 'A smooth voyage needs a calm sea.' I'm counting on his charts."

Chapter Three

Early Wednesday, Dr. Dennis Covino boarded American Airlines flight 809 for Washington. A cover-girl stewardess escorted him to his first-class seat. Throwing his suit jacket on top of the suitcase filed above his head, he settled in to await takeoff. Amid the sounds of folding newspapers, the creak of opening briefcases, and the smell of coffee, he watched the misty runway speed by.

Once in flight over Kansas, a male attendant approached with the plastic ingredients of a cup of coffee and a copy of *The Washington Post*. Dennis smiled his thanks, grateful for a way to fill some time on a day that prohibited window gazing. As the passenger behind him snored in oblivion, he unfolded the paper on his lap.

This was a habit his Colorado schedule didn't permit. Reading for him was confined to daily reports and an occasional journal. Work on his textbook favored the writer at the expense of the reader. Just as well, he thought, as he spotted the usual array of calamity spread across the front page: a hurricane named Gary was menacing the Gulf States. Workmen still toiled on the Supreme Court steps shaken to rubble by another explosion blamed on Syrian terrorists. Israel was making another frantic call for military safeguards against their poised eastern foes. Racial tension and lack of air conditioning had set off riots in an overcrowded Florida prison. The ambassador to Moscow, Philip Trusedale, a personal friend of the President, was dead at age fifty-two. Services were to be held today in Maine, with President Snelling among the mourners.

Dennis folded the paper and placed it on the vacant seat to his right. The vision of James Snelling as a mourner stuck with him: a tall figure surrounded by blank-faced Secret Service guards, paying final respects to a friend. From all accounts, bachelor Snelling had few close friends. He was an energetic introvert, more at ease with a tight band of lieutenants behind closed doors than out among the people extending his hand for votes. Or for sympathy. An ideologue with a large axe to grind, a man who filled orders for dangerous weapons daily, and at whose harsh banner a frustrated country would rally on call. For all his John Wayne diplomacy, the President today was just one among many dark-suited mourners for a fallen friend.

Once again Dennis thought of the President of the United States as his boss. Not since his seminary days had he worked for a superior. The word sounded silly, even then. It implied not only an authoritarian tradition long since discarded, but more often than not an unwarranted value judgment. He settled back into his seat, recalling a string of "superiors."

Father Henshaw came to mind, the Church Militant's finest drill sergeant. Taking Ignatius Loyola's words to heart, he never tired of reminding the young scholastics that "we are soldiers of God." It was Henshaw's dogmatic discipline and cruel self-assurance that made Dennis question the promise he had made to his mother that had brought him to the red-brick prison. Only the excitement of science classes had made the trial of three A.M. prayer bearable.

Gazing out the window at clearing skies that greeted sunrise over the Mississippi, he could see Father Lobel, his pious confessor, who had done his best to save the young man's shaky calling. "Prayer," the good man had said, "prayer, and listening to that guiding inner voice." At age eighteen, Dennis found himself impatient for those voices that somehow remained inaudible, and that were certainly of no help during exams on the East-West schism. Meanwhile he collected awards in biology and astronomy. His final year at St. Ignatius found him teaching New Testament studies to freshmen at the provincial high school in Queens. This was the spirit of sacrifice Father Henshaw demanded of his troops for the greater glory of God. Obedience, he learned, was the Order's highest virtue.

In the fall of 1960, Dennis left New York for graduate study at St. Anselm's. To his delight, the Arizona seminary housed an observatory and a renowned science faculty. The young man's reputation had preceded him, and the new superior, Father Maxwell, quickly placed him in charge of the McArdle Observatory, where he spent hours alone with a bright new world of astronomy.

The summer of 1961, television pictures showed space for the first time from Explorer 6 cameras in earth orbit. The young scholastic was on fire as President Kennedy's space program unfolded with furious speed. He observed, wrote, and compiled, working mostly at night and pushing himself through the days. The observatory became his library, his studio, his refuge. Papers he and Father Maxwell published on spectography, meteor showers, and deep space velocities carried McArdle's reputation far beyond the American Southwest. The duo regularly traveled to Los Angeles and to Chicago, helping what later would become NASA to verify its work on the new frontier of space. In 1963, Dennis received the prestigious Warrington Medal for astronomical research on Encke's comet.

That same year, Father Francis Manville came to St. Anselm's to replace the retiring Maxwell. The new superior frowned on Father Covino's passion for the stars. He called into question the young man's neglected vocation, his one-sided preparation for the priesthood. He demanded Dennis's active participation in advanced theology classes. There would be more attention paid to spiritual duties and less to scientific pursuits. Dennis rebelled. He made frequent visits to the infirmary. He overstayed visits to the University of Texas and to Palomar. Once he left the seminary without permission to attend a conference in Phoenix. On his return, he found the observatory locked. Nothing could have prepared him for the reason. Father Manville, with poorly disguised regret, read him the Provincial's letter: McArdle and St. Anselm's had been sold to the U.S. Army. All scholastics were to be transferred. If he chose to take the Order's decision personally, Manville told him, he could consider it punishment for a defective vocation. He left St. Anselm's with the superior's blessing and advice to examine his conscience. If the Church had no use for his credentials, the brotherhood of scientists did. For twenty-six years afterward, through four universities and two institutes, Dennis Covino had been his own superior.

"More coffee, sir?" a stewardess approached to ask.

"No. Thank you," he said, feeling a slight turbulence that brought him out of the past.

"We're a little behind schedule," she added. "The captain says meteor showers."

"Meteor showers?" He sat up.

"A little radio interference. No problem."

Dennis thought it strange this time of year. His mind flashed to Lyle's sky sweep. Meteor showers. He'd need to check on that.

He looked out the window at a brightening sky over what had to be the Ohio River and entertained a warm feeling of satisfaction at having been chosen over a Nobel-crowned MIT physicist and a Silicon Valley boy genius. He shifted in his seat until he found a plastic program sheet in the pouch before him. He plugged himself into the prerecorded world of Count Basie and after twenty minutes joined his travel mates in engine-induced slumber.

THE NEXT VOICE HE HEARD was the pilot's, giving a pitch for further travel "the American way" and announcing the local time as one P.M. Dennis set his watch ahead.

At the terminal a man looking for all the world like a young Bill Moyers hailed him and reached out for his free hand.

"Dr. Covino. Larry Jerard. White House. Welcome to the District. This way, please."

A black Cadillac rushed the pair through a warm drizzle along the George Washington Parkway, crossing the gray Potomac at the Fourteenth Street Bridge. Jerard slowed down at the Mall between the Washington Monument and the Capitol. He focused on his backseat passenger in the mirror. "Not a tourist day," he said. "Sorry. Have you had lunch, Doctor?"

"No. Slept right through it."

"Just as well," Jerard said. "Pryor'll have lunch for you at the House."

Dennis smiled at the young man's light Southern accent and his easy reference to the executive mansion. "Do you work for Ron Pryor?'' he asked to make conversation.

"No. Executive Escort Service."

"In civilian clothes?"

Jerard shrugged good-naturedly. "Informal. Yeah. Not like the uniforms they had back in Nixon's time."

"I remember," Dennis said.

"You come at a good time, Doctor. It's quiet now. The boss's out of town."

"You mean?"

"The President. Yeah. We call him 'the boss.'" Jerard braked at the Constitution Avenue lights. "Damn shame about his friend's death. The ambassador. He's up in Maine, you know."

"Yes, I saw that."

After a pause, Jerard's eyes reappeared in the rearview mirror. "Damn Russians poisoned him, I hear."

"Poison?"

"Radiation, someone said. Do you know anything about that, Doctor?"

"No, I don't," Dennis answered, disturbed by the question.

"I thought that might be the reason for your visit."

"The paper said cancer."

"That's the press release. Word close to the House, though, is radiation poisoning."

"When will the President be back at the House?" Dennis asked, surprised by his own instant familiarity.

"You never know," Jerard replied. "He bombed out of here Sunday night madder'n a hornet."

The car eased over the White House South Gate's bump. Jerard signaled to a raincoated guard and, without stopping, drove to the South portico. The limousine halted with a dip and a squeak. Jerard got out to open the passenger door as Ron Pryor descended the steps to greet the administration's newest appointee.

"Dr. Covino, welcome to Washington." They shook hands. "Larry will take your things to the hotel." A quick hand signal dismissed the car.

The two men passed a stiff Marine guard at the door. Inside, Pryor escorted Dennis down a beige corridor to an office Dennis assumed to be home base for the quick-stepping chief of staff.

"Please be seated, Doctor. Have you had lunch?"

"No."

"Good." Pryor took a seat behind a large desk. "I've ordered us a little something. How was your flight?"

"Fine," Dennis said, admiring the impressive sur-roundings. The office was plush, formal. A high ceiling gave the intended sense of grandeur. The room seemed untouched, used only for show. The thick blue carpet muted Pryor's short history of the room, whose walls displayed large portraits of Truman, both Roosevelts, and the framed photograph of a submarine.

"The *Kennedy*?"

"Of course," Pryor replied, as if the surging Trident needed no introduction.

Behind the polished desk, the youthful chief of staff beamed, looking like a tennis pro, suntanned and confident in a light brown suit with tiny gold eagles winging up toward the knot of a brown tie. He brushed back a handful of sandy hair.

"I congratulate you on your appointment, Doctor," he said. "And for your patience." Despite the welcoming smile, his formality matched the room's, and Dennis could feel an efficient tension in Pryor's words. "There'll be a press ceremony and a swearing-in for you next week when the President gets back."

"He's in Maine," Dennis verified.

"Yes. He'll be home in a few days, after a short stop in Boston. You've heard about the ambassador's death. Personal friend. It's thrown us all off. Cancer."

Dennis nodded, recalling Jerard's theory and making note of Pryor's clipped, detached reference to the official cause of death. "It's unfortunate," he said. "Mr. Pryor—"

"Ron."

"Ron. I don't want to appear overeager, but where will my office be? Here?"

"No. Next door. Executive Office Building. Third floor. I'll take you over there to meet the staff later."

"How large a staff?"

"You do like to get down to business, don't you?" Pryor smiled. "I noticed that in your file. Quite impressive, I might add. Ah, a staff of sixty, I believe."

Dennis nodded his satisfaction. "I am anxious to start."

"You can move in next week if you like."

"Ron, is there much unfinished business I'll need to clear up, or do I start from scratch?"

"As I mentioned over the phone, the staff has wrapped up most of Seymour White's work. You'll start clean slate." Pryor paused, tugging on an earlobe. "The boss has a few projects for you already, though."

"Oh?"

"Yes. There's a file on radio jamming he wants given top priority. Soviet antennas in the Persian Gulf have been raising their usual havoc with military communications. They're jamming codes and interfering with allied channels, specifically NATO."

"Isn't that routine?"

"Well, we both do it, if that's what you mean. But lately they've broken a long-standing pattern. It's a tough nut to crack, frankly. We've allowed them to get away with a lot for diplomatic reasons, but each time they respond to our warnings by shifting power, boosting some installations, turning off others. One in particular. Riga. Ever hear of it?''

''No.''

''They're daring us to make a move, and the President is ready to act.'' He paused. ''After consultation with you, of course.''

''You'll want a review of this?''

''An update. We're looking for an overview to help the President make clear why we're sending new equipment to Israel.''

Dennis recalled the arms deal vaguely from news accounts. He made a quick mental note to contact Dr. Adam Ames at Fordham for background on radio technology. He eyed his host for a moment, then asked, ''I report to you?''

''Exclusively.''

''Then let me ask you, Ron. Can I forget about Executive Order 047?''

''What do you mean?''

''Can I use my own sources to get data on radio jamming?''

Pryor sat up in his chair. ''That won't be necessary,'' he said. ''We've compiled everything you'll need. There's no research involved, just prose. As for 047, I don't want to appear cozy with you, Doctor, but I'd advise a low profile on that.''

Dennis's eye caught the picture of the surging *Kennedy*. ''Why?'' he asked.

Dennis could see the word was not one the chief of staff was used to hearing. Pryor spread his hands wide on the desktop. ''Let's say 047 is still a sore spot right now.''

"A problem?"

"We'll leave it at that. Okay?"

Dennis shook his head. "No. Let's not. Check my file again. If this appointment is ceremonial, there'll be no swearing-in next week. You are being cozy. I expected a briefing today, and so far you've offered lunch and advice not to touch 047. I won't work that way."

Pryor scratched his chin.

"I appreciate your directness," he said. "The President planned to meet with you himself today. Unfortunately, Trusedale's funeral prevented that. So I'm afraid you'll have to get more answers from source one. But my advice is sincere. The President is serious about 047."

"So am I."

"That's good to hear," Pryor said. "And your appointment is far from ceremonial, I assure you."

The remark didn't convince the scientist. "Look, I might as well tell you I'm used to working around that ban. Nondomestic scientific data is essential. I just don't want to cause any embarrassment."

Pryor shifted his eyes, then lowered his voice.

"In case you haven't heard, 047 is the reason for the vacancy you've come to fill. Seymour White couldn't handle it."

"Is that a warning?"

"Just good advice, Doctor. We use domestic data here."

A knock at the door announced the arrival of lunch. Over salad and Chablis, the two men explored the personal territory of careers and backgrounds. The chief of staff showed an appreciative grasp of the scientist's portfolio: his multiple degrees in astronomy and biology, his close association with Nobel laureates worldwide, his acclaimed books, his comet.

Dennis learned of Pryor's local roots: of his successful fund-raising operations for the senator from Maine who had set his eyes on the White House back in 1987. Pryor had hitched his wagon to the Snelling star early, placing his Georgetown law degree at the senator's disposal while he was staff counsel to the Armed Forces Committee, which Snelling had chaired. Ron Pryor represented well-established Washington. He would prosper under any administration, using family contacts and his evident gift of persuasion.

The lunch warmed the atmosphere to the point where Dennis decided to sound out the chief of staff on why and how his predecessor had failed the administration.

"What's the real story about Seymour White?"

Pryor avoided the scientist's glance but not before Dennis noticed a quick tightness in his expression. It seemed like minutes before Pryor turned back to answer. "White burned out," he said. "I guess after ten years in Washington, and at his age, he was entitled. Between you and me, he's had a breakdown."

"A breakdown? I had no idea."

"The family requested we cover it in the papers." Pryor's words fell like those of an undertaker, family-centered and delicately past tense without the slightest hint of sympathy. "He wrote his resignation from a private sanitarium in New York. Did you ever meet him?"

"Once," Dennis replied, "in Chicago."

"He was a brilliant man. Too brilliant. I could never understand a thing he said."

The remark, Dennis could tell, was not meant to be a criticism, but to underline the need for less erudition in the new man.

"I'm sorry to hear it," Dennis said. He placed his wineglass on the desk. "What was it about order 047 he couldn't handle?"

Pryor looked down this time, once again showing discomfort in answering a direct question. He checked his watch.

"This *is* a briefing," Dennis reminded him.

Pryor sighed. "He and the President disagreed on certain parts of the Israeli arms deal. He thought the President had gone too far and was going to push Israel into a new war. They had a blowup, and White lost. It was out of my hands."

"So White fell apart and you went looking for someone more apolitical?"

Pryor smiled as if a new level of understanding had been reached. "In a way," he said. "We think we now have a simplifier, a man of the world as well as a man of science."

"Someone not so brilliant?"

"I fought for your selection, Doctor. As an administrator. The last thing the President needs is another conscience."

"What are his plans for Israel?"

Pryor went into what sounded like a press-release defense of sending a billion dollars' worth of equipment and technicians to the Persian Gulf. Dennis asked if his first assignment was meant to put the finishing touches on a project already in the crates and awaiting shipment on some nearby Air Force tarmac. Pryor assured him this was not the case and once again said the post of science adviser was anything but ceremonial. The President needed hard facts on jamming operations, operations he intended to stop with Israeli help.

"So certain radio towers are being targeted?" Dennis asked.

"Riga is the question mark. We believe this one complex is the master center for all radio interference in the Gulf. Before we target anything, we have to be sure how Riga fits in."

"And White had no answers?"

"He took it upon himself to confer with some Soviets in Spain. Defectors who wanted to tell him all about Riga. He found nothing. When he got back, he and the President had a shouting match. If he hadn't agreed to resign, he would have been fired."

"So he chose to resign?" Dennis said.

"As soon as he violated 047, he was gone."

Dennis considered Pryor's somber tone. As much as the chief of staff wanted it to appear as background, it was a warning. Disobedience was the mortal sin. Snelling might tolerate incompetence, but he would not tolerate defiance of an Executive Order. He thought of his own anger at Norton Lee when the young assistant had taken the disturbing initiative with Hendley; not an act of disobedience, but a clear if well-intentioned violation of procedures. He understood the importance of giving and taking orders even as the scientist in him cried out for the freedom that had tripped up his predecessor.

After Pryor expressed pride in having secured the services of "the right man," Dennis thanked him and took advantage of the lunch-hour cordiality to drop a name.

"Have you ever met Bill Hendley?"

"No, I haven't." Pryor sipped his wine.

"He's the fatcat who wants to track the comet you showed some interest in."

"I know. He's also a big contributor to the President's opponent."

"Is that why you called me about his latest project?"

Pryor blinked his response. "As a matter of fact, yes. We were glad you nixed that comet probe. It made it easier for us."

"I blocked it for scientific reasons. I assume yours were political."

"Revenge, you mean?" Pryor asked. "Not really. He'll always get his share of military contracts. No. We were more concerned about public alarm over an approaching comet during a reelection campaign. Distracting, wouldn't you agree?"

"If it exists. Comet fever, like Halley's apparition."

"Apparition, it's called?" Pryor laughed. "Halley's barely appeared."

"We say apparition even when only astronomers can track it. You're right. Halley's was a disappointment for stargazers. We were out of position for a real show. Better luck next time."

"In..." Pryor tried some quick addition.

"In 2061," Dennis said. "You and I'll miss it."

Pryor settled into his leather chair. "Doctor, what are the chances for a close comet? Another apparition, one we could all see?" he asked.

"Very slim," Dennis explained. "And at the same time, constant. Sighting one, I mean. Every year about six new comets are spotted by amateur astronomers."

"Six. That sounds like a lot."

"Many more come by unspotted, but they're so small that only a few people ever know about them, or care to."

"And meteors?"

"Mostly debris from dying comets. They penetrate our atmospheric blanket regularly, bringing out all those UFO fans." Dennis smiled, enjoying Pryor's interest in his specialty. "A meteor shower will set the town buzzing, but comets like Halley's are overrated."

"Your own comet—in 1971, was it? How close did that come?"

"Pretty close. About nine million kilometers. A speck."

"How did you find it?"

Explaining the details of his discovery twenty years before, Dennis stressed the luck involved and the sleepless nights, the chilly vigils, the doubts. He mentioned the frustration of passing clouds, the maddening equipment failure, and the obsession that had made him physically ill. Would he go through it all again? No, he said with certainty, even as he felt a distant twinge of pride.

"So you came across it by chance," Pryor commented.

"Pure luck against astronomical odds, so to speak."

"You don't give the same odds to Hendley?"

"My sighting cost the observatory twelve thousand dollars a day for five weeks. A questionable bargain for boosting the ego of a single scientist. Hendley's shot would cost eight times that much just for the rocketry."

"It really is a shot in the dark, then," Pryor said.

"It's foolish for the return of possible benefits. Besides, we scientists are still digesting Halley data from ground equipment."

"Some people I spoke to still criticize your Institute for not okaying a space shot to Halley's in '85."

"I'm sure the President and I share the same detractors."

"True."

"As it turned out, we have more than enough data on Halley's to keep us busy until it returns."

"Would your fellow scientists agree with you on that?"

Dennis shook his head. "Some will never get over it. Their appetite is insatiable. I still get hate mail."

"After all this time?"

"It was a once-in-a-lifetime shot," Dennis said. "While we're on the subject, how seriously is a comet probe taken here?"

The President's aide rose from his chair and stood in front of the fireplace. Glancing at his watch, he replied, "The Pentagon said yes, pending your Institute's approval. The President says no, not till after the election."

"So it is political."

"That's where it stands now."

"That's all?"

"There's more. Some State Department officials agree with Hendley's intelligence that the Russians may have detected something between Saturn and Jupiter. An anomaly."

"A perturbation?"

"That's right. Something they evidently came across by chance. Sound familiar?" Pryor paused, taking a step closer to Dennis. "It's on hold until we can confirm the same effect here."

"Who's looking into it?"

"No one," Pryor said. "It's on hold."

"Why didn't I know of any of this before?"

"Classified information. Last week you were a civilian. And between you and me, you'd still be if you'd said yes to a comet probe."

Pryor returned to the desk but did not sit down. He hovered above Dennis, seeming to enjoy looking down on the new appointee the way an upperclassman enjoys a hazing. His self-assurance and the reluctant way he parted with information disturbed Dennis.

"I assume I'll have access to anything you have on a comet," he said.

"Of course. We want your assessment. But first the President wants more on the jamming thing."

"On Riga?"

"That's right. We realize comets are your specialty, but it'll have to wait. First the jamming."

"Not both?"

"Only if you believe the Russians have a comet we haven't found yet. You told me you didn't believe it. And neither do we. In fact, military intelligence is working on a lead that it's all a rumor and your friend Hendley is an unsuspecting plant."

"Some kind of agent?"

"No. He's too much of a successful capitalist for their taste. He's just been fed information the Russians wanted him to hear, and then they let his natural greed run its course. To the Pentagon, then to you for your blessing as a disinterested third party."

"I see. Hoping to . . ." Dennis searched for a reason.

"Divert us? It's a plausible scenario they've tried in the past. The Reds place great faith in our wildfire press. Looking for a new comet could shift attention away from whatever they're up to in the Gulf. Even interfere with the election."

"The election? That's a year off."

Pryor nodded. "So would be the sight of a comet now out near Jupiter, correct? Anyway, that's the operative theory. We see it as a diversionary scheme to explain silence at Riga. But the Soviets are hiding something more dramatic than a comet scare. The important thing is that we won't allow it to work." Pryor clapped his hands together. "And I'm glad you're on the team to help us unravel the mess."

"First the jamming," Dennis said.

"That's correct. The silence at Riga. You'll be filled in on it in detail next week."

"I won't be of much help until I know as much as you do," Dennis said.

"You'll be deluged after your swearing-in," Pryor pledged with a grin. He checked his watch again.

At first Dennis took this as a nervous habit, but then it struck him as the in-person equivalent of hanging up the phone. A brush-off. He wasn't sure just why, but in less than an hour he had come to dislike this Ivy League Presidential lieutenant. He rose to a surprise invitation.

"I hope you'll join me at seven-thirty at Deke Ziebert's for dinner," Pryor said.

"Thank you."

"In the meantime, Larry has delivered your bags to the Watergate. By the way, he's on call for all your transportation needs."

"Very kind."

"Executive treatment," Pryor beamed. "For one of the team."

They shook hands at the door. "I've taken the liberty of arranging a tour of your new offices at four," Pryor added. "That way you'll be able to see who's really working a full day over there. No one knows you're coming."

Dennis now knew why he disliked him.

"I'll pass it up for today," he said. "But I will see you for dinner at seven."

"Seven-thirty."

"Seven-thirty." Dennis turned at the door. "Oh, don't worry. I'll let you know who's working over there in my first report."

"Suit yourself," said Pryor, spreading wide his arms. "No tour. Larry is here and at your service. Until tonight."

Larry Jerard was waiting outside the office, as if Pryor's territory were off-limits to the help. Dennis thought a moment about asking him about this, but changed his mind as the two entered the Cadillac. The drizzly rain had stopped. Through the window, as he watched the White House recede, try as he might, he couldn't shake a sense of being out of his league, of playing a game whose rules he only partly understood.

Chapter Four

"Ladies and gentlemen," the President began, "with today's appointment I make good on my pledge to assure strong cooperation between the scientific community and this administration. In the trying times to come, this position will grow in importance, and I'm sure the day will dawn when even my critics will applaud the appointment I make today. Dr. Covino is an expert administrator and a well-respected scientist. A man whose reputation and credentials are of the highest order."

The Indian summer breeze scooped a tuft of graying hair onto his head as he turned smiling from the tangled mass of microphones before him to focus on the cameras.

"Our distinguished science adviser comes from Colorado. And even though I look forward to defeating the equally distinguished governor of that beautiful state, I am confident this will be the only point on which we might disagree."

A tide of chuckles rose from behind the President. He looked back into the crowd and smiled at Dennis, who in turn glanced at Sandi at his side.

"Now if David Henderson wins," Snelling continued, "both Dr. Covino and I will be unemployed, perhaps unemployable. So with this fact in mind let's put to rest any question of his allegiance. The good doctor assures me he is eager to take up his duties, as am I to profit from his advice. Thank you."

Amid applause and a photographic handshake, the President brought Dennis forward again. Afterward, he escorted Dennis and Sandi into the White House for a private luncheon. He was shorter than Dennis had imagined and more nervous than TV cameras allowed. His steely eyes blinked when he spoke, then widened as he listened to Sandi's compliments on the surroundings. When he released Sandi's arm at the top of the stairs, Dennis noticed how he patted both pockets of his jacket, as if unsure what to do with his hands.

The trio entered the ceremonial Roosevelt Room. Lunch was Atlantic salmon, which Snelling more than once boasted about. The President ate rapidly, mixing light chatter with compliments for Sandi and adding an occasional remark that disclosed a layman's admiration for science.

"I still can't tell the difference between fission and fusion," he said. "Atomic fission, I mean." He chuckled. "Now with a man of your caliper to advise me, looks like I'll never need to."

Sandi shot Dennis a look of embarrassment at the faux pas.

"Mr. President," Dennis said, "I can explain that if you like."

Snelling raised a hand. "No need. Science I leave in your capable hands." Touching her arm, he turned to Sandi and said, "Miss Whitman, I have a surprise for you. You're going to have a private tour of the White House while Dr. Covino and I confer."

The three separated in the hallway, Sandi leaving for the upstairs rooms with a pretty uniformed hostess. Executive Escort Service, Dennis thought as he followed the President past several busy offices where groups of badged people moved in and out, conferring in muffled tones.

The President stopped at a doorway and began fumbling in his pockets, clucking quietly until until he produced a key. Security was more than a priority with his new boss, Dennis thought, amazed. It was a mania.

The Oval Office appeared as it did in photos, stark and impressive: a blend of historic permanence and temporary occupancy. Two large flags stood at attention, sandwiching a broad, dark desk. Behind the stately high-backed leather chair, sunlight penetrated through a triple window and brightened an enormous rug that displayed the presidential seal. The walls held several plaques with lettering too small for Dennis to read and another portrait of the submarine *Kennedy*, this time in oil. His eyes settled on a delicate replica of the presidential yacht *Zephyr* on the mantel above a closed fireplace. Behind the boat, and serving as an appropriate backdrop, the familiar Rockport Motif Number One enlivened a beige wall. Beyond a grouping of five richly upholstered wing chairs circling a captain's table, a framed doorway dominated the curved far wall.

Ron Pryor emerged from this door, carrying under his arm what appeared to be a record album. The cover's bold black and yellow stripes gave away its top security status.

"Doctor, you already know Ron Pryor, my first mate," the President said. The two men shook hands.

"That's the homework I was told about?" Dennis asked good-naturedly. The President took a seat behind his desk and pointed a finger at the disc Pryor placed before him.

"This single disc," Snelling said gravely, "contains all our data on Soviet jamming operations. Never let it out of your sight or out of this building. My computer room has been set aside for you to take all the notes you need. Ever use the Beta-X model?"

"No."

"I'll have someone set it up for you." He pointed to his chief aide. "See to it, Ron." Pryor left the room by the same side door, which Dennis noticed needed no key. He was surprised by the President's hurried tone. Gone was that smile evidently reserved for television cameras. A stiffness replaced the President's former expansiveness. Fatigue, stress, maybe even campaign overexertion showed in the lines around his gray eyes. Dennis excused his abrupt change, charging it to the recent loss of his friend.

"Mr. President," he said, trying to establish eye contact. "Is there any other source of data at my disposal?"

"You mean at the Science Department?"

"No. I mean, can I use other sources of intelligence, besides these reports?" Dennis reached for the disc.

The President shook his head wearily. "There's no need to," he explained. "What you have in your hands are NASA, State, and Defense Department reports. Updated and complete. All we know. What I want now is a concise report on what in hell it all means. What the Soviets are doing in the Gulf, scientifically and in plain terms." He paused. "Between us, Dennis, I have too much information from too many sources. I need it all broken down so that voters can understand what we're up against."

"I understand."

"The Russians are up to something. It may be harassment as usual or, with the election coming up, it may be more serious. They've been jamming us at will. Now they are silent. I want to know why." Snelling hesitated to inhale. "I have personal intelligence on the importance of Riga. You'll find our sources have narrowed it down to this one complex. You have a free hand to pull it all together. And fast."

"There's a deadline?"

"There's always a deadline. We'll need your report within two weeks maximum. With a coded copy to go to the Secretary of Defense as per 047," he added pointedly.

"Two weeks," Dennis nodded.

The President came around from behind the desk.

"I don't need to underline the top security status of this work," he said, his tone confidential. "I have a deadline too. A crucial commitment for November. The Israeli arms deal. What you find out could determine how we carry out our pledge to defend interests in the Persian Gulf." He paused once more with a shrug. "Welcome to the front."

"Mr. President, you'll have my input within two weeks," Dennis said. "However, I'd like to know if I can tap scientists outside the country."

Snelling moved away, to sit again at his desk just as Ron Pryor came in from the adjoining room.

"You may not," Snelling ruled, folding his hands. "Security won't allow it. One question dropped in the wrong ear could compromise our whole network. I won't allow that to happen." He shook his head for emphasis. "Do you understand?"

"Frankly, sir, I don't," Dennis said.

From the corner of his eye, he could see Pryor closing both of his in despair. The President rose and leaned forward over the desk. His two arms anchoring him in place, he said, "I cannot afford even the perception of counting on the other side for anything. Order 047 stands. Discount any information that doesn't come from our own secure sources. Do you understand?"

Not waiting for an answer, he turned to Pryor. "Ron, didn't you go over this? No matter what the papers say, the race is on, and any slips could put us all out of work. No talks with scientists not on the 047 list."

"May I expand the list?" Dennis ventured.

"No, you may not."

"Can I confer outside the country?"

"What do you think this is, Simon Says? Go by the list, Doctor," Snelling commanded. "And kindly pass that word along to your colleagues. Some are in violation, and we'll get to them. I'll say no more to you on the subject."

Pryor shifted nervously. Dennis lowered his gaze, seeing no advantage in probing further. Snelling nodded his head jerkily. "This is a damn house of cards and no one realizes it," he said. "I just lost a friend to some kind of death beam, for chrissake. Radio-induced carcinoma, Bethesda says. Do you know what that is? I'll tell you. I buried a skeleton up in Maine. That radiation came from Riga. First it's on, now it's off. They will not be allowed to turn that thing on again. Get me that report, Doctor. On my terms."

"Two weeks," Dennis repeated.

"No more," Snelling ordered.

"Good day, Mr. President," Pryor said, signaling Dennis to follow him out of the office. Snelling had turned to stare out the window, and Dennis noticed the tight knot he made of his fists behind his back.

The two men entered a dimly lit room dominated by a large conference table. In the center hummed a television monitor filled with an indecipherable jumble of winking numbers and letters. The computer, fed and ready, vibrated its stand-by status. To one side of the screen lay a stack of yellow legal paper and an orderly row of like-colored pencils.

Pryor pulled out the room's only chair.

"Doctor, let me give you some advice. Never tell the boss you don't understand. 'Do you understand' is his signal for the end of a conversation."

Dennis knew he could have made their first meeting go smoother. All the same he resented the poor timing of Pryor's advice.

"He is very much the boss, isn't he?" he said.

"Is there any other way?"

"I guess not," Dennis agreed.

"The President is under a great deal of stress. He's counting on your help with this. That's all. Just help. No bucking. No resistance. He counts on your advice, Doctor." Pryor let the words sink in. "That means cooperation, from day one."

"You're right, Ron," Dennis said with contrite sincerity. "Chalk it up to experience. But in the future, I'd appreciate being told beforehand."

"Keep your ears open. I warned you."

"So you did. Trusedale died of cancer. Too many cigarettes?"

"Look, we appreciate your determination. Just apply it to this first assignment. If you need anything, I'm down the hall. Captain Lawrence is here to help you with the machine."

"Would you tell Sandi I'll meet her at the hotel for dinner at six?"

"Sure," Pryor said, forcing a slow smile. "It's the deadline that's important on this, okay?"

"I understand."

"Good. And good luck."

The door's cushioned thud sealed Dennis in the room. He removed his suit jacket. A gentle knock at the opposite door produced a tall, black Marine who introduced himself as Captain Lawrence. He inspected the computer, checking the disc placement and adjusting the focus on the viewing screen, and instructed Dennis on how to open the file bank. It was a simpler job than he had expected. The Beta-X was first cousin to the computer he used at the Institute. With an ironic smile, Dennis noticed the deck's silver H trademark. Beta-X was a product of Hendley International Industries.

"This machinery can do everything but erase and copy," the captain said in a measured drawl. "This button retrieves data chronologically entered. This is the interface mode. And this—RS—is retrieval by source." Lawrence backed away. "I'll stand by."

"Thank you, Captain. I can handle it."

"Yes, sir. I'll be at the doorway anyway. I have to refile the disc."

"It can't leave your sight?" Dennis asked.

"That's right," Lawrence replied. "And I'll need your signature here."

After Dennis scratched his initials on the security clipboard, Lawrence left to take up his station outside the door. He was dead serious about the disc not leaving his sight. The man was a babysitter under orders to keep the door opened a crack.

Dennis settled in at the keyboard, following instructions printed on the table. He studied the first electronic page, whose contents he recorded on the yellow pad. Riga complex—FILE XY9-119226A. After four or five technical paragraphs, he stopped and threw down the pencil. He called up page two, searching for more. Page two— data and fewer numbers, a stream of National Geographic prose. Bland accounts of visits to the complex and secondhand information compiled by names Dennis didn't recognize. He copied the names. All military, none above the rank of captain. Page three—more numbers,

more jargon in the form of a report from a Captain
O'Leary, USN. "RIGA (09771–BT) Baltic port. Latvia,
U.S.S.R. PMB-status: 4X. File 20R/047. Since 1975 site
of the highest-security radio complex in U.S.S.R. Model
for satellite installations placed subsequently in Turkey,
Syria, Iraq, Afghanistan? (1978–1982). Also coordinates
radio data from installations (three or four) in Kirovsk and
at other points within the Arctic Circle. Director: Dr. Illyich Sarantof(v), Minister of Radio Technologies: (1976
Marshal Dubrov)." Well done, Captain. Solid stuff.
Classified secret in 1982. Refiled top secret in 1983 on the
recommendation of the CIA.

Dennis called up the next page. "US ARMY INTELLI-
GENCE/Sector 14. 2/8/78. RIGA. ZAX–047. File: RA-
DIO."

"Thirteen years old," he said out loud. "God."

Page five—more of the same: outdated surface descrip-
tions written in terse, military style. More prose, pages of
it, swept by in tourist-diary style. Stored newspaper clip-
pings and articles now defunct appeared. He shook his
head in bewilderment. Here in the White House, at the
center of supersensitive intelligence that everyone seemed
to take seriously, it was hard not to imagine he was in the
basement of some public library.

This must be some kind of joke, he concluded, a hazing ritual meant to test his sense of humor. Only the door,
opened a crack with Captain Lawrence beyond, and the
President's admonition about top security held back a
smile. How can this stuff be intelligence?

With a frustrated stab, he ordered Beta-X to display the
files again. All sixteen frames, this time in chronological
order from 1973 to 1988. For some reason all documen-
tation stopped at 1988. His eyes caught a NASA report
dated 1987. A recent one, he scoffed. It was an account of

a 1986 on-site visit to Riga by a Dr. Abrahamson of the Jet Propulsion Lab in California. The report was sketchily drawn in half-sentences, scientific notation, and cryptic jargon that was either illegible or long since out of date. "Six towers, master console seventy meters underground. Reinforced concrete installation. Antenna dish display mobile, tracked like Very Large Array in New Mexico. Transmission and receiving capabilities (00–3930/424). Nearby radio antennas of Z-type under construction and off-limits to all but cleared technicians o.k.ed by Sarantof(v)."

A courtesy visit before the security curtain came down in 1988. Nothing more than a guided tour three years old, with no follow-up and no interpretive data. Dennis took down the numbered code, then tapped on the machine's cold frame. Abrahamson was evidently an engineer and more interested in concrete than in the inner workings of the Riga complex. Dennis shrugged his frustration to the empty room. Just then the idea hit him that Abrahamson could still be reached. Surely he had his own notes. Three years ago is not ancient history. He jotted down "JPL," then noticed more numbers on the screen: "d. 11/12/89." Abrahamson was dead, his legacy a mute, five-page flickering entry among the top-secret files of the President of the United States.

Dennis's eyes began to tire in the dark room. He squinted to steady the strange shapes dancing crazily before him. He rechecked his notes. After two hours and an insistent pinch in his lower back, he dropped the pencil onto the yellow pad and stood up to exhale his fatigue.

Updated and complete, he remembered the President saying, Never let the disc out of your sight. Good God. Riga is just as cloudy a spot on the map as it ever was. An intelligence fortress, as secure in 1991 as it had been sixteen years ago when its first antenna was turned on. Can the President be as in the dark as these frames show? he wondered. Not a single clue that Riga was the jamming center the President claimed it to be. Not one giveaway as to why Riga would be shut down.

Jamming aboard Trident submarines near the Gulf, space shuttle transmissions to SkyLab Da Vinci temporarily blacked out, embassies wired and bugged, NATO codes scrambled: these incidents were as routine to any informed person as box scores were to a baseball fan. But where's the link connecting it all to Riga?

Dennis jotted down the names of several colleagues who could supply more information with a simple phone call. The President can get all he wants on jamming, but he won't find it in his own house.

He tapped on the door where Captain Lawrence was guarding top-level, high-tech disarray. Dennis wondered if any of his colleagues, if Seymour White, knew about this embarrassment within the White House. Seymour White. Not a single entry from the former science adviser. No wonder the President needs to know what's up in the Gulf. How many months had passed since the last documented visit to Riga—forty? In any one of those time blocks, a single Soviet policy change could, probably had, turned these Beta-X files into a specimen for the National Archives.

Dennis pulled his jacket on as Captain Lawrence entered, turned on the lights, and headed for the desk. He retrieved the disc and turned off the machine.

"All set, sir?" he asked.

"Yes, Captain. I won't need the disc again. Thank you."

"You must be a speed reader," the Captain said with cordial admiration.

"Is Mr. Pryor still here?" Dennis asked.

"No, sir. Any messages?"

"Tell him I want a meeting when I've collected all the data I need."

"Yes, sir."

Dennis took a last glance at the useless data file the Captain couched securely under his arm.

"Oh, Captain," he called. "You said Beta-X cannot be erased."

"Or copied. That's right, Doctor."

"Can it be transferred to a twin?"

"Only on the President's orders," Lawrence answered.

"Thank you, Captain."

THAT NIGHT OVER DINNER at Joe and Moe's, as Sandi talked enthusiastically and in great detail about the minutiae of the White House, Dennis found it difficult to share her bubbling mood. Finally, over dessert he told her about his day.

"The President put you to work the first day," she remarked.

"He sent me to the library. Top secret."

"Really?"

"A computer library. Guarded. He wants a report in two weeks on radio interference."

Sandi raised her eyebrows. "Any problems?" she asked.

"No. So far it's a book report."

"Sounds easy."

Dennis nodded. "Too easy," he said. "His files are in sad shape. I've got to dig. Carefully though, until I'm more sure of my footing. The President is uptight over a place called Riga, in the Soviet Union. He claims they killed the ambassador with some kind of radiation. 'Death beams,' he called it.''

"What does he want you to do?"

"Explain what they do there," he said with a shrug. "And why they've shut down. He gave me a James Bond routine on how secret his files are. They're nothing but scattered notes. And the complex isn't even active. He wants me to find out why."

"That's all?"

"No. I can only use an approved list of scientists."

A puzzled look crossed her face.

"Like ground rules?" she said.

He nodded. "And I found out what happened to my predecessor."

"White?"

"He's in a sanitarium. He had a run-in with Snelling, then he resigned."

"That's quite a record. The ambassador dies, Seymour White is committed. I hope one of the President's retirees gets to go off and write his memoirs."

Dennis reached across the table and placed her hands in his.

"Maybe I'll be the first," he said softly.

Chapter Five

While the presidential reelection party made a precampaign swing through the South, Dennis was busy setting up his new office in the shadow of the White House. He made the rounds of his departments with Richard Lohmann, an executive branch official whom Dennis soon came to call his mentor.

Their first encounter had been a disaster that both men could now recall with good humor. Dennis had been on two phones at the time. In one he was having words with an abusive architect. In the other he was accepting a lengthy apology from the head of Goddard Space Center, who had never heard of Riga. He looked up at an impeccably dressed man with a flower in his lapel and a critical look in his eyes, who stood before his desk. The man seemed to be waiting for a formal introduction.

"Who the hell are you?" Dennis snapped, a phone in each hand.

"Richard Lohmann," the man replied. "National Security Adviser."

"Jesus."

"I cannot walk on water, Dr. Covino, but I will forgive a most uncivil greeting. I'll come back tomorrow."

He did, and after drinks at a nearby pub Lohmann recommended, Dennis was glad for the friend Ron Pryor had assigned to help him in his first days. On their first tour, the staff showed off a state-of-the-art wonderland of instant communication. A preprogrammed telephone bank filled one whole room, where Dennis could convene a meeting of experts in any field. Around the corner, two secured meeting rooms stood ready to house the top minds in the scientific community at a moment's notice. At a simulated run-through of his computerized directory, Dennis stopped to punch numbers that within seconds sent a video greeting to the surprised director of Pasadena's Jet Propulsion Laboratory.

As the two men strolled from office to office, they talked amid electronic wizardry that Dennis could only have dreamed of at the Institute.

"It is amazing, Dennis. All this technology. The building hums. Way over my head, I'm afraid. As for Beta-X," Lohmann said, pinching his lips like an Oxford don, "just two Greek letters to me. You say it had nothing after 1988, nothing from Seymour White?"

Dennis nodded. "And its contents can be traded only on the President's orders," he said.

"Could be CIA. I'll check on it. But you'd best see Pryor first."

"When he's in town." Dennis shrugged.

"Oh, yes. The A team is on the road again, isn't it? Mississippi or Alabama, I think. I can't keep up with the schedule. Sorry I can't be of more help. See Pryor when he gets back," Lohmann advised, "or send a memo."

"How about the Pentagon?"

"The Pentagon?" Lohmann looked up from the carnation he was fondling. "No. Stay away from there until you get a good compass. Dennis, our responsibilities here are clearly defined and monitored. You stay with the National Science Foundation, the Science Advisory Board, your colleagues. Get that jamming report in on time. It's routine, but then most of what we do is ongoing. Just go with it."

"If you could have seen that file—" Dennis began.

"I can imagine. Sometimes I think that's why so much is classified secret." He smiled, reaching into his jacket to pull out a plain envelope.

"What's this?" Dennis asked.

"Routine. Instructions for Mt. Weather, in the event of nuclear action. You're one of the lucky four hundred who get to join the President in time of crisis."

Dennis took the envelope. "Thanks, I think."

"Now I'll leave you to your computers," Lohmann said. "Give me a call. Anytime."

"I will."

DENNIS RETURNED TO HIS OFFICE, passing Lohmann's envelope to a secretary and glancing at the morning's schedule printout. At the top appeared the name Dr. Lyle, Smithsonian Astrophysical Observatory, and a number that he dialed himself. After accepting his colleague's best wishes on the new post, he asked about the meteor shower on his first flight to Washington. Lyle replied authoritatively. "Yeah, we had some light from Alpha Aurigids a couple weeks back. The usual."

"Nothing special?" Dennis asked.

"Nothing. Pons Winnecke remnants have faded, so it couldn't have been that. It's too early for d'Arrest's comet, if that's what you're wondering. You got my latest chart?"

"Yes. Thank you."

"What are you looking for, anyway?"

"I'm not sure," Dennis replied. "Nothing near Jupiter?"

"Should there be?"

"Look, Walter. I need to be the first to know if there's a new comet."

"Comet? You get our weekly updates."

"Yeah. But I need more, and before confirmation. I want to be the first to know of even a single sighting report."

"Are you expecting something?"

Dennis paused, then said, "I've heard the Soviets might be tracking an anomaly out near Jupiter."

"A comet?"

"A possibility."

"We'll check. Do you want us to alert our amateur network?"

"That won't be necessary."

"Just sightings."

"That's all," Dennis said. "And before confirmation."

"Okay. Sounds important."

"Could be."

"Security matter?"

"Not yet."

"But you can't say more."

Dennis smiled. "You got it. We'll just keep an eye on the skies."

"Eyes," Lyle corrected.

"I appreciate it, Walt."

"You've got the address, for our fund drive?"

"Yeah. My check'll be in the mail."

Lyle chuckled. "Just kidding, buddy. But we could use a good word now and then. Washington's tight as a drum these days."

"So I'm finding out. Keep in touch, will you?"

"Sure thing."

Dennis felt better for the call. Lyle would keep "eyes" on the sky, while he struggled to fill in pieces of the Riga puzzle. Lohmann, for all his good intentions, supplied next to nothing on the White House files. And dealing with the State Department proved to be even more frustrating as he awaited an explanation that he knew would never come on why State should be involved in a Soviet radio installation. The few calls returned brought only secondhand apologies from evasive bureaucrats. As the days went by, he was left with the unsettling feeling that he was the Riga expert.

THE COVINO REPORT was completed within ten days. Dennis took no pride in the scant seven-page document. He had simply reordered the scattered bits and pieces available in the White House and recommended monthly updates on the Riga complex. Output equals input, he told himself. At the same time, he vowed never again to place his name on so unsatisfactory a report.

Yes, Soviet jammers were active in Iran-Iraq, on the Turkish border near Yerevan, and at the North Pole. Yes, Israeli complaints of interference were legitimate. No, he did not know which jamming incidents matched which sites, but he would find out. No, there was no hard evidence from documents presented to explain why Riga was now silent. He would assign a team to solve the mystery.

Despite disappointment over the report, he accepted the compliments of his staff, who were impressed at the new adviser's organization. They, like Ron Pryor, seemed content that a deadline had been met. At least now he had an idea of what the President was working with and what ammunition his own new arsenal held. A starting point, he mused as he watched the courier take up the report from his secretary's desk for delivery to the Secretary of Defense.

Amid workmen renovating several offices and bright new phones that rang unpredictably until they could be debugged, Dennis got down to work on other matters. He ordered a second opinion on an Agriculture Department proposal for solar-powered irrigation stations in Nebraska and listened to the Secretary spit fury into the phone over another delay. The cursed phone lines kept both Nebraska senators on hold. Dennis wrote to them instead, expressing his regret for the double inconvenience.

He initialed several funding grants for the cancer foundation and signed his name to a kidney research bill for a grateful surgeon general.

He lunched with his five male department heads and enjoyed their loose banter over drinks. It took less than two martinis apiece to soften their reserve and bring on a round-table rush of rumors and office gossip. At a small Eighteenth Street Italian restaurant, he learned that the Vice President was about to resign before the campaigning incumbent dumped him; that receptionist Sally Waters was as discreet at the office as she was great in bed; that the ''orange list'' he had noticed taped to nearly every department desk posted the numbers of high-ranking cranks whose calls could be ignored. And that twenty percent of the staff was overpaid while the rest languished in need of a long-overdue raise. Taking the hint and mindful of first impressions, the new adviser made a point of dividing the check six ways.

Within two weeks, Dennis had achieved his goal of meeting personally with every member of his new staff. They returned this courtesy with an in-house joke that the new science adviser's door was always open. In fact, it had been removed, its empty frame awaiting a new one promised any day.

The day the polished oak door arrived, he was on the phone with Richard Lohmann. The National Security chief surprised him by announcing that through State Department friends he had secured a visa for Dr. Cho Chan, the Nobel astronomer, head of Nanking's Purple Mountain Observatory, who was anxious to meet him.

"China," Dennis commented suspiciously. "Will Executive Order 047 let me talk with him?"

"You don't need my permission. Anyway, the guy's an invited guest of the Department of Education. He's got a visa for a university tour. And he's going to be at Georgetown at the end of the week."

Dennis was excited by the news. When others were storming the Evergreen Institute in 1985, demanding an American-financed international space probe to Halley's comet, Dr. Cho Chan boldly lent his considerable support to Dennis's plea for earth-based tracking. He would be honored to meet the scientist, he told Lohmann, who agreed to see to the details.

"How'd he get around 047?" Dennis wanted to know.

"A favor from the Pentagon."

"Pentagon?"

"Happens all the time," Lohmann said. "General Wainwright arranged it."

"Wainwright? Special Technologies?"

"Top brass."

Dennis didn't need to hear any more. His excitement dampened at the name that brought back Hendley and his "innovative" Pentagon contact. Cho Chan wanted to see him about a comet.

THE TWO SCIENTISTS MET in a partially completed conference room next to Dennis's office. Cho Chan, a diminutive, almost fragile man, bowed politely to his host and accepted one of the plastic-covered chairs. He gazed about the room and smiled at Dennis's apologies for the dust and wood shavings at their feet.

"Dr. Chan, I'm pleased to meet you at last."

"Thank you, Doctor. And congratulations on your appointment. I hope it will mean easier contact for us in the future."

Dennis kept the same hope to himself as he took a seat and offered his guest tea, which his secretary had provided.

"You are eager to learn about a new comet, as I understand," Chan said.

If it had been anyone but Cho Chan, Dennis would have resented the word. Wainwright was eager; he was wary.

"Is it real?" he asked.

Cho Chan sipped from his cup. Two black eyes stared at Dennis over its white rim. Very deliberately, he placed the cup on a table, folded his hands, and spoke slowly. "We have evidence that Sarantof at the Moscow Institute has detected an object. An unexplained perturbation they say they can see."

"Have you detected the same object?"

"Not yet. However, we have information that Soviet scientists—astronomers, I should say—are doing little else these days but keeping an eye on what could be a comet."

"A stray?"

"Something that shouldn't be there," Chan said. "We are tracking as best we can in Nanking. So are the Japanese. But with so little to go on, you can understand the futility of the task."

Dennis shared his colleague's nod, imagining the search for a single grain of sand somewhere on the Pacific coast.

"How can the Soviets detect an object at that distance?" he asked.

"That's the easy part. The French."

"The French?"

"Sarantof has purchased three Lapierre Electro-graphic-Nine cameras to go with the latest radio astronomy equipment available. They were evidently studying a quasar when something got in the way. They say it's a comet." Chan hesitated. "You look surprised, Doctor."

"I am," he replied with a tense smile. "As you can see, I'm new to this office and I have a lot of catch-up work."

Cho Chan tilted his head, a gesture Dennis hoped came from unfamiliarity with the expression rather than from disbelief at such a lame excuse.

"I mean, I have yet to get to that file," he added.

"A Lapierre Electrographic-Nine," Chan continued, "captures images to the thirtieth magnitude."

"So I've heard."

"The French will not sell one to us. The Soviet Union has enviable leverage with their magnificent pipeline. Their trade agreement leaves us out, so we're using a Griboval."

The thirtieth magnitude, Dennis thought. Then he thought of the Naval Observatory's twenty-five magnitude Electrographic, an instrument that could literally show a candle flame at one million kilometers.

Chan went on. "The Soviet instruments can pierce into deepest space to watch eruptions on Io. I've seen the pictures. We believe they may have at least two Electrographic-Nines in earth orbit. This could explain their finding of a distant comet. Even a cometary fragment or a dark apollo object the size of this teacup can fill their viewing screens."

"But why haven't they announced?"

"I suppose their findings are tentative. The object must be very, very small and dim so far away from the sun. Something we couldn't see for months, if ever."

Dr. Chan reached within his suit for a package of Winstons and held it out, as if asking permission to smoke.

"Please," Dennis said with dazed attention. He dug out a workman's ashtray from the table.

"Thank you," Chan said. "Doctor, if I may be so direct, you know nothing of this, do you?"

Dennis was about to follow his first instincts and deny the remark. Instead, he paused, wondering if Cho Chan thought him as incompetent as he felt. Was the Evergreen Institute such an isolated ivory tower? What else had Executive Order 047 been keeping from American scientists? He watched a blue smoke ring hover over Cho Chan's head, then confessed, "I'm in the dark so far."

Chan's eyes widened. "Then may I be perfectly frank?" he asked.

"Please tell me all you can."

Chan inhaled more smoke, then dropped both arms onto the arms of his chair. "Dr. Covino, Sarantof, up until this comet work began, was busy altering the earth's magnetic field."

"What?"

"In stages, to be sure. But with remarkable success. His team is charged with altering polar bias to accomplish a Circular Error Probable of several meters."

"For missile accuracy?" Dennis gasped.

"Yes. The last we knew, he had succeeded with a CEP of ten meters."

"Ten meters! They can fire missiles over the North Pole and land warheads ten meters from a target?"

Chan nodded solemnly. "At least fifty percent of the time," he said. "About six months ago, all Sarantof's experiments stopped. We've heard nothing since. There can only be two reasons for this silence. Neither one comforting, I'm afraid."

"Yes?"

"Either a CEP of ten meters is satisfactory to the Kremlin or all magnetic-field work was halted to track a comet they think may cause trouble."

"Trouble?"

"A close apparition, yes. It is speculation, of course. And I'm sure your Defense Department is monitoring the situation closely. However, I am surprised by your reaction, Doctor. Surely you know this much. I am offending you."

Dennis cursed his inability to hide the impact of what he was hearing for the first time. He could feel Cho Chan's penetrating gaze.

"No," he said. "I'm just new to this job, as you can see."

He lowered his head, remembering the secret White House files and hearing an inner voice repeating "Circular Error Probable." Missile accuracy. CEP ten. Eliminating polar bias would end the arms race once and for all. If what this man said was true, the President was playing games with him. Why was he hearing this from a foreigner? He raised his head.

"A comet six hundred million kilometers away, and it's still a secret?"

"Until someone else confirms it," Chan said.

"Or a CEP of ten meters has been achieved," Dennis continued, almost to himself. "Can you tell me who can verify what you say?"

"Your Defense Department, surely."

"Another scientist?"

Chan hesitated before speaking. "Pardon me, Doctor, but as a guest in your country there are certain restrictions I've agreed to."

"047?"

Chan nodded. "My visa is specific. No exchanges—"

"Nothing's exchanged. You're telling me. It's one way. Let 047 be my problem."

Chan thought a moment, then smiled. "Dr. Franz," he answered.

"From Laval?"

"Yes."

Chan leaned forward to put out the cigarette. "Dr. Franz was in on the development of the Lapierre Electrographic-Nine," he said. "And Dr. Horowitz at the Weizmann Institute. David Horowitz."

Dennis recognized the name. "Horowitz," he repeated. "Israel. And the comet?"

"Always a possibility. But we know of it only indirectly. Until we have proof, it is a rumor, and who knows where it might be after six months? All I can say now is that the Soviets have the equipment to know. If a comet exists, detection at this time is a major scientific feat."

Second only to a Circular Error Probable of ten meters, Dennis thought.

"On the other hand," Cho Chan continued, "it may be a bluff, a diversion from their bias work. This is in the political realm, and our capabilities at Nanking go only so far even with a neighbor."

Dennis felt a sinking sensation in his stomach. A bluff. A rumor. In twenty minutes he had compiled more hard data than in two hours spent with the files of the President of the United States.

"I obviously have a lot of work ahead of me," he said. "I appreciate what you've told me, Doctor. Please see me if you would like your visa extended."

"Once out of the country, can I come back in?" Chan asked with a wide smile.

"As long as I have nothing to exchange, you have my word on it," Dennis said. "May I call on you again?"

"By all means."

As Chan rose to leave, Dennis cut short the handshake to ask, "Oh, Doctor, where did you say Sarantof was doing his bias work?"

"I didn't."

"But you do know."

"Why, yes. It's no secret. The complex at Riga."

AT TEN O'CLOCK, Dennis stood before the presidential chief of staff. In his private room adjacent to the Oval Office, Ron Pryor pumped and counted leg strokes from atop a shining exercise bike. He brushed aside his agitated visitor's demand that they call back the adviser's first report.

"It's a sham," Dennis shouted over the whirring wheel. "A damned embarrassment."

Pryor pointed to a red Queen Anne chair. He stopped pedaling and wiped his face with a towel wrapped around his neck.

"Easy, Doctor," he said, out of breath. "Who's embarrassed?"

"I am," Dennis said, refusing the offer to sit.

"What could possibly embarrass you?"

"I submitted trash I'm ashamed of to the Secretary of Defense."

"Oh, he doesn't read it. Relax. No harm done."

"I got more information from a colleague in ten minutes than from an afternoon with the President's secret files. You had me go through an exercise. For what?"

Pryor pulled off his damp T-shirt.

"Doctor, I read your memo."

"Death beam, for chrissake. Was that meant to comfort the President? You knock out Riga to make up for the ambassador's death?"

"Don't be silly."

"Silly, huh. Does the President know the Soviets are screwing around with the earth's magnetic field?" Dennis asked, clenching his fists.

"Yes, of course," came the calm reply.

"Does he know they may have discovered an errant comet?"

"Do you?" Pryor got off the machine. "Have you discovered another comet?" Dennis's face reddened at the question. Pryor continued to wipe the sweat from his face and neck. "Dr. Covino, you did what you were asked to do. Any new information should be properly filed. The President will be briefed on anything of importance."

"Who determines importance?" Dennis shot back.

"I do. Now calm down. What do you want me to tell you? Your feelings are hurt because your first assignment was routine, is that it?"

Pryor went to a wall closet and put on a new shirt. Dennis followed him across the room.

"Look," he said, "either you don't care that your secret files are a joke, or all your intelligence is over at the Pentagon. I know nothing. I will not be embarrassed again by a foreigner knowing more than I do."

"A foreigner?"

"Dr. Cho Chan, a Nobel astronomer, who tried for three months to tell me what I learned this morning."

"Is he on the 047 list?" Pryor asked.

"Who the hell cares? He has more information than your damn Beta-X."

"He's also nondomestic."

"Riga is a scapegoat."

Pryor showed no sign of hearing the charge. He moved toward his desk. ''What did you learn?'' he asked.

''Oh, you are interested.''

''Of course.''

''According to Cho Chan, Soviet jamming has been halted because they may have picked up an object near Jupiter. A possible comet.''

''We've heard that rumor before, haven't we?''

''Where was that in those files that never leave the White House? That are supposed to help the President?''

''There's a lag,'' Pryor admitted. ''We're still compiling Army reports.''

''A three-year lag?''

''It's been worse.''

''Do you really expect my complicity in firing on an inactive Soviet radio complex?''

''All we want is a clear report, a recap of what we have on file, in case Congress becomes curious. It is an election year.''

Pryor turned away as if in search of something to hold. He flexed his hands tightly behind his head, then moved forward in the chair. ''Doctor, what do you think is going on at Riga?''

''Nothing.''

''Nothing?''

''I'll take six-month-old intelligence over your three-year-old secret files any time.''

''That's a stupid thing to say.''

''Is it? Riga is shut down.''

''And what does that tell you?''

''A high-powered radio complex is turned off because a mission has been accomplished. Not because some Red Jedi warriors have zapped a friend of the President's. If they spotted a new comet, they'd shut down power.''

"And so what if they have?"

"We might want to know where it is, if it's going to light up the sky." Dennis caught his breath in time to know he was being baited. "I'm going to find out."

"Oh, are you?" The chief of staff tapped his fingers noisily on the green desk blotter and stared at Dennis. "Well, that is your job," he said. "But let me tell you something. If you come into this office like a wild man again, I'll personally bounce your ass the hell back to the hills where you came from. I brought you here. Don't forget it."

Dennis held his ground. "You make it sound like a favor," he said. "For the record, you called me. You've got yourself an adviser, not another office-holder."

"Okay." Pryor waved a hand to concede the point.

"You may be the official White House bouncer. I don't care. But if you think you're protecting the President by withholding information from me, it won't work. I'm going to try to confirm what Cho Chan told me. If what he says is true, we may have problems the President needs to know about right away."

"Problems at Riga?"

"Problems right here, for God's sake! You can tell Snelling I'm disregarding 047. If he wants to fire me, okay. This place is so filled with secrets that my days are numbered anyway. I'm not being told everything here. Maybe I can get the facts he needs elsewhere."

Dennis turned to leave. As he did, Pryor jumped from his chair.

"Wait," he called. "You will be fired. I could do it right now. What do you want?"

Dennis took a step closer to him and studied a face he did not trust. "I can work inside or outside," he said. "But I won't be caged by a presidential order because someone around here wants to start a war. There may be a comet out there. An uncharted one is a potential menace. I need to know what the Russians have found.''

Pryor stared back. ''Not a comet,'' he said, pinching the ends of his mouth. ''They've found a CEP of ten meters. They've come up with a way to defeat magnetic-field resistance so that ICBMs can glide in from east to west. Riga has given them a new accuracy on missile firing over the pole.'' He shrugged. ''They can drop a nuclear warhead within a few meters of any target they choose.''

''If it's true,'' Dennis corrected.

''Shall we make believe it isn't? Or shall we wait till it's too late?''

''Where's that in the White House file?'' Dennis asked.

Pryor's answer was his silence.

''At the Pentagon,'' Dennis guessed.

''They've confirmed the bias work. The President's been meeting weekly with the Joint Chiefs on it. The Israeli arms deal calls for secret countermeasures.''

''Secret from me?''

''Who do you think you are?''

''I am not the resident asshole. Why have me go through the motions with an incomplete Riga file?''

Pryor looked up from the floor. ''I told you it was routine.''

''You wanted my blessing?''

''I told you what we wanted. A report. Something official for Congress.''

''A disinterested third party. I see. Who would argue with an expert? Someone who agrees we have to show the Russians how tough we are. Before they land the first punch.''

''That's closer to the truth than you know.''

''Since you're dispensing truth, you must be right.'' Dennis's heart was pounding. He was being used, an unsuspecting plant who was expected to grease his assigned wheel in a plan to provoke a Soviet response. He cleared his throat.

"Mr. Pryor, you've made a terrible mistake. The installations at Riga are already targeted, aren't they?"

"It's a military operation, and it's in the works."

"That's not the mistake I mean."

"Oh?"

"You're wrong if you think I'm a disinterested third party."

"Doctor—"

"I know. It's in the works. 047 makes it none of my business. Check with the Pentagon, then play make-believe with Congress."

"It's no longer a matter of science," Pryor insisted. "And there's no comet, for chrissake. You said so yourself."

"But if you're wrong about why Riga is silent, then no countermeasures are needed."

Pryor's eyes darted back and forth from Dennis to a corner bookcase.

"What problems could a comet cause?" he asked at last.

"In the first place, I've never heard of keeping a comet a secret. Chan told me the Soviets have orbiting telescopes that could spot one long before we even knew where to look. If one comes close before we're able to track it, it could start a panic."

"You told us in Colorado that wasn't possible."

"I've been wrong before."

"I'll remind the President."

Dennis could sense another brush-off in the words and in the way Pryor fixed his eyes on him. "Let me get what I can on Riga," he said, "from scientists. Give me time to get this straight before any buttons are pushed."

"We have all we need."

"Then why don't you sound convinced?"

Dennis waited for a reply. He had already made up his mind to see Dr. Franz in Canada. Pryor's cooperation would make that easier, but even without it he was prepared to disobey a direct order to remain "disinterested."

Finally, Pryor sat up in his chair, his back straight and his eyes intent.

"I'll give you two weeks," he said. "No more. The President is all set to announce the deal before Thanksgiving. It's in the fire."

"The election?"

"That's right. The Israeli deal goes with the reelection statement. November twenty-third. He won't allow a word of it to be changed." Pryor paused. "Dennis, your swearing-in had an oath. To serve the President. What I'm going to say puts us both on thin ice. Give me a report on Riga in two weeks. One copy, just to me. Confirm a comet or drop it."

"Agreed."

"I'll cover you on 047. Just tell me where you're going and who you'll see. We count on your discretion. After two weeks, I don't want to hear any more about a comet."

"You'll be the first to know," Dennis said.

"I'll be the only one to know. Check in with me." His voice trailed off as Dennis reached the door. He looked up to add, "If the boss finds out about this, we'll both be out on our ass."

Chapter Six

A chill north wind slapped Dennis's face as he left the cab
and mounted the steps to the hotel. The dry snow
crunched loudly under his feet. He could see the late
afternoon's first lights flickering within Québec's majes-
tic Château Frontenac, a welcoming granite beacon, and
in the distance he could hear the ice floes churning below
in the angry St. Lawrence. The hotel's lobby was an inviting haven of warm, dark wood. He moved briskly
across an ancient Oriental rug to the long reservation
counter to check in, using neglected textbook French that
the pleasant bilingual receptionist acknowledged with a
smile. An elderly porter appeared at his elbow to carry his
single bag to the ninth floor. In the elevator the man commented vacantly that monsieur would not be staying long.

Not long at all, Dennis thought. Hours, if I can help it.
He was ashamed to feel guilty about his hasty trip to see
Franz. Yet guilt it was. He felt strangely allied to Pryor,
his accomplice in a matter best kept from the President.
Was it reckless determination or merely a sense of irony
that had made him leave the country? After all, it was
Snelling's confining paranoia about nondomestic intelligence that had made the visit necessary. If only it weren't
secret, he mused, uneasy as the elevator's ancient arrow
clicked nine. He stepped out, following the old porter.

Ever since his arrival at the tiny provincial airstrip, he
had fought a feeling of being watched, a feeling that the
walk down the S-shaped corridor only amplified.

Sounds preceded their source by what seemed minutes. A woman's soft voice rose to the closing of a door somewhere. Dennis turned to look behind him at an empty corridor.

The porter handed Dennis his bag at the doorway. With a toothless grin and eyes aimed at the floor, he awaited a tip. Dennis put a dollar bill into his sparrow-like hand. Pocketing the money, the old man nodded. "M'sieur."

"Mercy," Dennis pronounced.

Inside, he phoned Dr. Normand Franz at Laval University. To his dismay, Franz had to be reminded of their dinner appointment at the Château. "Shadow," Franz called it, in a hard-driving English. He would be over in half an hour. The professor's voice sounded distracted and distant, as if his colleague's invitation had come at a bad time. Dennis lowered the phone, wondering if there was ever a good time to disobey a presidential order. He dismissed the thought, charging it to a slight case of nerves in a new surrounding.

He showered quickly, then watched a youthful tele-vised couple in camp-counselor blazers skip through the day's headlines. CBC News flashed a clip of Colorado Governor David Henderson addressing a crowd in Houston—Dallas? The candidate, a Kennedy look-alike, was scolding the incumbent for rearming the Persian Gulf at a time when dialogue was needed. His candidacy would "open doors," bring stability, and assure continued prosperity. All at the same time. With a jabbing finger, the governor pressed the crowd to help him bring a "changing of the guard" to Washington. For an instant, Dennis wondered what it would be like to serve his boss's opponent. The camera panned to a wildly applauding crowd.

The sound of a door closing outside brought him suddenly to his feet. He listened for voices or footsteps. Silence. Shrugging off the now-silly feeling that he was some kind of spy, he snapped off the television, grabbed the bilingual "Do Not Disturb" sign from the dresser, and opened the door to place it on the doorknob.

He had left Washington only three hours ago for this one-day trip north. Only Ron Pryor, Sandi, and his secretary knew his destination. Still, he felt watched and uneasy. He flopped onto the too-soft bed and stared at a network of ceiling cracks that spread like nerve endings. Would this trip fill in the blanks on Riga? Could its risks justify the secrecy?

He had never met Dr. Franz, Laval's famous physicist, yet his new directory had confirmed Chan's words that this was the man to see. Informal, unpredictably independent, and well connected with the scientific community that was officially off-limits to American colleagues, Franz's specialty was astro-optics. If anyone knew what Soviet scientists had in their sights, it would be Franz.

THE PHONE RANG, announcing Franz's arrival in the lobby. Dennis took the elevator and crossed the lobby toward a tall figure standing at the main desk.

"Dr. Franz," he asked. The figure turned quickly. With a polite but puzzled look, the husky stranger conveyed an apology in rapid French.

"Yes, Dr. Covino," said a quiet voice from behind. Franz rose from the couch where he had watched the faux pas with bemused detachment. "Ici Docteur Franz," he said, extending a bony hand. "You'll excuse that fellow's surprise. He's waiting for a hockey player." Franz chuckled good-naturedly. The two men moved to the hotel's dining room.

Dr. Franz looked fortyish, his tall frame capped by a bush of curly ashen hair. A raincoat draped over his long forearm covered a wrinkled gray suit that was more used to being hung than to being worn. The pair sat at a corner table softly lit by the glow of a copper-topped lantern. Dennis gazed around the crowded dining room.

"Expecting someone else?" Franz asked.

"No." Caught off guard by the remark coming from a man who appeared more like the house detective than a scientist, Dennis repeated, "No."

"There's someone who seems to know you." Franz tilted his head toward a table across the room. "Over there." He whistled discreetly. "Not bad."

Dennis turned to notice a man and a woman seated at the table, quietly finishing their meal. The woman returned a sideward smile in their direction. Was it his imagination, or was she distracted by their presence?

"She's been eyeing one of us," Franz added. "Or the wine rack."

"No one I know," Dennis said.

A waiter arrived, blocking the view between tables, and Franz turned to the wine list, ordering a Riesling with the boyish excitement of a man on the town.

"Are you married?" he asked with offhanded curiosity.

"No."

"Ever been?"

"Never."

"I was." Franz grinned. "Until yesterday. Today the divorce is final. My first day of freedom, and I'm dining with a man." His expression fell. "Grizzly damn business. Grizzly. Two beatup losers, three mixed-up kids, and three fattened lawyers later, it's final."

"You sound relieved."

"I am, but we're not here to celebrate my liberation. How can I help you?"

"First I'd like confirmation on what Dr. Cho Chan has told me about a comet," Dennis said, welcoming the cordial invitation.

"A comet? I don't know anything about comets. Aren't you the expert?"

"Cho Chan mentioned your work on the Lapierre Electrographic-Nine for the Russians."

"For the French," Franz corrected. "Have they found a comet? Small wonder. With that piece, they could spot the reflection of Voyager 2 out beyond Uranus."

"Is that true?"

"Absolutely. The Nine is to radio astronomers what Galileo's telescope was to seventeenth-century star-gazers. Incredible. Whatever you heard from Chan about the Electrographic-Nine is true."

"You were in on its development."

"A consultant," Franz said. "That's right. I verified some optics for Professor Lapierre four years ago. Then we lost touch."

"Can you tell me if the Soviets have the thing in orbit?"

"For a fact, no. But if they've spotted a comet with it, it's probably in earth orbit." He paused, lowering his brows. "Have you fellows found a comet?"

"No," Dennis admitted.

"Then they may have beaten you to the punch, huh?"

"It's possible."

The wine arrived. Franz tasted it with ceremony. He smiled his satisfaction with its bouquet and greenish-white color, then signaled the waiter to pour.

"Dr. Covino, if the Reds have spotted a comet, why haven't they been crowing about it?" he asked.

"I have a better question," Dennis replied. "Why have they been silent at Riga?"

Franz smacked his moistened lips.

"That is a better question. Picking up a stray comet would make me shut off magnetic-field work too."

"What do you mean?"

"As a precaution."

"A precaution?"

"You better believe it. Riga's signals have been punching large holes in the magnetosphere for years. Thanks to them, we now have a wobbly magnetic field that they've been changing at will." Franz waved his fingers in a fishtail motion. "Ask a transatlantic pilot where magnetic north is this month." He smiled.

"And now it's turned off," Dennis said, thinking aloud. "Would they close down if they suspected a close apparition?"

"They'd be crazy not to. That blanket is full of holes. Every one is an open door inviting possible damage. Cosmic, gamma rays, meteorites, who knows what else could come crashing through?"

"A comet?" Dennis inserted.

Franz twisted his face oddly. "Even a comet," he said. "But you tell me, what comet comes so close as to pose a threat?"

"One deflected by Jupiter."

"Doctor, what's this got to do with Russian cameras?"

Dennis sighed, unsure of his answer. "Maybe nothing," he said. "Tell me, could an Electrographic-Nine in orbit show a comet-size object six hundred million kilometers away?"

"Easily. As I said, the Nine could show you car headlights on Venus if..."

"If?"

Franz cracked a smile. "If you knew there was a Buick on Venus."

"That's what I thought," Dennis said, sensing a dead end.

"Dr. Covino, there's no longer a problem in seeing an object anywhere there's light. I mean anywhere. A proton. A red giant. The problem is knowing where to look."

"The odds," Dennis said to Franz's nod.

"The odds of catching a new light in the space between here and Jupiter? Well, you tell me."

Dennis adjusted his napkin, waiting for his embarrassment to fade. Of course, what has no light is invisible. He didn't mean to ask for a picture of nothing, but he could tell that that was just how it sounded.

"We can't take a picture until we know where to aim the camera," Franz said with diplomatic simplicity. "As for Riga, the Russians have been warned again and again. You know, in Geneva. But they go right on altering the field."

"Until now," Dennis offered.

"So I hear."

Dennis took a sip of wine. "What's your theory for the shutdown at Riga?" he asked.

"Not a comet," Franz replied gently. "I think they're toning things down until they're more sure of what your President'll do to get reelected."

"In the Gulf?"

"That's right. They're afraid of Snelling, ever since they saw him whip you Yanks into shape after the *Kennedy* fiasco. I'd say they're keeping the West guessing. Turning things off and on to see what the response will be. Showing off a bag of tricks."

"Doctor, our reports on Riga are in need of some updating. Can you give me background?"

"Background? Sure. Where to begin."

"Make believe I'm a student."

"You?" Franz laughed. "Science adviser to the President of the United States, a student? I'm flattered."

"Don't be. Just start at the beginning."

Franz emptied his glass and poured himself another.

"Riga is the brainchild of Marshal Dubrov, a counterintelligence officer from the Stalin days. He set up shop with a staff of four hundred in 1975, I think it was, with a lab all to himself. He was given all the resources to construct a master center of radio communications. Two centers, really. Both located at separate sites near Riga on the Baltic. One center receives radio signals from all over the world. The other transmits and interferes with radio signals. It's the largest network of frequency variable waves we know of."

"Anywhere?" Dennis interrupted.

"Anywhere. You said it. Riga can monitor the whole known spectrum. It listens in on every signal from a country-and-western station in Edmonton to talk between your space shuttle astronauts."

"Have you ever seen the complex?"

"No one's seen it since '88. They have a list of only twenty or so people who are even allowed on the grounds. Everyone else is shot on sight."

Dennis watched Franz's eyes carefully, wondering how much of this report would be fact, how much editorial.

"This is only phase one," Franz continued. "You used to be bothered by your Moscow embassy being tapped. Remember the microphones behind the seal? Even the new building was wired for sound. Sending and receiving. That was a Dubrov production too. Then a new program extended the capability to all embassies, even ours. They remembered Canada's help to you Yanks when Iran took over your embassy. All conversations are recorded for study in Moscow."

"But we have jammers, signal scramblers."

"Oh, yes," Franz agreed. "We can counter this phase. We jump all over the radio band and escape the ear. It's become a safe game. Fortunately, unselective receiving is very expensive. So in 1982 they put all their money on transmitting. Dubrov's transmitters beam in on a signal, any signal apparently, and screw it up, delay it, even change the damn direction." Franz leaned closer, lowering his voice. "That's what they did to the *Kennedy*. You remember that near-collision of two Tridents off the coast of Greece?"

Dennis nodded.

"Riga interference made each invisible to the other. Only on-board sonar averted a nuclear accident. And the unexplained Red Alerts at NORAD during Carter's time—"

"Riga?"

"Yes. It was called computer error. I understand it took two weeks to debug, to establish another frequency alley."

The stories came back in headline form to Dennis. The near-misses, the accidents, the studies his Institute had prepared, the official explanations announced to buy correction time. He remembered Trusedale's death. At the embassy. And the driver Larry Jerard's words: "Radiation poisoning." Was Riga really the President's target number one for personal revenge, or was it chosen out of righteous anger? Were the Russians just cooling off a hot situation with their silence?

"How about space?" Dennis asked. "You mentioned astronauts. Riga carried into earth orbit?"

"And beyond. Their dishes are not as large as ours in the West, but they have the power to pinpoint and interfere with extraterrestrial frequencies, yes."

Dennis recalled the President's recent warning to the Presidium about jamming space shuttle missions. Snelling had come one step from declaring an ultimatum after two astronauts returned from SkyLab Da Vinci with nausea lasting for days.

Franz inhaled, looking around the room as though impatient to order dinner. Dennis, with no appetite, tried to make sense out of what Franz was telling him.

"So what we have is a radio center capable of setting up a party line between earth orbit and Houston," he concluded.

"Party line," Franz chuckled. "That's good." His face suddenly softened, his expression grave. "It's more than capable," he said. "Riga is a proven veteran."

"Dubrov then moved on to magnetic-field experiments?" Dennis asked.

Franz shook his head, eyeing the approaching waiter. "Not Dubrov," he explained. "His successor. Dubrov died five years ago or so. I will have the trout, please."

As the waiter jotted down the order, Dennis couldn't help admiring the scientist's ability to change subjects without missing a beat. His stomach churned, not from hunger, but from nerves.

"Shrimp salad," he said. "That's all, thanks."

"So that's phase one, Doctor," Franz continued, folding his long arms on the table. His look awaited further questions.

"When did Sarantof come on board?" Dennis obliged.

"In 1982. By that summer, Riga's signals began playing with the electromagnetic field, throwing off navigational equipment. They even threw themselves off at first, with forays into Norwegian waters. And we have proof at Laval that Riga has also killed millions of migrating birds. The towers jam some kind of biological clock in terns and storks. They're beamed off course and land hundreds of kilometers from food supplies. You recall the kamikaze drop off East Africa last winter? Thousands of migrating flocks falling from the sky over Port Sudan."

Dennis's face paled.

Hesitantly, Franz added, "Some of our biologists believe Riga jamming has done the same damage to dolphins and whales."

Dennis now felt a tightening knot in the pit of his stomach. He shifted in his chair to relieve the discomfort.

"What are they experimenting with?" he asked.

"We suspect they're developing a series of frequencies aimed at altering human metabolism. They've run experiments to throw off the internal synchronization between humans and the earth's rotation."

"Like jet lag?" Dennis was now visibly queasy. The question came out painfully, and he winced as Franz went on.

"A bit. We think it could lead to some kind of mind control. Phase one is the easy part. Phase two is dirty. These are not nice people. They conduct experiments from time to time on selected small populations. Signals beamed on villages, in Afghanistan mostly. We have more than one defector who claims he's been to remote villages where people are suffering from nausea, blurred vision, and wounds that don't heal. The Russians tell us it's malnutrition and that we should send more wheat. They're still compiling proof on most of this at the Weizmann Institute."

"Israel?"

"Yes. Dr. Horowitz. Do you know him?"

Dennis shook his head. "Just the name."

"Bright man. He's the man to talk to about Riga these days. That is, if you can find him. No one seems to know where he's been for over a year."

"That's strange."

"Strange. Or simply your CIA," Franz said. "He's been on and off that payroll. At any rate, he's among the missing."

Dennis sighed his frustration, then said, "Dr. Chan said Riga has changed polar bias to the point of having achieved a Circular Error Probable of ten meters."

"You mean for ICBMs?" A hint of surprise crossed Franz's face. "Could be. That's military intelligence. All I know is they've stopped transmitting. If it's because of the bias problem, Horowitz would know. If it's because of a new comet"—he smiled, seeing his food arrive—"well, that's your specialty, isn't it?" Franz hesitated before starting his meal. "You know, a man could lose his appetite talking about this."

"I appreciate what you've told me."

"I'd feel a lot better if it wasn't news to you. You guys in the States don't share anything anymore."

"We've gone far afield of comets, haven't we?" Dennis said.

Franz smiled assuringly. "Well, it's really not to worry. If the Russians are tracking anything with an Electrographic-Nine and it's coming our way, whatever it might be won't be visible for months."

"And when it is visible," Dennis thought out loud, "it won't be anybody's secret. It won't be a Tunguska surprise."

"A what?"

"Tunguska. A comet collision in Russia. No warning. A bright sky, then a nuclear explosion."

"Nuclear? From a ball of ice?"

The repeated word knocked Dennis out of his trancelike mood.

"No. Not nuclear, of course." His words came slowly. "But like a nuclear event." Like a nuclear event. The statement echoed in front of his mind for the remainder of the meal.

DENNIS EXCUSED HIMSELF from the table early and went up to his room where for several fitful hours he sorted out at least two things Franz had made clear; not certain, but clear. Riga was silent because the Soviets held a secret. Were they tracking a comet? Or were they crowning years of research at Riga with an endgame nuclear threat?

He kicked off his shoes and began making notes at the desk, scribbling on scraps of paper, shifting them like odd-shaped pieces of an enormous puzzle. He immediately scratched out his colleague's bag-of-tricks theory and tossed that paper to the floor.

He got up to pace in his stocking feet.

If Riga contained radio telescopes, that would support the extraterrestrial theory he couldn't shake off. Only high-altitude reconnaissance could confirm the unmistakable shape of concave ears tuned to the silent stars. Was that worth recommending, worth the risk of another Soviet attack on spy planes? And if pictures revealed no evidence of telescopes, would that mean Riga was being retooled to make way for warheads, as Franz had hinted?

Silence was the enemy. Silence on both sides. The Iron Curtain had turned into a more secure metal— lead. Wasn't that what they used to line coffins? Iron to lead, in the same sad progression of bronze to iron. Space-age man still peered out through a helmet onto landscapes only vigilance and force made his for as long as the will to fight and die remained strong from generation to generation. Politicians held the torch high, a torch men like him and Franz helped to light. *Plus ça change,* Father Maxwell used to say. While Leonardo's fragile pen sketched details of the human body, his patron clamored for an underwater war machine, an ultimate weapon that advisers assured him would bring peace: the feasible submarine, promising dominance and peace. Leonardo's triumph now cruised the oceans, and more than one was certainly on a silent course toward the Baltic.

He understood the President's direction, but his own was not so certain. Although he hadn't mentioned it to Sandi, he had entertained thoughts of quitting, of returning to Colorado. But as long as the possibility of a comet loomed, he would stay and dig for answers. Even if the questions seemed foolish and brought only ridicule or half-answers, he had to find out what was going on at Riga. A death beam? An innocent observatory now silent? Or a tracking station alerted to a new Tunguska?

He put away his notes and before going to bed made two vows: to look into his files on the Tunguska Fall, an eighty-three-year-old documented comet collision with a Siberian village, and to find David Horowitz at all costs.

Chapter Seven

Dennis circled the twenty-third on his November desk calendar. Thirteen days to go before the President's re-election kick-off. Less than two weeks to contact the elusive Dr. Horowitz. It was proving to be a time-consuming task. So far, three calls directly to the Weizmann Institute had produced nothing. "The doctor is not here," a distant voice announced, each time with less patience. "Yes, I'll take your number." Even his White House connection didn't help open the line. Like any other bureaucrat, he left a message.

He checked the 047 "Secure Scientists" list again and found David Horowitz's name under two headings. He sent two unanswered cables to the Israeli scientist's listed home address. A fourth call to Weizmann brought a prepared reply from a new voice. "I am instructed to tell you, sir, to contact your State Department's Agency for International Security. Dr. Horowitz is not here."

State Department, Dennis thought. A strange forwarding address for a nuclear scientist. Agency for International Security? He called Richard Lohmann at the White House, only to learn that his mentor was at the President's side in Cincinnati helping to dedicate a string of newly opened arms plants. Each campaign sally tapped a rotating pool of administration officials on call to accompany the President. It was Lohmann's week to travel.

If his boss could collect a team, so could he. Early Tuesday, he called a meeting of his top staff and asked each department head for an hour a day of extra work. Their bowed heads and sideways glances told him the request came as an unwelcome break from past practice. The seven men and four women filling the main conference room sat silently taking notes while he stood to outline his dilemma.

In two weeks he would file a second report for the President. He needed to know exactly what Riga was capable of, and he wanted their best guesses on what could make it inoperative. He watched eleven sets of eyes scan the room apprehensively as he announced assignments. Fielding and Marsh would explore magnetic fields: "What confirmed changes in the magnetosphere could be attributed to artificial forces?" Hawley and Graves were in charge of radio technology: "What are Riga's precise jamming capabilities?" To Swanson and Keyes went the biological assignment: "What documented mass physiological alterations are on file anywhere?" Ecological concerns fell to Dr. Levin: "What atmospheric changes can be traced to Riga?" Fortes would report on the current status of the Circular Error Probable. Reynolds, Johnson, and Myerling, whose specialties shielded them from direct research, were responsible for synthesizing all reports.

Dennis fielded an objection from Dr. Keyes.

"Doctor, excuse me. When you say on file 'anywhere,' do you mean—"

"Yes, I do. Use any source that will help."

"And 047?" Keyes asked.

"On this you can forget it."

Dennis then briefed them on what he knew of Riga, telling Swanson to investigate the ambassador's death and ordering a profile of Dr. Sarantof from Jan Fortes.

''What I'm calling for,'' he announced, ''is a complete picture. My first report was preliminary. This time, we'll get it right. I'm sorry to be retracing steps. It serves me right for not having your help from the start. I'm still learning.''

Jan Fortes waited until the others had left.

''You'll have to excuse our lack of enthusiasm, Doctor,'' she said. ''We're just used to a looser rein.''

''I can tell.''

''Seymour's style was more laid back.''

Dennis smiled. ''This is a real tight ship, huh?''

''Deadlines haven't been our specialty,'' she said.

Her half-apology revealed a desire to play by more demanding rules.

''Do you know if Seymour White left any of his files here?'' he asked.

''I'll check.''

''I'm curious to see anything around the time of his trip to Spain.''

''To Spain?''

''Yes. Maybe last spring?'' Dennis studied the puzzled look on his colleague's face. ''What's wrong?'' he asked.

''I never knew he went to Spain.''

''See what you can find.''

HE SPENT THE NEXT TWO DAYS punching the directory's buttons for the Smithsonian Astrophysical Observatory in Cambridge—Cometsville—and received yards of printout sheets describing the coordinates of all verified comets reported in the last twelve months. A cross-check revealed nothing new, nothing unexpected. He called back for twenty-four months, just to be sure. Apollo objects, meteors, satellite debris, asteroids: all their trackings fell under his gaze with predictable results. All plotted, all charted. God's in His heaven, all's right with the world.

Dennis called a colleague at Mauna Kea in Hawaii. "All's well," reported the volcanic watchtowers that enjoyed one of the earth's most favorable viewing sites. The same at busy Kitt Peak in Arizona. Nothing new. Nothing to report. The Jet Propulsion Laboratory in California assured him that the heavens were presently "clean," devoid of any mystery. Dennis was rankled by the low ranking that comets held there. "First December's solar eclipse, then back to quasars, then Air Force, then the Army," he was reminded. Fifth on the list was comets. Encke expected within twenty months. Don't call us, we'll call you.

A Mr. Warren from the Agency for International Security returned his call a week later. David Horowitz was officially on assignment. Could the science adviser leave a message? Dennis checked his anger, left the number, and then asked where the scientist was. Warren repeated, "On assignment, sir. I am not authorized to say more at this time."

Dennis hung up. So much for instant communication. What was it Mark Twain had said about the first telephone system? "Amazing, but what will Indiana have to say to New York?" An amazing array of silicon chips surrounding him, a switchboard of touchtone immediacy, plugged in and flashing, providing contact but no information.

One call from Dr. Loren Gray at the U.S. Naval Observatory supplied no lead on Horowitz but a guarded belief that Riga contained a radio telescope. Another rumor? Gray called it "a working assumption" and suggested the adviser check it out further with the Pentagon.

The next day, Dennis did just that. And waited for a cleared response. Two weeks, he was told.

He knew it was unlikely that a center filled with radio transmitters would also house a telescope. Observatories prize their isolation, their closeness only to clear skies. A radio telescope on the Baltic Sea was an anomaly. Not the first he had encountered since coming to Washington, but another puzzle. He tried to imagine a fogbound observatory and would have dismissed the idea but for the memory of Tycho Brahe's primitive sixteenth-century observatory on an island in the North Sea. Johannes Kepler's sometime-mentor was a mad, dogmatic tyrant whose mathematics the young student had unwound and spun into the three basic laws of planetary motion. Kepler's calculations helped explain the orbits of comets—from an isolated rock in the north. After four hundred years, was there another advance about to emerge from those same distant mists?

Not from this office. Dennis shrugged. He shook himself out of the hazy past and ordered his secretary to pull a file for him. While he waited for Richard Lohmann to return his calls, he reread the notes on Tunguska.

On the morning of June 30, 1908, a piece of the sky about the size of New York's Shea Stadium fell on the Russian village of Tunguska. Farmers noticed to their horror an enormous fireball falling to the horizon. An explosion followed that instantly incinerated two thousand square kilometers of forest. The blast sent an atmospheric shock wave twice around the world. On July first and second, London was covered by the explosion's fine dust, soot that literally turned day into night.

Survivors of the Tunguska "event" reported a great noise, like stones falling from the sky; a hot hurricane wind; a mushroom cloud; and an earth that trembled with

Old Testament fury. Years later, when the dust returned to the atmosphere and officials were permitted in to inspect ground zero, they found physical devastation and human trauma, which they attributed to every cause from God's wrath to a spectacular extraterrestrial accident.

Eighty-three years later, most scientists agreed with the latter explanation. A part of Encke's comet had struck the earth at that time and at that location. Only the object's orbital angle and the earth's rotation had saved the city of St. Petersburg from total destruction. A dense collection of ice and dust weighing over a million tons had been captured by the earth's gravity, which then pulled the steaming mass to the planet's surface at a speed of 117,000 kilometers an hour. On impact, the ice melted, the dust was dispersed upward, and everything in the way was shaken or destroyed. Tunguska was indeed an extraterrestrial accident, a one-in-one-hundred-thousand shot. In 1908, the earth was in the way of cosmic physics, and that tiny inhabited dot in central Russia suffered the powerful consequences.

The only difference between this fall and a twentieth-century one-megaton nuclear blast was the aftermath. At Tunguska there was no impact crater and no radioactive fallout. After more than eighty years the earth had healed itself. The errant earthgrazer had collided, then vanished in a puff of smoke like some cosmic magic trick. To future generations of scientists was left the task of piecing together what had happened at Tunguska. In the meantime, others were busy developing their own magic, in the form of nuclear fission.

The chances of another Tunguska event were one hundred thousand to one. But in the age of nuclear weapons, could a like event be mistaken for a nuclear first strike? In the eight minutes between nuclear detonation and programmed retaliation, would the world's leaders—would Snelling—agree to suspend the final holocaust until scientists could determine that it was not a comet fall?

He closed the file at the sound of a knock on the door. His secretary came in to remind him of his pledge to leave the office by five o'clock and asked, "Will you take a call from William Hendley?"

Dennis glanced at his watch: 5:07.

"No," he answered. "Ask him to call back."

"He's called before."

"Have him call back, please. Heather, any luck on reaching Richard Lohmann?"

She shook her head.

"Good night," he said.

Before leaving the office for home, he left another message at Lohmann's White House number.

Hendley—the Wizard of Oz, he thought, inching his way through Georgetown while "Somewhere Over the Rainbow" played on FM. What could Hendley be on his trail for? Lobbying? Not likely, since his new position meant hands-off with government contractors and their agents. A new scheme? More wonders? Hendley and his secrets. God, how this crazy city loves secrets. Everyone has a data processor and no one has data. Evidently, power lasts as long as secrets can be kept, stored as in a battery. Keep what you know to yourself. Divulge only what's been cleared. You stay charged until you've opened up, losing power as you use it.

He turned his lights on, defeating dusk on the Key Bridge behind a slow-moving line of commuters. Are some people really able to unwind on the way home? He couldn't see how, as disappointment tugged at him, weighing him down.

IN TEN DAYS HIS BUSY STAFF had come up with nothing substantial on Riga. On November 20, they were still running into the same roadblocks that he was hitting in a State Department runaround. He felt outmatched. Secrecy, baptized "security," kept all the doors locked and unlabeled, and this made him angry. Angry at Pryor and disappointed at Lohmann.

He remembered Lohmann's advice to stay in his science pasture, write his routine reports. But something wasn't routine about Riga, or about the President's Israeli connection. Why was it none of his business? He recalled with bitterness Pryor's question: Who do you think you are?

If the nondomestic Horowitz could come through, he would serve the answer to Pryor on a plate. Meanwhile, Pryor's deadline was three days away, and the chief of staff had not bothered to call about the second report. That promised report was a dead end—like the White House files.

He arrived home exhausted again. After another quiet dinner, Sandi kept her distance while he added some notes to his new book. At eleven o'clock he went upstairs. Sandi was reading in bed. Dennis blamed himself for the silent treatment he'd been getting since they had moved to Falls Church. To Sandi had fallen the chore of setting up house, arranging for the yard work, and keeping a light in the window and a meal in the stove until he got home. She was killing time at work in Senator Browning's research office till spring, when a teaching position in biology at Georgetown would be hers. They had always allowed each other room, that necessary space that two busy people require to keep from crowding each other's career world. But in the last five weeks he knew he had abused the agreement. Room was becoming distance.

He crawled into bed next to her and searched for some opening that might elicit sympathy instead of the scorn he deserved. His touch brought no response.

"Sandi, I'm getting nowhere." His voice fell to a sigh. She folded her magazine and did not reply.

"Did you hear me?" he asked.

"I heard you." Her voice was strained. "You're getting nowhere. I can tell."

"I have nothing to report to Pryor. I'm making a fool of myself and all I know is what I can't understand."

Her silence continued.

"Why does Riga have a radio telescope if it's only jamming signals, or used to?" he asked himself.

Although Sandi seemed to concentrate on the magazine, Dennis could tell it no longer held her attention. She dropped it to the floor, turned to him, and said, "Tell me what's the matter."

Dennis told her about the Tunguska fall. Not the ideal topic to regain contact, but a start. She listened with interest, but her expression showed confusion.

"Dennis, why is it so important to verify what Dr. Cho Chan told you?"

"It's only a theory."

"So why? Why suspect the worst? A new Tung—?"

"Tunguska."

"Why think of a comet collision when there's no comet?" she asked. "You didn't believe it in Colorado."

"Yes, I did."

"You did?"

"Yes. I believe in the possibility," he explained.

"Isn't that what's called a Jesuitical distinction?" she asked with a softening smile.

"I suppose so," he admitted. "Just the same, it's the possibility that keeps me alive."

"I don't understand."

Dennis turned to her face on the pillow. He brushed a wisp of hair gently from her forehead.

"There's something you should know about an old comet-seeker like me. When I first spotted a speck of light in 1971 and no one could explain to me what it was, I made it a comet. I wished it to be something no one had ever seen before. A piece of heaven all my own. And after it proved to be what I hoped it was, I wasn't happy. I was crushed. I lost what was mine.

"I spent twenty-four-hour days alone, like Doctor Faustus. Alone, and alive with a light. I never felt so alive. And when it was confirmed a new comet and given a number and my name, I was disappointed. Not because it went away forever, but because a part of me left the solar system with it, gone forever.

"All the greatest scientists have a piece of the moon named after them, dust, a crater. And none of them knows it. They were spared my vanity. I am no great scientist, and I have a piece of heaven locked in here." He tapped his heart. "This'll sound crazy," he continued, "I know what the Wise Men felt at Bethlehem. Not the stable, not a new king, but a touch I'll never feel again. It saddens me even more to know no one will feel it for thousands of years. Who will be here when any light returns? No one. And I also know why the ancients worshiped comets. Do you?"

Sandi shook her head.

"Because," he said, "because comets ruin science. They overthrow established order and throw out mathematics. Aristotle refused to believe in them. They spoiled his orderly universe, so he explained them as illusions. They didn't exist so that his world could. But people keep on seeing these intruders, and whenever anything appears that shouldn't, because our understanding says it isn't possible, we cling to the understanding like a baby to its mother. And we agree to disbelieve.

"When I was two years old, some scientists reinvented the sun at Los Alamos. A nuclear reaction all our own. We stole fire from the sun and kept it a secret at least for a few years. People still fear lights in the sky more than a man-made nuclear event. And I fear those people."

"People like the President?"

Dennis shook his head. "Even following a comet lead is 'on hold.' He doesn't want to know one way or the other."

Sandi reached over to touch his hair.

"But you have to," she said.

"Sandi, I'd love this job to be routine. We owe that to each other. We wanted Washington, and here it is, not on our terms."

"I could join a bridge club."

He smiled. "I know this agreement isn't fair. I'm working too hard, the staff is . . . has a deliberate pace. I come home just to sleep, and I can't even do that."

Sandi moved her hand across his chest. He could smell the scent of lily-of-the-valley and feel the day's tensions falling away as one finger etched tiny figure eights on his stomach.

"The President is so sure," he said. "And I'm afraid of his certainty."

"Uncertainty."

"That's what makes Cho Chan a great scientist. He can live with uncertainty. I can't sleep, so I search."

He turned his face to hers. "I search."

"And what will you find?"

"Just more uncertainty," he replied, turning and matching her touches with a gentle hand that glided to remove her silk nightgown.

THEY AWOKE EARLY and had breakfast in the large family dining room, where they talked for the first time in a week. Dennis promised to be home early that night, only to learn that it made no difference. Sandi and her friend Lisa were going to stay in the city for dinner and a show. He gulped down a sense of disappointment as she explained that the plans had been made two weeks before as a way to combat nights alone.

At the office he arranged a time-zone call list. Somewhere in academia there had to be a scientist who knew of Dr. David Horowitz. He started with MIT and Brandeis, then Fordham and Columbia. Newmarck at Princeton said he believed a Horowitz had died somewhere in the Orient in 1974. Rangoon? Plane crash? Dennis thanked the Einstein professor and made the Midwest calls: to Leventhal at the University of Chicago, to Dorian at the University of Texas. Regrets, puzzlement, and assumptions made that morning longer than any he could recall. He had lunch at his desk while he continued the unsatisfying search with calls to Cal Tech and Stanford. Nothing. Horowitz was a name and, with each call, was becoming an embarrassment.

At two-thirty his secretary announced Dr. Myerling's arrival with the staff's Riga report.

Dennis could tell from the sour look on Dr. Harold Myerling's wrinkled face that the day's frustrations were not over. Myerling approached the desk with a silent scowl and handed him a thin folder: his second report, weighing in at half a pound and, Dennis guessed, holding at most a dozen pages. Its dark blue cover sported a label that read: RIGA, FACT OR FICTION?

"A joke?" he asked the somber geologist.

"You said it. I didn't."

Myerling made no apologies and no attempt to hide his irritation at being a party to a waste of valuable time. He waited as if for permission to get back to Utah's soil erosion problems. Just then Jan Fortes appeared at the door.

"That'll be all, Harold. Thank you," Dennis said.

Without a word, Myerling passed his colleague in the doorway.

"Have a seat, Jan." Dennis gestured with the folder in his hand. As she sat, he turned to the section on Circular Error Probable. He looked at her.

"Jan, two pages?"

"We don't have the security clearances we used to have. The best I could do was a question-and-answer letter from Strategic Services. I was even lucky to get that much in writing."

"No specifications?"

"Classified."

"No oversight reports?"

"None available," she said. "I was told CEP was an Air Force matter. Top security."

"Was information any easier to get before Snelling's time?"

"Like night and day."

Dennis threw the report onto the desk in disgust.

"Damn."

"Doctor, why is this complex important to you?" Fortes asked.

"The President thinks he has all he needs on Riga. I suspect there's more. His security blanket tells me he has enough to justify military action. I think he might be wrong.''

Dr. Fortes folded her hands, looking disinterested, as though she wished she were somewhere else. ''Well, that isn't for us to say, is it,'' she said. ''We just advise.''

''Do you really believe that, as a scientist?''

''If I were a scientist, I'd be working on a grant in my laboratory. Doctor, policy isn't made here. We carry out orders.''

''And what happens to truth when information is withheld?'' He paused, answering his own question in a loud voice. ''Half-truths. No science. We play guessing games.''

Fortes lowered her eyes. After a moment, she looked up and said, ''This is all Seymour White left.'' She handed him two worn manila folders. ''A calendar, some doodles, and numbers.''

Dennis flipped through several yellow sheets torn from a legal pad and a single striped printout filled with numbers.

''What's this?'' he asked, holding up the printout sheet. Fortes leaned forward to take the paper.

''Looks like a phone number, repeated,'' she said, ''or a code. I've never seen it before.''

Dennis stared at the repeated series of numbers, a neat block of digits filling six lines. After twelve numbers, the series repeated itself down half the page. He handed the file back to Dr. Fortes.

''Run those numbers through our cross-reference decks, will you please?'' he said. ''Tell me what it is.''

''Another mystery?''

''Too damn many mysteries around here.''

''We aren't really equipped for this kind of research,'' she said defensively.

Dennis checked his anger. "I know that, Jan. This isn't an institute. I don't mean here. I mean Washington."

He sat back, swiveling his chair, and looked directly at Dr. Fortes. She smiled self-consciously.

"What was Seymour White like?" he asked.

"What was he like? He's not dead, is he?"

"No."

"He's in the hospital."

"Yes, I tried to reach him. They told me their policy says family only."

"Sounds bad off." Her dry reply made it clear she was not close to the former adviser.

"'Severe depression' is all they'd tell me," Dennis said. "How was he as a boss?"

"An odd duck. He stayed to himself and let us do pretty much as we pleased. He was—" she flapped her long fingers, searching for a word.

"Aloof?"

"Aloof. That's the word. We really ran things at our own pace."

"Until I came?"

"Until you came." She grinned.

"How'm I doing so far?" He laughed.

"Well, discounting those who placed office bets on Robinson and Switzler and who are still making believe you never came—"

"Myerling?"

"He's one. Consensus says you work too hard, you keep too much to yourself, and you answer questions with questions. On a scale from one to ten, you come in at, oh, about a four, I'd say."

"Four!"

"Seven before the Riga report," she was quick to add.

"Seven. Almost a point a week. And then the report."

He glanced at the Riga folder. Fortes was more at ease now. She spoke with the ease of a confidante. "We're used to doing our own thing," she explained. "Give us more time. Dr. White was nowhere near so organized. He hated numbers. Wendy Reynolds had to do the budget for him."

"Hated numbers?" Dennis sat up. "Yet his last file is numbers."

"Doctor, I'll break the code. And I have an idea on how to get you back up to a seven."

"You do?"

She stood up to leave. "Burn that Riga file and take us all out to lunch."

He rose with a smile. "Tomorrow," he said.

The next day, Wednesday, he treated the department heads to lunch at Victor's, on Fifteenth Street. Jan Fortes was right. His attempts to solve the Horowitz-Riga mystery had come as a shock to a system that was used to an independent pace. What made his quest automatically theirs? He needed to regroup his forces, to ease back on the reins with these temperamental specialists. After all, there is life after Riga and other projects as important as jamming. He decided to make a fresh start, just as soon as he found Horowitz.

He ordered shrimp on his secretary's recommendation, then, leaving his martini untouched, he excused himself and headed for the men's room. Ancient black and white mosaic chips covered the cracked floor. A mirror serving as one wall reflected a bank of overscrubbed stalls. A familiar pungency wafted outward from white, wall-mounted sanitary cones, whose tubing released colorless perfume into each of three urinals with IV consistency.

A large bald man in a brown tweed suit stood with his back to him in front of a noisy hand-dryer. The machine stopped. The man knocked it again, and it started up with an angry whirr that drowned out the exhaust fan overhead.

Dennis unzipped and turned his head absently toward the man, who had left the machine running and was now hunched over the middle sink. Dennis caught the man's upturning glance in the mirror. With one hand on the horizontal flushing handle, he froze at the sight of William Hendley's smiling reflection.

"Dr. Covino. What a coincidence," he said. "Wednesday really is Prince Spaghetti day." He straightened up, addressing his words to Dennis in the mirror. Dennis turned and stood by him at the sink.

"Mr. Hendley."

"Surprised?" Hendley asked.

"If you're here to lobby, you picked a hell of a place."

"Lobby? No. I couldn't even get your help when you were able to give it. I'm having more success with your successor. Lee's a sharp kid."

Dennis agreed stiffly, as the faucet sprayed his hands with lukewarm water. He moved to the hand-dryer and poked it on.

Over the loud hum, Hendley spoke. "I know it's too much to expect any thanks from you for arranging Cho Chan's visa, but now I understand you're looking for Horowitz."

"And you know how to contact him?"

"Doctor, no sarcasm, okay? Let's be more civil. My hatchet is buried. I'm just here to see friends."

"At the Pentagon?"

"That's where all the action is." Hendley smiled. "When I found out you were knocking down walls sniffing out Horowitz, I thought I'd look you up and give you some advice. Save you some trouble."

The hand-dryer fell silent.

"Doctor, don't bother looking for your man. There is no Horowitz."

Dennis stared into Hendley's eyes. The man's expression was sincere.

"It's a code name the Israelis are using," Hendley added quietly. "The man died last year."

"Do you know a Dr. Franz, from Canada?"

Hendley shook his head no.

"Ever hear of a Lapierre Electrographic-Nine camera?"

"No. Should that mean something to me?"

"How about a place called Riga?"

"I don't know what you're talking about."

"So there are limits to your international contacts."

"All I know is you're beating your head against a stone wall. There is no Horowitz." Hendley checked his tie in the mirror.

"You got that from the Soviets?" Dennis asked.

"Please. It's legit. Take it or leave it."

"Like your comet."

"That's legit too. And we'll be going after it, you'll see."

Dennis turned to leave. "Mr. Hendley, there may be a comet. But *we* are not going after it."

"Then I hope you find it fast." Hendley sighed. "Horowitz can't help, believe me."

Dennis returned to his table. The shrimp was disappointing, the conversation was falling into a stale drone of petty bitching, and seeing William Hendley had taken away what little appetite remained. The man had his nose into everything, and no two men could be farther apart. For Dennis there was no comet, but there was a Dr. Horowitz. And Hendley had gone out of his way to maintain the exact opposite with a certainty that, if it weren't so grating, would be enviable. President Snelling would be better off with Hendley as science adviser. They deserved each other.

THAT AFTERNOON, Dennis called the Israeli embassy once more. This time the conversation on both ends was less diplomatic—and shorter. Before he got past the first deputy ambassador, he had learned the Hebrew word for "drop dead." He called associates at the Pentagon, who put him on hold while they conferred with superiors. Back to State, then finally a video transmission to Richard Lohmann. The National Security Adviser, with his carnation but minus his David Niven calm, glared from the screen like a man unable to handle a sharp rise in blood pressure.

Before Dennis could say a word, Lohmann stormed, "Dennis, this is my desk. See this paper? This is my paperwork. Message slips from everywhere. Tel Aviv, State, the Pentagon. What in hell are you up to? Are you trying for the Guinness record for shortest tenure in office? Have you seen the papers?"

"What do you mean?" Dennis asked, half amused at Lohmann's histrionics.

"You've singlehandedly blown the cover off Israeli security. David Horowitz!"

"What?"

"You want the *Times* or the *Post*?" Dennis saw him reach and raise both to each side of his heated face. "David Horowitz is the code word for all Israeli intelligence in the Western Hemisphere. It says so here in the paper. Haven't you been in touch with Pryor?"

"No. I—"

"Well, he'll be in touch with you. You've torn the top off the President's security network just when he's set to announce the Israeli arms deal. You're a regular hurricane."

Dennis tried to remain calm. "I'm looking for Dr. Horowitz, the scientist," he attempted to explain.

"He's been dead for over a year, Dennis. If it was any of your business, you would have known that. His name was recycled as a security cover."

"A secret," Dennis concluded bitterly.

"Not anymore. Somehow the papers found a memo someplace and discovered that Horowitz—the real one—is dead and that the name is—was—a pipeline."

"I didn't know a thing."

"You will. Check the papers. Heads are going to roll. Get ready."

"Thanks for the warning, Richard," Dennis said sarcastically. He shut off the picture of the still-puffing security adviser.

Shit! More secrecy. What have I done? Followed a lead in search of data the President needs. And swam right into a security net. Before he could gather his thoughts, Ron Pryor was blinking on his phone deck. His voice was calm but simmering.

"Dennis. Dennis. Didn't I tell you to check in with me?"

"Check in! For chrissake, how can I keep up with you?"

"Easy now. We're controlling the situation. Did you see the papers?"

"No. I haven't seen the papers."

"We're preparing an official explanation. That's not why I called."

"Do I get an explanation?"

"On Horowitz?"

"Of course on Horowitz!"

Pryor hesitated. Dennis could imagine him reaching for a prepared release. To his surprise, the chief of staff's reply was strangely confidential.

"David Horowitz," he said, "passed away quietly in '90. At the time, the CIA advised a simple cover by keeping the name, referring to him to mean Israeli intelligence. It helped protect other sources for a while. We were about to change it anyway."

"Listen, what have I done?" Dennis asked impatiently, less interested in the background than in the verdict.

"Nothing serious. In fact it might help. That's why I called. You're to meet the President in L.A. for the re-election announcement."

"My number was drawn?"

"That's right."

"You want my picture taken with the candidate after this fiasco?"

"That's just what we want. The papers are getting the story that your Horowitz search was to give Science Department approval to the Israeli deal."

"A lie."

"Swallow it, and say nothing to the press. We'll handle it here."

Dennis did not reply. He wavered between relief and confusion. Pryor assured him that the President, while not pleased, was persuaded to see the whole affair as a pre-announcement plus if handled properly. Dennis's role was the easiest: just remain silent.

"You can really turn an ass into an asset," he asked.

Pryor chuckled. "Be in L.A. at the Marriott-Hilton tomorrow afternoon for a meeting at four. We're going to put you on TV and treat this whole thing lightly. Let them laugh with us, not at us."

"You mean laugh at me."

"Wear glasses and a moustache," Pryor joked.

Dennis was not smiling. After a brief pause, Pryor's tone changed. "It's the twenty-second," he said. "No report?"

"No."

"And no comet. So we drop it as agreed."

"Okay," Dennis said. If he were superstitious, he would have crossed his fingers. Instead, he repeated "Okay," and assented to a second lie.

Chapter Eight

Dennis saw the Washington papers later that day. Mercifully, the afternoon editions had moved the "headstrong adviser" story to page three. The front pages now carried pictures of the waving President bidding farewell to Chrysler workers in Detroit. According to accounts, the Motor City had turned out in great numbers on a cold day to cheer the incumbent's latest attack on Governor Henderson as the antibusiness candidate.

The Washington press corps called the President the "Easy Rider," harking back to the movie of the late sixties that depicted a hard-driving motorcycle hero in search of America. But James Snelling had already found America. He knew the hum of its vibration, the rumble of its moods. He mastered the throng, playing each assembly with custom-made tools: a shot of humor to tone down international fears, a twist of sarcasm to stun the opposition, an occasional dose of flag-waving, and, for fine tuning, always the lowered brow of vigilance to help keep the real enemy in view. Whenever campaign enthusiasm wavered, he pulled out a favorite slogan designed to touch a common nerve.

He called this relationship "our trust," and crowds from coast to coast shouted assent with almost Islamic fervor. Wall Street slapped his back, workers—upstate or downtown—stopped to listen to his message. Grant-rich universities filled the stadium, and blacks gathered for the man who had placed one of their own "one heartbeat away."

The President mounted public opinion, riding it like a charger. And it was the electorate's job to keep up. Following the campaigning President around the country was a hectic affair. No glamour, just reporters scrambling madly from airports to hotels to word processors, describing a plant opening in North Carolina, a defense contract awarded with more ceremony than substance in Denver, a flood-control complex in Illinois, a new stadium in Phoenix. As Thanksgiving Day approached, the news photos blurred into a monotonous sameness, and the prose strained to distinguish San Antonio from San Diego.

The country gave thanks for a booming economy and an energetic, if restless, Chief Executive who never dropped in unannounced or empty-handed. Like a rich uncle, Snelling always arrived with presents and left with the promise of more where that came from. The show played to rave reviews from Seattle to Miami. Not one local congressman from either party would miss the chance to be photographed next to the magnanimous leader. Lukewarm legislators took a glance at the latest polls and rushed to the airport to be first in line greeting the President as he stood on the steps of Air Force One and waved at the cameras.

It was only the most cynical newsman who dared refer to the President's excusable penchant for traveling with a rotating crew of young female attendants and his less excusable disdain for the country's first black Vice President.

For months Raymond Lattimore had fanned rumors that he would bolt the Snelling team. Black leaders pushed the former San Diego mayor to cut himself away from the administration's string of empty pledges. Only

that spring, Secret Service agents in St. Louis had overpowered and disarmed a black assassin embittered by
Lattimore's official rhetoric about promised jobs for mi-
norities. An uninjured but shaken Vice President admitted to the press what some had already written, that he was
actively examining his options for 1992. The President
sent Lattimore a note after the incident. They had met,
but Snelling's office issued no further comment.

ON NOVEMBER 23, Los Angeles's Marriott-Hilton ballroom was filling up steadily. Businessmen, politicians,
and frantic reporters vied for each other's attention,
shaking hands and smiling in all directions into lights and
cameras. The last of a security team was whispering final
instructions into walkie-talkies from corner checkpoints.
The camera's red lights flashed on at six o'clock in time
to catch Dr. Dennis Covino following a line of men who
needed no nametags up to the bright temporary stage,
where an incongruous bed of yellow iris hid the podium's
presidential seal.

In front of the science adviser, Commerce Secretary
Steven Woodward grabbed two hands at once and tossed
drawled hellos into the pressing crowd. Behind him
pushed Press Secretary Tom Miller, who was doing his
best to shed a beautiful NBC reporter's microphone. At
the head of the line, gesturing for more room, marched
Secretary of Defense Dean Newcombe and, at his side,
Presidential speechwriter Wayne Ryan. Both men were
surrounded by several dark-suited Secret Service agents.
More wired agents rimmed the slow-moving cortege all
the way back to the doorway. The visiting dignitaries
weaved their way up to the podium and stared through
strong lights into the noisy crowd. The room clamored for
the President's arrival with a ballpark chant.

Someone was missing, Dennis thought. The Vice President. Lattimore was not onstage. Dennis scanned the throng and noticed a tight circle of blacks at the far wall near the entranceway. Lattimore waved from the center to a group hidden behind two network cameras. Holding back, Dennis supposed, waiting to follow the President to the podium.

The crowd stilled, then mounted the unmistakable applause that could only signal the Chief Executive's presence. The pinstriped President moved deliberately behind a phalanx of sternfaced agents to accept the charged crowd's greeting: "Snel-ling! Snel-ling!" The President waved from the podium. After several minutes, he officially announced his intention to run for a second term. He reminded the country of his restraint during the 1989 Soviet invasion of Iran-Iraq. He recalled the death of a personal friend at the hands of "heinous forces behind the Iron Curtain." The audience was hushed in respect and anticipation as the President's voice cracked slightly. He underlined America's longstanding commitment to defend Israel and the need to safeguard economic interests in the troubled ally's neighborhood. "Never," he pledged in a loud voice, "will the United States allow further Soviet attempts at dominance to loosen the close ties between Washington and Tel Aviv."

He then disclosed the details of the arms deal: five hundred million dollars in new military aid, five hundred million in technicians' payroll, and nine hundred million for strategic electronics. One point nine billion dollars. "An overdue investment in international security," he announced, his voice ringing into a new wave of applause. In remarks aimed at his opponent, he warned of the folly of talking with the Soviets "while they pursue their course of mischief in the Persian Gulf." "My challenger keeps saying 'talk, talk.' Well, now I assure you we have something to say.''

In remarks directed at the Soviet Premier, he announced the expected ultimatum: any further jamming events traced to Soviet sources would be countered by an Israeli-American nuclear strike against the offending sites. The necessary equipment was in transit via a secret route, and the President said he expected to hear within four months that the technicians had everything in place to insure compliance. Dennis joined in the applause, his head still reeling at the nearly two-billion-dollar figure. He looked up at a sudden movement coming from the back of the ballroom. He saw Vice President Lattimore say something to a bearded man to his right, then exit with a dozen blacks while the room exploded wildly at the presidential initiative.

After a drawn-out camera session, the presidential party—now a campaign troupe—made its way upstairs. Dennis accompanied Ron Pryor to the reserved room, stopping along the way to shake hands with several local notables whom the chief of staff introduced quickly by name and title.

"See," Pryor said, "you are an asset."

Feeling out of place and, despite the remark, like an add-on, Dennis followed Pryor into the third-floor presidential suite. The beds and chairs were already claimed by well-dressed men and women whom Dennis recognized from newspaper photos.

Secretary of the Treasury Roy Meeker lounged across a twin bed and feigned listening to speechwriter Ryan while shooting rapid glances at a comely campaign pollster's cleavage. The Interior Secretary was poking the lapel of Assistant Press Secretary Owen Willins, who retaliated with a volley of cigar smoke. In the next room he could see the dome of the tall Secretary of State, who was listening to the slurred speech of a man Dennis didn't know but could tell had arrived long before the other revelers. The campaign was in full swing.

"Where are the damn sandwiches?" someone yelled. "Ron, where are the sandwiches?"

Pryor ignored the question. Dennis fixed himself a drink and moved to a corner near the door, where he introduced himself to the bespectacled congressional liaison officer he had met at dinner.

"Jane DeLuze?"

She nodded. "So you're the Horowitz hunter," she said with a teasing smile.

"My one claim to fame. Yes."

"What put you onto that trail?" she asked.

"Orders."

"Orders? Don't tell me. Secret, right?"

"Not anymore," Dennis replied. "I was looking for new data on Riga. I followed a bum lead."

"The boss doesn't seem too upset," she said. "But between us, Doctor, more than one senator is talking about looking into it."

Dennis smiled. "I wish them better luck than I had."

"What's Riga?" she asked.

Dennis took a sip of his drink. He was about to answer when the President entered. His tie already loosened, he took off his jacket and tossed it to an outstretched arm. With one hand he wiped an offered towel over his face. With the other he accepted a frosty Scotch and soda from Wayne Ryan. He twirled the mixture with a finger and joined the roomful of happy aides in a toast for the day's triumph.

"Hail to the Chief!" Pryor crowed, raising his glass to the President. Snelling bowed and spread his arms in acknowledgment of the applause. Speechwriter Ryan lifted a gin and tonic. "Well done, Mr. President," he said joyfully. "All the networks were there."

"Naturally," Snelling nodded. "And no antinuke demonstrators. Imagine that."

"Oh, they were there, sir," Ryan clarified. "Lining the highway from Los Alamitos, screaming at the dummy motorcade." He grinned. "The news teams just got your speech, no demonstrators."

"Wonderful," Snelling said. "Out of sight, out of mind." He took a swallow of his drink. "Ron, any response from Henderson?"

"Nothing," Pryor replied, switching TV channels.

"Good. Good."

"He'll hit you hard on the arms deal, though. Get ready."

"We're ready," Snelling declared triumphantly. His smile broadened. "The polls will leave him in the dust on that one." He took another sip of Scotch. Turning to Ryan, he asked, "Do you have that list of his advisers, Wayne?"

"Yeah. Nobodies." Ryan handed him a typed list. Snelling glanced down the list of names. "Ron, what are the chances of his using the mistress thing against us?"

"Slim," Pryor was quick to answer. "Maybe it'll surface as postconvention desperation, but it isn't a present worry."

Snelling eyed a pretty pollster stretched out on the bed. "Henderson's looking for the White House harem," he scoffed. "Hey, Roy, watch where you put your hands." He laughed as the red-faced Treasury Secretary sat up obediently.

The President called to Ron Pryor. "Are we going back to Washington or on to New Orleans directly?"

"New Orleans tomorrow. Crime prevention," Pryor said. "Then New York with job training."

"Then Washington?"

"Right. Sunday."

"Get me a morning with Governor Toms as soon as we get back, will you," the President ordered. He looked around the room.

"Where's the Black Stallion?"

"Here the rest of the week," Ryan answered. "Chicago on Thursday."

"Just keep him on the move," the President told Pryor. "Was he in the ballroom?"

"Like a seismograph," Dennis commented. "One tremor, and things go boom." He imagined the flashing "ready lights" aboard the *Kennedy*. Eighteen seconds to oblivion. Snelling turned away.

"I think they know better than to risk that," Pryor said reassuringly.

"The risks have been worked out. They'll cooperate. You'll see," Snelling said with a wave of the hand.

"We can do without all this heavy talk," Pryor said. "This is a party."

Dennis welcomed the opening as Pryor took him by the elbow. Dennis excused himself to the President, and the pair walked toward the door. Pryor stopped.

"Look, Dennis. You don't have to agree with what we're doing, but you took an oath to carry out orders. I realize you have experience breaking vows, but the campaign has started. So we'd appreciate your cooperation. Keep any reservations to yourself—and out of the papers. I covered you on 047, we're mopping up the Horowitz thing, and frankly you're becoming one pain in the ass."

Dennis's mouth tightened. He tugged away from Pryor's grip on his arm.

"I told you the President couldn't do without you," Pryor continued. "That's not flattery. It's fact."

"What are you talking about?"

"We're going to dump the Vice President. And that's got to be our only defection. I know you appreciate the direct approach, so here it is: stay at your desk and do what you're told."

"More advice?" Dennis quipped.

"Last advice," Pryor shot back. "Let's call it an ultimatum."

The chief of staff moved away and into the crowd. Dennis stood alone, feeling more than ever like the odd man out.

Chapter Nine

The fiasco was soon forgotten. While the President's science adviser had enraged half of Washington's bureaucracy in his search for Dr. Horowitz, the other half laughed at a maverick rookie a bit too eager to impress. He was the butt of the capital's top comic's routine and, as he and Sandi made the rounds of holiday parties, he tried to maintain his good humor. Yes, he had turned over sensitive stones in search of a man who didn't exist. Yes, he confessed over sherry and punch, he felt like a bull in a china shop. Or was it a horse's ass? But after two weeks or so, even the radio talk shows dropped the Horowitz affair in favor of plumbing public opinion on the ultimatum.

The name Riga never appeared in the papers. Nor did congressional opposition, stilled by a long Christmas recess. As expected, Henderson slammed away at "a fragile economy based on confrontation" and "a banquet for the military while domestic needs look through the window." The headlines went to Snelling, who amplified his Thanksgiving ultimatum to crowds in the Midwest, reassuring the lukewarm and recharging the faithful. When small bands of antinuclear demonstrators jeered the President in Newark and Memphis, he wisely campaigned from the safety of the television studio.

"The Soviets are checked," he announced electronically from Houston. "And free men throughout the world can celebrate this holiday season with new confidence in the words 'Peace to men of good will.' "

In the Middle East, American and Israeli technicians erected secret installations behind the silent sentry of the sixth fleet. The Gulf, Snelling reported, was being "wired for freedom" with the help of cooperative allies "dedicated as one to stopping further Soviet jamming." Public opinion showed a nearly unanimous fervor for the commander-in-chief and his bold initiative. Three weeks passed with neither a single jamming incident nor a Soviet response to the President's ultimatum. By Christmas, the press noted that James Snelling was enjoying the highest level of popularity for a Chief Executive since 1984.

Dennis came to resent this acclaim as much as he resented Pryor's orders to stay at his desk. And that crack about "breaking vows" rankled him too. He was a soldier, not of God this time, but of a man whose rashness and certainty disturbed him more than he wanted to show.

Sandi remarked on his irritability on the sands of Aruba, where they spent Christmas week.

"Still pouting?" she said.

Dennis squinted at the sparkling ocean. "I'm not pouting. I just don't want to go back."

She covered her eyes from the glare. "Who does?"

"I mean it, Sandi. I'm pushing research on a flu virus one day and okaying MX components the next, making believe they're both important."

"Aren't they?"

"Yeah. Life and death," he said, grabbing a fistful of warm sand. "Lohmann says the President's dangerous. And I think he may be right."

"Snelling, dangerous?"

"He's determined to fire on the Soviet Union, and he expects my help. I'm supposed to stay in my seat while he starts a war. Chained in place, locked up till I'm needed. I didn't know how happy I was in Colorado."

"But you said yes."

"I said yes to the priesthood, too, once."

Sandi sat up. "Oh, so it's God's punishment," she said sharply. "You're unhappy, at Christmastime, because the President's planning a showdown. World War III will be your fault. God's revenge on you."

"I'm chained," he said. "Chained, and used."

"You signed up. Eyes open. Why shouldn't you be used? Washington is politics. What did you expect?"

He stared back at the ocean, angry at himself for having no answer and angry at Sandi for being so right.

At sunset they walked the beach hand in hand. The sun and the water had refreshed Sandi. She was now counting the days till she could give notice to Senator Browning and start work at Georgetown. Dennis squeezed her hand tighter and envied her her impending freedom.

RETURNING TO WASHINGTON the week after Christmas, Dennis found himself long on time and short on staff. Those not away using up vacation time milled around the offices, routinely cleaning files and answering the few calls that came in from offices as deserted as his. He received a holiday card from Seymour White's wife thanking him for his wishes and informing him that her husband's condition remained unchanged. He checked in with Jan Fortes for progress on the numbers found in his predecessor's file. Fortes had passed the printout code on to an assistant, who would get to it shortly. Her matter-of-fact reply, along with the office's disarray, brought out a rough edge.

"Sooner rather than later, okay?" he told her.

Friday he met Sandi for lunch before leaving to address a meteorologists' convention at the Commodore. Sandi presented him with a surprise gift, a book, *Stress and the Mature Executive*. Stress, he learned, was a killer of men over fifty. He took the hint gracefully and, over a second martini, agreed to greet the new year on more peaceful terms. He told her he would take more time impressing visitors and leave the hard decision making to the higher-ups. Maybe Sandi was right. Maybe this was a reward position. The Christmas polls promised at least four more years of job security, his for the taking with everyone's blessing. A reward, he tried telling himself.

On the President's behalf, he assured the meteorologists of two new weather satellites before year's end.

Making good on the New Year's resolution he made to Sandi, he geared his schedule down to a more manageable routine for 1992. He cleared up a California irrigation plan that had occupied two office tables for over five weeks. In less than a day he helped streamline the FDA's method of approving life-extending drugs. Afternoons he spent with his top staff, relying on their reports to fill him in on progress on particle beams and kinetic weapons research.

He left the Executive Office Building promptly at five-thirty, not minding being part of the impossible exodus to Virginia behind the wheel of his new blue Volvo. Unwinding time, he called it, turning stress into programmed relaxation, according to the authors of *Stress and the Mature Executive*. He spent it listening to "All Things Considered" on the radio or to the beat of an Oscar Peterson tape.

One afternoon, creeping in Arlington Boulevard traffic, his thoughts took him to the far-off Evergreen Institute.

He missed the country pace, the freedom, and even the isolation of Colorado, where people would need a map to find the Baltic and where stress was a big-city worry. Was the new director happily installed amid frantic yet harmless academics, as Lee's Christmas card had hinted? He made a mental note to call Lee while it was on his mind.

That opportunity came the next day. His calendar showed white until a meeting at two with the tedious Science Advisory Board. He telephoned Colorado. To his surprise, the director himself answered.

"Hello, Norton. Dennis Covino here."

"Dennis," came a cheery voice. "Dr. Horowitz here."

"Oh, don't make me go through that. Please," he groaned. "So you've heard."

"Yes, indeed. Henderson's made a big thing of it out here. How've you been otherwise?"

"Good, Norton. Very good. And you?"

"Busier than ever. Lagrange misses Sandi, though. Can you send her back? Or take him off my hands?"

Dennis laughed. "Tell him she's staying here," he said. "She has plans to be Secretary of Agriculture by '95."

Lee did not respond right away. After a moment he asked in a serious tone, "You've called about Hendley?"

Dennis blinked at the unexpected name.

"Hendley? No."

"Oh, I thought you were ready to lay into me for okaying his space shot."

"You didn't," Dennis's voice dropped.

"Yes. He's in. If at first you don't succeed—"

"Norton, he's taking you for a ride. The Institute's going to be burned."

"Dennis, there's been a change of heart somewhere down the line. I've got two wires from the Pentagon asking when, not how much."

Dennis felt a sudden blow, like a door slammed in his face. Someone was making decisions, leaving him on the outside. Dammit to hell!

"Why the reversal?" he asked. "Who's pushing it?"

"General Wainwright."

Norton went on to mention the financial advantages to the Institute, the backing of the Air Force, and the modifications of the original plan to spot a comet. This time a comet search was not part of the flight plan. The new project was a satellite reconnaissance mission over Eastern Europe. It was a rush order, Lee said, and Special Technologies officials were calling almost daily.

With each word Dennis's head pounded. A military operation. Science was consulted only as an afterthought. The important thing was the launch.

"What launch?" Dennis asked.

"It sounds to me like a dummy, like they want anything in orbit," Lee explained. "Just to get it up."

Dennis's mind flashed with a sudden idea. He grabbed a notepad. "Norton, what camera equipment is in the package?"

"Stereoscopic TL-4s. The best."

"Is the setup the same as before, with just a lighter payload?"

"Yes. Why do you ask?"

"Then there's still room for another camera?"

"Why, I suppose so. What are you getting at?"

"Can we put a Griboval Electrographic on the telescope, aimed away from the earth?"

Lee hesitated. "What on earth for?" he wanted to know.

"For one eye on Jupiter while the Air Force keeps another on the Baltic."

"Jupiter? Dennis, this is a military mission. I need Pentagon approval for any changes."

"You'll get it. And I'll get you the camera."

"Now will you tell me why?"

"If it stays between you and me."

"Of course."

"Norton, I've received information from Dr. Cho Chan that the comet Hendley was looking for might be more than a Russian rumor."

"Now hold on," Lee broke in.

"They've shut down an important complex in Eastern Europe. Chan thinks it could be because of a perturbation beyond Jupiter. A comet is a possibility."

"You spoke to Chan?" Lee interrupted again.

"Yes. He says the Soviets have the capability to track anything to the thirtieth magnitude. They've closed down magnetic-field work and it could be due to an errant comet."

"Thirtieth magnitude! Dennis, what could possibly concern us at that distance?"

"I don't know when the Soviets did their tracking. I don't even know for sure that they have. But if it is a comet, it's a lot closer now. Maybe detectable."

"A secret comet?"

"I know. It's crazy," Dennis said. "If I get the camera, will you help?"

"I'll make arrangements here. Sure."

"Good. Is a launch date set?"

"It'll be weeks rather than months to a favorable launch window."

"From Holloman?"

"Most likely. It's going through final testing now at Huntsville. Say, Dennis, all this is cleared, I assume."

"It will be."

"I'm told the launch is an important part of the ultimatum. The President may even be at Holloman himself for a media event."

"That it's sure to be," Dennis agreed.

There was silence on the line for a minute. Lee was the first to break it. "Dennis, are we in for a close apparition?"

"You don't really expect me to answer that, do you?"

"Hey, until a few minutes ago I never heard of a camera that could reach to the thirtieth magnitude. Come on, Dennis. How close an apparition?"

Dennis sighed loudly. "First we have to find it. I don't know what the hell I'm talking about. I just need to know what I can't find out here."

"How can I help?"

"Make room on your end for a Griboval Electrographic. I'll set up the rest from here," Dennis said. "Keep everything routine. No commotion."

"Okay."

"And Norton—"

"Yes."

"I realize I'm asking you to stick your neck out. If you feel the need to be cautious, I'll understand."

"You bastard," Lee laughed.

"It comes with the office, doesn't it? Like a shirt and tie," Dennis said, happy his former assistant had taken the dig in its intended spirit.

"Dennis, I'll do all I can, without embarrassing the institute."

"I appreciate it. Either this launch can confirm the rumor, and we go from there, or else the Russians tell us what the hell they're up to."

"Do you have any Soviet contacts?"

"Are you kidding? The blackout is darker than ever. The last time I bucked 047 I bumped into Dr. Horowitz."

"I might try," Lee offered.

"Please feel free. And Norton, secrecy, as much as possible, will minimize any panic."

"I understand. Caution."

"We're just gathering more data. If we find nothing, it'll be easier to cover our tracks if there's no mention of a comet."

"I got you. And Dennis, for what it's worth, I still think I got the best of this deal."

"You may be right," Dennis said limply. He hung up feeling more than ever like a conspirator. At least now he had an ally.

BEFORE THE WEEK WAS OUT, Dennis had ordered a Griboval-XF for installation on Alpha-One's telescope. The spec sheet he made out for Norton Lee identified the last-minute change as an experimental strategic search module, the kind irresistible to Special Technologies. Wainwright snapped at the bait. A call to Richard Lohmann secured the correct clearance code, and soon technicians in Alabama were setting the camera into its gyro cradle and running the prescribed simulations. Alpha-One was checked, packed, and shipped to Holloman Air Force Base in New Mexico for a February seventh launch.

The same day his Alpha-One report left the office for White House filing, Dennis received an official invitation to the not-so-secret desert launch. His campaign number had been drawn again.

Chapter Ten

The dark February night was cold enough to suspend breath in cartoon-caption clouds. Dennis climbed the lighted gangway of Air Force One, exchanging puffs with a stern sentry who looked as if he was expecting some unnamed trouble. At the top of the entranceway, Dennis made a nervous salute, then presented his credentials for inspection. Satisfied, the young captain handed back his yellow ID card and stepped inside.

"Dr. Covino," he announced to a shadow inside the plane. "Step up, sir."

Ron Pryor emerged from behind a dark-blue curtain.

"Dennis," he said a bit stiffly. Then to the guard, "We're full, Captain."

The door slammed shut.

Dennis followed Pryor inside the famous "Cloud Palace." The craft's interior was enormous. Its discreet lighting reminded him of a comfortable television studio, the kind he used to visit in Denver in '85 for the talk shows. The main cabin was a series of plush, open offices, a floating lounge. All the windows were curtained, each one sporting a small gold presidential seal against a blue background. The soft swivel seats, a lighter blue, were living-room spacious, and beside each sat a lighted work table more suitable for conversation than for study. Each furniture grouping included a generous-size coffee table and matching hassock. What would have been aisles in another plane were carpeted corridors three feet apart here. Dennis felt like a newlywed touring a furniture showroom.

Pryor pointed to a seat in the center of a huddle of men murmuring softly. Of the group, Dennis recognized only Secretary of Defense Newcombe, who looked up as Dennis greeted three generals introduced by Pryor as members of the Joint Chiefs of Staff. Pryor took his coat and briefcase without a word.

"Gentlemen," he called out, "the President will be with you right after takeoff. Our flight will touch down at Holloman at 2330 hours local time. Launch time is set for 0600 hours. I'm sure you'll excuse the short notice and the inconvenient hour. The President will explain the reasons. Please make yourselves comfortable in the meantime."

Two uniformed stewardesses appeared from behind a hedgelike planter at the back of the plane to take orders for snacks and drinks. Following the lead of the generals, Dennis ordered a Scotch and water. Dean Newcombe approached the group, hands extended in greeting.

"Well, well," he said in a loud voice. "This is Dr. Covino. Dean Newcombe, Defense. Generals." He made a bow that the generals took as a signal to depart. "Doctor, this is a pleasant surprise, sharing the ride with a civilian, I mean. Tell me, how much notice did you have for this flight? If you say any less than the forty-eight hours I was given, we can never be friends." His face opened into a full smile.

"A day," Dennis replied.

"Well, anything more than twelve hours is a distinct compliment."

"So I've heard."

Dennis followed the Secretary to the forward seats away from the others. Somehow he was drawn toward this cordial man.

"I got the word on another plane," Newcombe said. "Seems I'm not allowed to touch ground these days. Or else it's a plan to keep me away from Washington until after the election." He smiled. "And you?"

"I got a memo," Dennis said.

"On campaign stationery, I'll bet."

"I think it was."

"Everything's on reelection stationery now, even memos, huh?"

"Right."

"Nice tan," Newcombe commented breezily. "I understand you've been out of the country." Dennis wondered which way to take the remark. He settled for innocence with a simple "Thank you. Vacation."

The drinks arrived, and as the two men settled in to await takeoff, Newcombe raised his gold-rimmed tumbler. "Cheers."

Dennis accepted the toast, wondering if the Secretary had planned to be his traveling companion and if the genial, bow-tied giant really felt out of place among the military brass he commanded.

Newcombe's next words cleared up both questions. "I've left orders that we are not to be disturbed, until the boss arrives, that is. This your first trip?"

"Yes," Dennis said. "It's quite a plane."

"A castle in the sky. A regular palace. This is my fourth midnight raid."

"Why shouldn't we be disturbed?" Dennis wanted to know. Newcombe leaned closer. "I thought we could exchange notes on this launch," he confided. "Frankly,

Doctor, I've been puzzled about something since I received a report from you awhile back.''

"You read it?''

"I read everything,'' Newcombe assured him. "Including a last-minute data sheet handed to me this afternoon on the Holloman launch. Why the camera add-on?''

Dennis sipped his drink. He could feel the muscles around his neck begin to tense. So much for secrecy.

"A scientific experiment,'' he said.

"That much is clear. Go on.''

"That's all. We have the space to make this launch a dual shot. Two for the price of one.''

Newcombe blinked at the reply. "You ordered an electrographic camera beamed outward, from what I understand. Strange on a mission meant to keep eyes on Riga, wouldn't you say?''

"Mr. Secretary, it happens all the time. Holloman launches are designed to be economical. Military as well as scientific.''

Newcombe placed his glass on the table deliberately and folded his arms in a way that told Dennis he had stepped on sensitive toes. "Dr. Covino, your first report to me was a real wonder. I understand you were embarrassed by it.''

"Output equals input,'' Dennis answered defensively. "Believe me, it won't happen again. My direct orders were to gather and update files on jamming. It was a book report, I admit. You're not expecting an apology, I hope. I did what I was told.''

"As do we all. But why did you go to so much trouble reporting what anyone can get from the papers?''

"Look. We all know it was some kind of test, a loyalty test. Let's drop it there.''

Dennis showed his irritation by lifting his eyes and his glass upward. He wondered if he was talking to a friend or an enemy.

"Doctor," Newcombe said, "I'm just as in the dark as you seem to be. The new science adviser, top man, sends me press release intelligence. I ask why." He paused. "Until I see a change in Alpha-One's flight specs. A camera aimed at the stars on a mission meant for election headlines. Something's up."

Dennis was about to reply, to attempt to share some of his own confusion about the mission, when Ron Pryor announced, "Seat belt time, gentlemen. Ease in."

One by one the click of snapping belts filled the cabin, accompanied immediately by a slight vibration and then a deep drone from the far-off engines.

Dennis and Newcombe unsnapped their belts at the same time. Newcombe adjusted himself in the seat.

"We can speak in confidence, Doctor." His voice was hushed. "What is it you are looking for?"

"I can't say."

"Orders?"

"Let's leave it there, all right?"

Newcombe backed off with a shrug. "Okay, partner," he said. "I'll ask Pryor."

Just then Pryor reappeared with the President from behind a solid door at the front of the plane. The President wore a dressing robe over his shirt and loosened tie. His pants were wrinkled. He looked pale, his eyes distant and watery. He'd either been drinking or, more likely, Dennis thought, had been awakened from a fitful sleep. He moved toward the passengers slowly, looking at Pryor the way a patient eyes a doctor who insists he can now walk on his own.

The President blinked as if in pain, then spoke in a hoarse voice. "Gentlemen, you see before you a man racked by a flu my doctors tell me comes from Singapore, sent over by God knows what ill wind. I won't come any closer. If I sound a little faint I hope you'll excuse the effects of the wonder drugs that at least allow me to stand." He coughed and inhaled with effort.

"I owe you an explanation on why you were asked to leave hearth and home and join me in New Mexico tomorrow morning. I've disobeyed medical advice to be here myself. But I'm confident you will agree that the sacrifice—yours and mine—is a small price to pay for what we hope to accomplish at Holloman."

Snelling thrust both hands into his robe pockets and continued. "What is called a favorable launch window and new developments in the Gulf have conspired to supply us with the chance to bolster our ultimatum. I call on you to help me make this orbital mission a media success. In doing so, I am asking each of you to do something a lawyer in the crowd would call conspiracy. I want you to support an official lie."

He flopped into a swivel chair. His eyes scanned the silent cabin.

"After eleven weeks," he croaked, "the Russians have issued no response to our ultimatum. All we're getting on radio are some beeps. Flyovers have shown they are boosting power at installations rather than halting it. It appears likely they are preparing an active response we still hope to avoid. They are scoffing at us again.

"Tomorrow's mission is a show. The press will be there. There'll be pictures and questions. So I want to brief you all on what we're going to say." He drew a handkerchief to his nose. "For those with mental reservations, I want you to say 'no comment' and refer questioners to General

McKinnon. The story for tomorrow is that Alpha-One is top-security orbital surveillance of Soviet antenna emplacements. A shot aimed at showing our determination to zero in on jamming stations. The satellite is launched to coordinate what the Israelis are targeting. We are escalating the situation." His voice trailed off. "Of course this mission can do nothing of the kind. It's routine. A bluff."

Dennis exchanged a quick glance with Newcombe, who sat motionless with a lost expression on his face that told Dennis that he wasn't the only one in the dark.

Snelling went on. "Some will say that my timing is political, that I need a strong showing in the spring polls. If it were as transparent as that, I would admit it. The fact is that, short of nuclear firing, this is all we can do right now to show the Russians we are serious about the ultimatum."

He coughed. "Down the road, we are set to give Israel the go-ahead and, if need be, to call Red Alert if the status doesn't change. Our aim is to bring the Soviets to their senses, not to their knees. Alpha-One was not of course in the original game plan the Joint Chiefs and I developed. If there is any blame to place, I accept it. I didn't think it would be necessary to deviate from my November plan. However, I am advised by NASA that the next favorable launch window won't open up till late April. That, in our view, is too late. But as long as the Russians don't know this, we gain strategy time. So an unimportant space shot becomes quite important. As a message." He turned to Pryor. "Ron has a briefing outline for each of you. The story line for tomorrow. It's a show, gentlemen. Here are your parts."

With ceremonial silence, the chief of staff circulated a two-page sheet to each man. "We will collect and shred these before landing," Snelling said. "In the meantime please learn your parts well. Those who choose the 'no comment' route, and I can understand that, make sure you give your name to Ron before we land. I thank you in advance for your support. Now, the launch is an early one, six o'clock, so you should have at least four hours' sleep, anyway. I'll see you at 0600 hours."

The President rose stiffly and disappeared behind the door to his private room. Ron Pryor stayed behind, answering questions from the subdued officials. Dennis turned to a dazed Newcombe.

"Well, I'll be damned," the Defense Secretary exclaimed. "This is the reason for your camera. Big camera, no film. We're shooting with blanks." Before Dennis could deny the Secretary's conclusion, Newcombe bolted from his chair and headed back for Ron Pryor.

Alone now, Dennis gazed at the sheets Pryor had handed him. Alpha-One was a show. A bluff, the President had called it. No reconnaissance. No weapons. Blanks. He didn't know whether to be relieved or upset. The only part of the mission of any possible value was the Griboval Electrographic, known now to Newcombe and shortly, he was sure, to Ron Pryor. Despite himself the President had said more than he knew: "an unimportant space shot becomes quite important." If the onboard camera confirmed a Red comet, this launch would be the most important one of the decade.

He tried to collect his thoughts on what to say to Pryor. The computer hook-up to his office was complete. Pictures from Alpha-One would start to come in in a matter of days. Images from the telescope at Kitt Peak National Observatory would be relayed electronically to his viewing screen. He had also taken the precaution to order a backup link to the new computer-imager at Mount Hopkins. If Alpha-One showed anything unusual, astronomers would start buzzing and the clamor could be deafening. Then what will I do, he wondered. The Griboval Electrographic is in place awaiting focusing instructions only hours away. Any object that produces or reflects light will be recorded; then the detective work begins. Science is not always a logical process, he concluded uneasily, and the die is cast. He ran both hands along his pant legs, drying the moisture from his palms.

Pryor approached from behind his seat, sinking his fingers into the fabric of the adjoining chair. His knuckles whitened as his face flushed with anger.

"Dennis, can we talk?" Not waiting for an answer, he spun into the seat Newcombe had vacated. "What is Newcombe talking about? What's an electrographic camera?"

"I've ordered an additional camera for Alpha-One," Dennis said flatly.

"And?"

"And it will send us electronic images of objects between the earth and Jupiter."

"Looking for a comet?"

"Yes."

"My God!" Pryor shut his eyes, pushing himself into the seat. "Have you told anyone?"

"Just Lee at Evergreen. And Newcombe."

"No one else?"

"No. No one."

Pryor clenched his teeth. "Didn't we agree, no more comet?"

"It's a camera," Dennis insisted. "It scans and takes pictures."

"An add-on secret." Pryor spat out the last word.

"What's one more secret to you?" Dennis snapped. "The details are on your desk."

"If Snelling finds out, he'll have you shot."

"Is he afraid we'll find something? Afraid the Russians may be planning a hoax of their own?"

Pryor pinched his forehead and winced.

"How in hell will we know unless we can see for ourselves?" Dennis added.

"Know what?" Pryor challenged. "If the Russians see a comet, they'll announce it."

"Before or after Red Alert?" Dennis sat up in the chair and raised his voice. "What happens when one of their nuclear-powered satellites falls from orbit? Did they announce anything in '83? In '87? Ron, we could have a comet lighting up the sky soon. Shouldn't the President know?" He drew back in the chair.

"What makes you think now there's a comet anywhere near Jupiter?"

"I believe the Russians are tracking a speck of light. It could be debris from outgoing Halley's or part of a comet pushed off course by Jupiter. It could be the asteroid Hermes. We lost track of that in 1937, and it hasn't been seen since. Or," he inhaled, "it could be an uncharted comet falling toward the sun."

"Or it could be nothing."

Dennis nodded at the possibility. "Look, whatever it might be, real or imagined, until we see something we have to rely on their word."

"What word? They're silent."

"So it's all right if we're blind?" Dennis's response brought a deep sigh from the President's man. Dennis continued, "If the camera spots what they say they've found—"

"What you say they've found."

"Okay. It may be millions of kilometers away. The chances of its coming anywhere near us are minimal. Or it could be closer. Unless we know for sure if it even exists, how will we respond if the Soviets say it's on top of us? Hold on till we can launch probes to confirm? By then it might be too late. Can you see the panic whether it's real or a hoax?"

"It wouldn't matter," Pryor said.

"The panic would come from our having no explanation. Not from the Soviet Union. Don't you see?"

"Where are your colleagues on this?" Pryor asked with more curiosity than anger now.

"I've been stripped of colleagues. All I'm sure of is that the Russians have the equipment to know first. With luck, on this camera we might know as much in a few months."

"Months?"

"Jupiter is six hundred million kilometers away. That's a lot of space to cover. We need all the time we can get." Dennis paused. "Can I see the President?"

"No. He can't be disturbed."

"Will you give him a message then?"

Pryor seemed to consider the request, looking down at his hands. "All right," he replied at last.

"Tell him we need to talk to Soviet scientists."

Pryor closed his eyes as Dennis added, "If a comet is more than a rumor, he'll need to know as much as they do. Tell him Alpha-One is a start."

Pryor shook his head. "If you had told me about this, we could have used it as a cover for the launch."

"And pulled you off the campaign to contain comet fever?"

Pryor nodded, conceding the point. "What if your camera sends back nothing?" he asked.

"Then we start again. But with Soviet help."

"On a rumor? Never."

Dennis stood up and pointed to the presidential quarters ahead of him. "Ron, rumor has it the President is in there with a naked stewardess. I could barge in and find out, then tell the world. Ask Snelling what he would do if the Soviets tried the same thing with a comet scare?"

Pryor froze in place. He looked up to Dennis.

"I'll convey your message," he agreed. "After the launch."

"No later, for God's sake."

The shaken aide rose slowly. "Not a word about this," he warned.

"Another little secret," Dennis nodded, "between friends. I'm not making trouble, Ron. Believe me. And I'm not trying to screw up an election, either. Tell the President—tell him the odds are over a million to one against anything that could cause him trouble. I just need to know. I have to be sure."

Pryor moved toward the President's quarters. Dennis called after him. "And, Ron. Put me down as a 'no comment.'"

"That is understood."

THE NEXT MORNING Dennis felt hung over, unprepared for the dawn that took them all by surprise. He took no comfort in noticing that none of his fellow travelers had slept either.

Only the President looked better. Whatever medicine he had taken was indeed a wonder drug. Composed, even buoyant before the bright lights at Holloman Air Force Base's oversize viewing bunker, Snelling addressed dignitaries and press in front of curtainless reinforced windows. His voice had regained its strength, and his manner was as dominant as usual before the media.

"I do not usually rise from a sickbed to view an un-manned space launch," he explained. "However, to-day's mission brings us all together on a matter of grave national security. Alpha-One has been painstakingly engineered to perform a vital task for freedom. We have told the Soviet leadership repeatedly that the days of patient, diplomatic warnings are over. Our ultimatum of November last declares as much, and our determination remains strong. With today's launch, we urge those leaders not to underestimate our resolve. Today we move forward in the still-flickering hope that our message is a clear one. Thank you."

There was no applause. Snelling joined the generals while Ron Pryor rose to add, "Ladies and gentlemen, unfortunately our schedule is very tight and there will be no time for questions. I invite you to withdraw to the upper level viewing deck for the launch. You will find your media packs on the chairs in the reserved area. Any questions can be referred to General Richard T. McKinnon here at Holloman."

The green-buttoned dignitaries left the VIP Room amidst the bustle of shuffling reporters and cameramen who preceded them. The room cleared swiftly, leaving behind only the President and the eleven men who had been aboard Air Force One. Each man took binoculars from a small rack and one by one moved to the observation window. No one spoke.

Dennis focused on a clear sunrise already painting its kaleidoscope of pastels on the New Mexican desert. Above, the night's fingernail moon yielded its brilliance to the oncoming sun. The fast-fading darkness now revealed a broad canvas of pink and orange, spreading in all directions. He could see the distant gray-violet outline of butte and cactus stretching to the horizon, where a flock of dark birds swam skyward in formation. The openness thrilled him as an old cliché came to mind: this was a Godlike view of the world's first morning.

At his raised elbow, the President coughed just as the ceiling speaker crackled to life.

"T-minus three minutes, forty seconds," a voice announced. "All systems are go. Alpha-One is internal at one hundred percent." The same data flashed across a wall-mounted console beside the room's only anachronism: a face clock, whose red baton clipped the seconds. The President lowered his binoculars.

"Beautiful sight," he said. "Magnificent."

Dennis turned his binoculars onto the man-made launch structure half a kilometer away. It wasn't the world's first morning after all. His eyes moved up and down the tall white shaft. Growing white billows of steam gathered at the rocket's base. A far cry from SkyLab manned flights in Florida, he noted. But impressive just the same. Like a smoking erector set.

"T-minus one minute, eighteen seconds and counting," the computerized voice reminded the observers. "Alpha-One is clean and breathing. All is go."

Dennis smiled at the disembodied voice using human terminology. One automaton telling another that all is well in the language of man—the eavesdropper.

"...minus thirty-five seconds... We are go for A.T.... thirty-two, thirty-one, thirty seconds..."

The giant support arms separated lazily from the shining craft, exposing it to the shock of the fire building within its slender walls.

"...fourteen, thirteen, twelve..."

A mounting wave of vibration shook the window. Dennis twisted the binoculars' center knob to adjust his view.

"...eight, seven...six...five..."

The launch area ignited with a spreading orange explosion. The freed engines scattered storms of white clouds underneath the rockets. Dennis felt the whole room shaking through the soles of his shoes.

"...three...two...one. Liftoff."

The spacecraft lumbered upward from its skeletal moorings already scorched by the blazing heat. Alpha-One, set free at last, lifted in slow motion, a pillar of white fire. The observers gulped, clearing their ears of the room's increased pressure.

Dennis followed the stream of white upward as it chalked a long trail behind it. The stream froze in place, stretching, then melting in the upper atmosphere winds. Slowly the colors of the desert returned as Dennis lowered his binoculars. His naked eye could see only a white dot now, pill size and resembling a shooting star. Alpha-One disappeared, blending into a pale sky.

President Snelling followed the flash upward until binoculars were useless.

"It's up, gentlemen," he said. Then, with a quiver in his lower lip, he added, "Pray God they believe she's loaded with destruction."

Chapter Eleven

The return trip on Air Force One was uneventful, each passenger seemingly content in the isolation of his own thoughts. The men were more spread out, subdued. An occasional word here and there, an assenting grunt to an unheard comment broke the silence over the engines' pacifying drone. From his seat in the forward cabin, Dennis watched Ron Pryor shuttle between the President's quarters and Dean Newcombe's seat at the center of the plane. Newcombe, quiet throughout the launch, kept his distance now, as though offended by a meaningless mission and a science adviser who seemed more informed than he was.

The President as usual chose not to mingle. Dennis focused on the door separating him from his scattered guests. Like everything else on board, the door displayed the presidential seal, the silent screaming eagle, a don't-tread-on-me warning as ominous as a skull and crossbones. The lonely hunter. The man who stalked the enemy from afar. Locked in, no doubt, behind closed doors and gambling that the enemy trembled at his shadow.

It was the Snelling administration that denied the Russians food; their grain now came from Canada. It was Snelling's idea lock them out of access to high-technology components; the French and the Japanese eagerly filled that breach. Snelling then keyed on South America and the more secure countries of Africa as markets for American food and know-how. And business was booming; the Soviets' retreat from the Western Hemisphere as planned to concentrate on the Persian Gulf and the Strait of Hormuz made Japan a captive ally. It was East versus West. "We can go it alone," Snelling echoed his inaugural message. "We've done it before and victory will be our reward." The reward was prosperity.

According to the President and to a pliant Congress, the Soviets would suffer more from the realignment. However, all indications since 1988 showed the same unsatisfactory standoff President John Kennedy had known a generation earlier. For Snelling, the Soviet bear was the white whale and he the isolated Ahab, alone behind the locked door with the angry eagle.

I must speak to the President, Dennis decided. Not now, not yet. But proof in hand, I will need direct access, a way to penetrate Pryor's defenses. A way to confer with Soviet astronomers before the amateurs scream their excitement to the world. Was the comet a Soviet hoax, their own Alpha-One bluff? Has Pryor delivered my message to the President?

Pryor passed his seat once again, avoiding his glance a third time as he headed for Newcombe. Security talks, Dennis imagined. Even the Secretary of Defense doesn't enjoy direct access to the candidate. What are the chances for me, the Secretary of Rumor? He organized his thoughts, preparing for what could become a defensive face-to-face confrontation with the impatient President. Fact: Riga was silent. Fact: Soviet scientists can penetrate space to the thirtieth magnitude. Fact: Alpha-One will be sending back something or nothing within a week. And then? The Griboval pictures will show an unexpected fuzzy dot. A comet? Or the camera will find nothing. Horowitz revisited.

He shook off that nightmare with a tug of an earlobe. Calmly, he tried seeing the situation through Snelling's eyes. Fact: Reelection day nine months away. Fact: The ultimatum disregarded in favor of reciprocal silence. What's the old adage, you get back what you give out? God, I'm filled with vintage sayings lately. And the unknowns: Will Snelling push the Soviets to the brink in time to rally insurmountable support by November, as Henderson was claiming? Is a CEP of ten meters the basis of a Russian ultimatum? Is there a comet coming toward us with a Tunguska rendezvous? If I'm imagining things at their worst, best to keep quiet. Only a sighting would supply a clue. Fighting the plane's hypnotic vibration, he asked himself which would be better, a confirmed comet or a Soviet trick. In either case he knew the President would need his help. But would he accept it?

The seat-belt light flashed red. He strapped himself in, relieved that the long day's journey was nearly over. He checked his watch. Four-thirty. Sandi would be just arriving home. He imagined a supper by the fire, but just as that thought began to warm his mood, Ron Pryor bounded into the adjoining seat. He snapped his belt in place and pulled apart the knotted tie at his throat.

"The President's got your message," he said, thrusting his head against the padded headrest. "He's pissed about the stewardess crack, but he wants to see you. Tomorrow. Two o'clock."

AN EXECUTIVE STAFF CAR brought Dennis home. He felt tired, unkempt, rumpled in his travel-worn suit. A shave and a warm bed would make all things new and settle him down for tomorrow's appointment.

Sandi greeted him at the door with a kiss and a surprise. Her friends Lisa and Hal were coming for dinner. He frowned at the unwelcome news.

"I put it on our calendar," she insisted, pointing to the calendar they both used for social events. "They'll be here in half an hour."

Dennis showered and shaved away his annoyance at the night's intrusion. He knew Lisa from accounts Sandi brought back from the office. Senator Browning's personal secretary and Sandi were tennis partners as well as coworkers. They had hit it off from the first day, when Sandi explained her own working conditions to her new boss. Lisa, more used to traditional office protocol, spilled her coffee when Sandi told Browning she would require her own office—and her own secretary. Lisa ruined a new skirt with the next coffee spill when within a week Browning had delivered on both counts. The office was never the same. Dennis recalled Lisa as the one with the laugh that Sandi had tried to imitate for him. A high-pitched, girlish giggle, cute in a thirteen-year-old, but grounds for justifiable homicide in anyone older. He bit the bullet on this one. They would have to meet sometime, he and Lisa with—Herb?

"Hal," Sandi repeated from the kitchen. "Hal Tomlin. He's a professional pollster."

"A what?"

"A pollster."

"Like Frank Perdue?" he joked, dipping a finger into the shrimp dip as soon as it was set down.

Sandi slapped his hand. "Very funny. Open the wine, please."

Dennis obeyed. "I'll need more than one bottle," he said. He moved to the living-room table, clutching four wineglass stems in his fingers. He set the open bottle on the table next to a bouquet of violets, then dropped onto the couch.

"I can't say it was a hard day at the office, but seven hours in a plane, even Air Force One, is a grind. Sandi, you should see the inside of that thing."

"And the launch?" she asked.

"Beautiful. It was beautiful. And I finally got to meet Dean Newcombe."

"Old blood-and-guts?"

"The bald eagle."

"Is that what they call him?"

"That's what I call him." Dennis stretched his legs. "We were almost friends."

"How do you mean?" she asked, entering the room and pouring them both a sherry. She sat next to him.

"Thank you. Newcombe thought I knew something he didn't. Then when he found out we were both in the dark, he walked away. No dope, no friendship."

"Dope?" Sandi mouthed the word.

"Information. That dope. Generation gap."

She snuggled. "Know what?"

"What?"

"I missed you last night."

"I missed you too," he said, putting an arm around her.

When the doorbell rang Sandi jumped up, nearly spilling her wine. Dennis took the glasses to the kitchen, resigned to a shared evening.

"Lisa. Hal." Sandi greeted the guests. "Dennis Covino."

"Hello." Dennis smiled from behind the kitchen counter. God, they're kids, he thought. The couple's polished looks reminded him of models from a Sears catalog. It suddenly dawned on him that he and Sandi were lovers from different generations. His friends were either bald or gray, hers were kids. And dope no longer meant information.

"May I get you a sherry?" he asked.

Sandi took their coats to the closet and led them to the couch. After a minute Dennis brought the drinks.

"To us," he toasted cordially.

"Us," Sandi echoed.

As Dennis drank, he studied Lisa. She was very pretty, dark-haired and willowy, younger than Sandi. She was wearing a tight white dress, the kind designed by *Times* advertisers to accent firm contours. Hal, visibly nervous, appeared to be, at most, thirty. His dark blazer and gold tie gave him a private-school look.

"Have a seat." Dennis offered Hal his favorite red recliner.

"Thank you, Doctor."

"Dennis. Please."

"Dennis." Hal tried out the word. "It isn't easy for me," he said. "You taught me science."

"My book?"

"*Perspectives*, right?"

"Yes." Dennis smiled.

"I remember it from high school."

"I'm flattered. Really, but it's still Dennis," he said, tossing aside the temptation to ask how long ago that was.

When the couples sat down to dinner and talk about Washington's commuter mess, the conversation soon turned to matters closer to home.

"I understand you were with the President today," Hal said.

"I saw you on the news," Lisa giggled.

"Yes," Dennis admitted. "Quite a spectacle."

"You have what they call access, then?" Hal was eager to learn. "To the President, I mean."

Dennis hesitated, caught between the urge to impress and the impulse to play the cynic. He chose the middle ground.

"I'll be meeting with him tomorrow," he said. "But not even the Cabinet has access. I don't see him often, with the campaign and all."

Lisa seemed impressed, but Hal came back with another question.

"Is there any truth to the rumor that the President's ultimatum has backfired?" he asked.

"Sandi said you were a pollster," Dennis kidded. "I don't know about that rumor. I'm on the scientific end of things, not the political."

He hoped his reply would suffice, but Hal didn't seem put off.

"Sandi tells us you were once a Jesuit," he said.

"In a former life, yes."

"You were a teacher, then?" Hal pursued.

"For about six years, before I left."

"Why did you leave, if you don't mind my asking?" Hal said. The sherry had taken the edge off his nervousness.

"I had a problem with the vows," Dennis confessed with a smile.

"The one on chastity," Sandi teased.

"The one on obedience," Dennis corrected. "I had the run of the observatory. McArdle in Arizona. Right on the seminary grounds. Then one day my superior announced the Order's Provincial had received permission to sell the seminary to the Army. Vocations were drying up, and we were no longer cost-effective. So I was transferred to a high school in St. Louis. I dropped out instead."

"Married to science," Hal concluded.

"Well, I'd say a mistress."

Hal showed the good taste not to pick up on the word and link it to another presidential rumor. Instead, he seemed more interested in his host.

"Can you just stop being a priest?" he asked. "I mean, isn't that forever?"

"Final vows, yes. But I never took them."

"That's something," Hal said, nodding as if this were a revelation. Dennis decided to change the subject.

"And you, Hal. What does a pollster do?" he asked.

"Telemarketing," Lisa answered for him.

Hal sent a look of disapproval her way, then went on to explain. "I do charting mostly. Once the interviews are verified I run numbers through an IBM–2000 and come up with answers to questions."

"You work only for Browning?"

"No. I'm with Templeton and Simms. We tell anyone what's on everyone's mind."

"That's their motto," Lisa added.

"What's the opinion on the vice president's resignation?" Dennis asked.

"That Snelling'll do better without him," Hal said. "Black vote's still around ten percent. And Woodward will bring in a net gain of thirty electoral votes."

"You make it sound as if the election is all over," Sandi remarked.

"It's in the numbers."

"What are people saying about the President's ultimatum?" Dennis asked him.

"Best thing since the Grenada invasion," Hal replied. "Seventy-two percent approval."

"Do you have any figures on the risks of a Persian Gulf war?"

"With the Russians?" Hal's eyebrows lifted in surprise. "I don't think that question's come up," he said.

"A majority sees the ultimatum as Israel's problem. They're the ones at ground zero."

"And what is your opinion?" Dennis asked.

"I don't have one," Hal admitted. "It interferes with my work."

"You're serious?" Dennis said.

"Why, yes," Hal replied with a hint of offense. "Objectivity is an occupational given."

Dennis was stunned by the buzzword.

"Occupational given," he said. "That's incredible. Don't you interpret what you find, personally?"

"News editors do that," Hal explained. "We just give them the numbers."

"And no comment?"

"That's right. Our service provides standardized numerical quotients on any public issue. We ask the question the client wants answered, and we compute the results. With the ultimatum, Snelling's people asked us to monitor public opinion on rearming the Persian Gulf. So we indexed reaction to every statement Henderson's made on the issue on a Zimmer scale."

"Index?"

"A printout sheet."

"And what did you discover?"

"Numbers. Seventy-two percent positive for Snelling in this case. The media do the rest," Hal said flatly. "It's very scientific."

"I'm sure."

"Hal has opinions," Lisa said. "But on issues he deals with, never."

Dennis looked at Sandi for emotional support. He had never heard such nonsense delivered so sincerely. These kids, so favored, so polished, took pride in their objectivity. They didn't want opinions. They were technocrats, bright cogs in a machine they made no effort to understand. As long as ground zero was in someone else's backyard, they would choose to sit out any involvement. Born in the sixties, they were post-Hiroshima children who must believe their opinions worthless. Was it that that made them oblivious to a nuclear bomb? Were they too far removed, or too close, to Hiroshima to care? It made no sense to hold an opinion in a world programmed for destruction.

Lisa might have opinions someday. But for Hal it was too late. He did "charting" in a world that went by the numbers. He was a robot, an IBM–2000's accessory, a cipher. And there was nothing wrong with that because "it's very scientific."

After they left, Dennis tried to sleep. But instead he tossed next to Sandi's warm side until the clock radio's digits flashed three-seventeen. He tumbled in and out of sleep afterward, unable to close his eyes.

Chapter Twelve

It was a refreshing walk to the White House. The clear afternoon sparkled under a high blue sky and reminded Dennis of a Colorado day, except that the snow piled along the curbs was measured in inches rather than feet. The walkway was dry, any melting suspended by week-long below-freezing temperatures. He walked quickly past the West Gate, identified himself to the guard, and reported to the President's private secretary.

He entered the Oval Office, the secretary one step behind. She quietly retreated, closing the door, and he stood alone, wondering if the President, seated with his back to him, knew he was there. On the floor, an arrow-clutching eagle in the rug's presidential seal screamed furiously at the rim of gold stars that encircled him.

A loud snap of the swivel chair behind the desk broke the silence. The President whirled around, threw Dennis a cold stare, and pointed to a nearby chair.

"That was some crack you made—'naked stewardess.' I hope it was said in haste. To get my attention. Now allow me to get yours." The President pushed himself away from the desk. "You live with a woman who works for Senator Browning, who in turn feeds Governor Henderson. Can you guess what rumors I'm hearing?"

Dennis blinked as the President's voice rose.

"No. I can't," he said.

"I'm no mathematician, but I can spot a triangle of circumstances when I see one. Henderson is sniffing all around this city looking for dirty laundry on what he thinks is a harem in the White House. Is this supper talk at your place?''

Dennis reeled at the accusation. ''You've got to be kidding!'' he exclaimed.

''Kidding? Am I known for my sense of humor? Look, I don't know what in hell you're up to. Just remember this. Henderson and old Brownie are more desperate with each new poll. They're after my ass, and they'll grab at anything they think might help. Cheap shots about stewardesses and mistresses ricochet in all directions. In the future, keep sordid remarks to yourself. Do you understand?''

Dennis's jaw tightened. He gripped the chair's armrest.

''I've just taken the risk of dumping a Vice President. I will not risk a scandal.'' Snelling paused to catch his breath. ''I'm not as unbeatable as the papers say.''

Dennis shook off his astonishment. ''You believe I'm spending my time spreading scandal?'' he asked slowly. ''Mr. President, I could care less about your reelection. I have more important matters to discuss than the campaign.''

''Oh, do you?''

''Did Ron Pryor tell you anything else besides the crack about a stewardess?''

Snelling inhaled. ''He mentioned rumors. And talking with Russian scientists. You know that's out. What else do you consider more important than my reelection?''

''Alpha-One,'' Dennis answered.

''I understand you couldn't keep your nose out of that, either.''

''Mr. President, if what I'm about to tell you is true, you'll have no reason to fear a scandal.''

"What do you mean?"

"I mean that what I have to say has nothing to do with candidate Snelling. And I resent any references to my nose or anyone's dirty laundry." Dennis hesitated. He lowered his voice to add, "I'm making a report to the President of the United States."

The title, stretched out slowly, seemed to calm his accuser. "Go on," Snelling said.

"What I'm about to say is neither rumor nor fact. It's speculation."

"Speculation on what? Get to it."

"On a comet."

"I've heard all about that."

"What have you heard?"

"The Russians have found a comet. It's heading for earth. It'll land on New York City during rush hour on Wall Street or incinerate Camp David. Probably in time for my second inaugural. Is that what you've come to tell me?"

"Sir, Alpha-One is set to take pictures of space between here and Jupiter," Dennis said calmly. "If we find a speck of light traceable to any source not already plotted, we'll know whether or not the comet is a hoax."

"Are you telling me there is a comet?"

"No."

"But there may be one."

"It's a possibility."

"What shall I do with possibilities, huh?" Snelling asked with a sneer. "It's possible the Soviets are preparing a first strike. How's that for a comet?"

"Alpha-One will tell us yes or no," Dennis insisted. "If a comet's what's out there, we'll know its size, direction, and speed. But only if I can get a fix on it from Soviet astronomers."

"Drop it!"

"Sir—"

"Forget it, I said." The President stood up and moved away from the desk. At the windows he turned to ask, "You were the one who slammed the door on a comet probe last fall. You even had us sit out Halley's comet. What's changed your mind?"

"Silence at Riga, for one thing," Dennis said. "And an orbiting Russian telescope with an electrographic camera."

"Where did you get all that?"

"From Dr. Cho Chan and from Dr. Franz."

"Dr. France," Snelling scoffed. "The same man who told you David Horowitz is alive and well and living in Israel?"

Dennis deflected the President's scornful look.

"Cho Chan told me about Riga," he said.

Snelling turned to face him directly. He pointed a finger. "Let me tell you something. You may not like those files I let you see. They may not be up to your high standards. But that's what we go by. Not speculation from foreigners."

"The files are useless."

"I didn't ask for your opinion."

"Just a report."

"That's all. And no comet."

"I didn't mention a comet."

"You didn't mention CEP either. Now you know why Dean Newcombe thinks you're a clown. Look, you don't need to search any further. I appreciate the enthusiasm, Doctor, but your Alpha-One camera is a waste. A mistake. How much was it, anyway?"

"With link-ups to Kitt Peak, three million and a half," Dennis replied.

"That's a big lump to hide, but we'll cover it."

"Mr. President, it doesn't have to be a waste. It is money down the drain unless we get a fix on a position. To track."

"From the Russians?"

"Yes."

"No! We'll take the loss. God knows there's more to worry about now than a light in the sky." Snelling cocked his head. "You don't understand, do you? The comet is bullshit, a decoy to cover Riga's work on Circular Error Probable. You helped confirm this for us when you nixed the comet probe."

Dennis's eyebrows twisted in confusion.

"Yes," the President continued. "Don't look so surprised. Your rejection of Hendley's scheme brought us back to square one, to the only other explanation for silence at Riga. CEP ten."

"I had no idea of those consequences."

"Of course not. We needed a second opinion. Your rejection simply confirmed what military intelligence had been telling us all along. Riga's been our target since '86. And we intend to knock it out this year." Snelling paused, then sat. Dennis looked at him, cursing under his breath the man's use of selective intelligence. A secret file that wasn't secret, an Israeli ghost scientist, a phantom space shot, an Evergreen recommendation meant to be rejected, and a Chief Executive intent on destroying what might be a vacant Latvian laboratory.

Sensing from Snelling's finger tapping that the conversation was coming to an end, Dennis knew he must get to the point before it was too late.

"Cho Chan mentioned another theory," he said.

"A theory? Not a rumor?"

"Speculation. There's another possible reason for shutdown at Riga."

"Dr. Covino—"

"Please hear me out. Riga alters polar bias and warps the earth's magnetosphere. Radio waves of that power and frequency can damage the protective magnetic field surrounding the whole planet. Stopping transmissions would be a reasonable precaution if a new comet had been found."

"If."

"Their orbiting observatory makes them the first to know."

"But consider the source. A Chinese astronomer. A communist."

"He is a Nobel astronomer," Dennis said, stung by the slur.

"The Academy lets anybody in these days. What makes this second theory of his any better than the first?"

"Chan's integrity and reputation as a scientist."

"I see. And do you also vouch for Dr. France?"

"On space optics and astrophysics, yes, I do."

"I'll take the first explanation," Snelling said. "Even if you were to come in here with pictures of a comet, a comet the Soviets might or might not choose to announce to the world, what would that mean to me? Another possibility."

"It would confirm or deny the second theory."

"So?"

"Mr. President, if I'm not out of order, you're working on the shaky assumption that the Soviets are as cocksure as you are. You give them a lot of credit."

"I always have."

"Confirmation of a new comet, one that might approach dangerously close to earth orbit, would set the world on its ear. It could blow things sky high."

Snelling raised a palm from the desk blotter. A smirk appeared on his lips as he spoke. "This is beginning to sound like warnings we heard in '85. All that excitement for nothing."

Dennis resented the President's resistance to anything—even a theory—standing in the way of a fait accompli. It was obvious his mind was closed to any other explanation but his own for silence at Riga.

It was time for a scare, Dennis decided. Maybe the Tunguska precedent could cut through the stone.

As he began to explain the 1908 event, the President at first appeared to listen with guarded interest. Then he took to glancing at his watch and shifted several times in his chair. But as Dennis dwelled on the damage at Tunguska, his eyes became more attentive, his movements less frequent. At the description of the catastrophe's resemblance to a nuclear blast, he asked, "All that damage from a block of dirty ice?"

Dennis went on to describe the dust cloud, the eerie sunsets lasting for months, the furious heat generated by the impact's energy, the H-bomb-force winds. At the mention of damage to radio and electric fields, the President stopped him.

"In 1908?"

"Nothing compared with the mess it would cause today. For roads and horses, substitute satellites, air traffic, and all telecommunications."

"Blackouts?"

"Unprecedented chaos," Dennis said. "No one lives in villages anymore. Panic would be worldwide even before impact," he predicted, "and the four or five hours between verification of ground zero and impact would make evacuation a joke."

"So there is no preparation," Snelling concluded.

"None to speak of. Once the fireball is spotted in the sky, it would be the end of the world for anyone witnessing it. The last thing they'd see."

"A nightmare."

"Catastrophe one," Dennis said. "What happens next is worse."

"How's that?"

"The damage to nonhuman life is repairable. A comet is ice and dust. A meteor or apollo object would leave a crater, but not a comet. After impact, the earth would start healing itself. But before impact, with a light in the skies"—Dennis bit his lower lip—"it would look like a nuclear attack. Any nuclear-powered government might decide to respond with a strike that could end the world—on a mistake."

Snelling moved around in the chair, then fixed his glance on Dennis. "You've told me what could happen, Doctor. What *has* happened. Now tell me, if a comet is so dangerous, why was Halley's barely visible?"

"Halley's has a known orbit. It's predictable. A new comet is an unknown."

"You said that. I didn't." The President pulled a pen from its ebony stand, and from a side drawer he took a small legal pad. "Now what are the chances of seeing a new one?"

"In any given year," Dennis said, rather reluctantly, "one in ten. Assuming for the moment that this one exists and that it's somewhere this side of Jupiter, on or near earth's plane, and it shows a bright tail, one in a thousand."

Snelling added two zeros to the ten he scratched on the pad. "Four big assumptions," he said. "And the chances of a collision, like Tung—?"

"Tunguska." Dennis's voice dropped. "Mathematically, it's remote."

"How remote?"

"In a given year, one in two hundred and fifty thousand."

Snelling paused long enough to raise his eyebrows, then wrote the number. "Okay, and how about a warning? Once spotted, how long before we know if one will come close? Roughly."

"Once clearing the sun, at most a week."

"Assumption number five."

Dennis nodded, uneasy with the numbers. "This is speculation," he reminded the President.

"I should say. I assume that, like falling Russian satellites, hitting the earth would break things down to seventy-thirty water-to-land impact."

"That's correct. A large comet hitting the ocean at midsea would cause typhoon-size seas rippling to land. A hit anywhere near Hawaii would swamp a whole island. A water fall, in the Mediterranean or the Gulf of Mexico, would mean tidal waves. Tidal waves near any coastline. Old Testament-size tidal waves."

"Of course. And the thirty percent chance of a land fall, what odds there?"

"In any given year, one in a hundred thousand."

The President entered this figure on his pad. He looked up into Dennis's eyes. "So after seven assumptions, starting with if a comet exists, and then odds as high as a quarter of a million to one, you want to confer with Soviet scientists?"

Dennis answered, "There'll be no images from Alpha-One without their coordinates. Not knowing what the Soviets may know shrinks those odds." His eyes settled on the dark zeros beneath the President's hand. Snelling dropped the pen.

"So there we are," he said. "Back to earth, Doctor." Snelling sat back and placed his hands behind his head. "I've been called a fool before, but never an asshole." He looked down at his numbers. "I'd look better funding a search for the Loch Ness monster."

"My opinion is that you need to know before any Russian announcement makes us all go to pieces," Dennis said.

"It's all very interesting and I applaud the homework you've done to warn me. But surely you'll agree, as you once upon a time did, that this is very far from a dangerous situation. The National Security Council gives me more compelling odds every other day. In fact, any danger from even a confirmed comet is more psychological than real."

"Yes, of course."

"Then, Doctor, we agree again," he said, leaning forward. "It is a ploy. A psychological cover to explain Riga's shutdown and to protect CEP work."

Dennis wiped his palms together. "Sir, we don't know one way or the other," he said after a few seconds. "The danger is not in the numbers, it's in ignorance. If this is a planned hoax, any information we get from them will prove it."

Snelling shook his head. "Information they would share would just keep us on any track they choose, and support a different theory from the one we are going by. A light in the sky has always been a diversion. Let's not be fooled."

"I say let's be sure."

"I can't afford to spend any more time on odds like this. I know how you hate politics, but think of this: as the President's science adviser, what Soviet scientist could tell you anything of value without risking a career change in Siberia?"

Snelling placed both hands down on the blotter, deliberately, like a judge confident in his decision. "We have more important things to do than wait for the sky to fall on the word of Comrade Chicken Little. It'll be hardball soon enough."

"My responsibility is to inform you and to advise you," Dennis replied.

"No question. Your advice is to talk to the Russians, and I'm rejecting it. They're the ones who need to speak up."

"The ultimatum?"

"Theirs could come at any time," Snelling nodded. "Maybe election week. Wouldn't that be appropriate?"

This man was incapable of considering anything beyond the scope of his reelection. The numbers—polls and odds—ruled in this secure house where even the chimneys were capped. Dennis saw no way out.

"Mr. President, if you reject my advice, then I'm of no more use to you."

"Don't do that."

"Do what?"

"Threaten to quit. I've heard it before. I'm still not getting through to you, am I? You don't see why I can't talk to them, do you?"

"White tried to talk."

"Yes."

"He went to Spain."

"Against my direct order."

"Which he paid for."

"White's a sick man."

"Does everyone who disobeys one of your orders get sick or die?"

Snelling squinted as though stung by the reply. He reached into a drawer and pulled out a printout sheet.

"Sy White talked to defectors," he said, "who gave him this." He handed the sheet to Dennis. One look at the flow of numbers, like a bank statement run wild, was enough to make his jaw drop.

"You've seen it before?" Snelling guessed.

"I have a copy," Dennis said, recognizing the sequence. "We're studying it now."

"And what do you think it is?"

"A code," Dennis said. "Some kind of code."

"A damn good one too."

"White gave you this?"

Snelling nodded. "He dropped it here. More time, he said. More time to study. Well, you scientists have that luxury. I don't. I have no more time."

"Do you know what this is?" Dennis asked.

"His Swiss bank account, for all I know. He threw it on my desk and started shouting. When he became abusive, the Secret Service took him out."

"Shouting?"

"Stammering about 'Riga, Riga.'"

Dennis looked again at the printout. It was a duplicate of the puzzle he had given to Jan Fortes.

"So, you take it," Snelling said. "And this." He passed him the paper with Dennis's odds scribbled across it. "And get back to work. If you plan to hand in a resignation letter, whenever it reaches me, I'll dump it. You'll leave when I dismiss you, not before."

Dennis rose with the President, who placed a hand on his shoulder as they walked to the door. His grip was strong, his tone oddly familiar.

"I'd hate to lose you, Dennis. We've got lots of projects ahead of us. I've been making promises to farmers, fishermen, engineers, everyone, and I need your help on some very down-to-earth matters. So think before you act, will you? And don't worry about that three and a half million. I'll absolve it."

Dennis left the Oval Office numbed by a headache that had begun coming on when the President called for the numbers. His temples pounded with each step back to the Executive Office Building. He lifted his coat collar and moved quickly, smelling snow in the air. Heavy, dark clouds now filled the sky, and the wind had changed direction, turning afternoon into a wintry early evening. Not even four o'clock, and every light in the city seemed to be on. Cars and buses had their lights on too, as they honked impatiently to get to a safe port ahead of the storm.

Back at his office, he dropped his coat on a chair and called for his secretary. "Heather, get me an aspirin, please. And tell Dr. Fortes I want to see her right away."

He told Fortes he wanted quick action on White's number code. She looked at her watch, but was smart enough not to comment on the hour. She left with the printout that the President had given Dennis and with a promise to have the numbers processed within thirty-six hours.

Dennis reached home in time for dinner, and even before Sandi could ask, he told her about his conversation with the President.

"Sandi, I offered to resign today."

She made no reply.

"The words just came out," he said. "I told him he doesn't have the information he thinks he has and that my advice is to get more from the Russians."

"He wouldn't hear of it."

"That's right," he replied lifelessly. "It seems Seymour White tried to tell him the same thing. So I concluded he had no more use for me."

"And what did he say?"

"He won't accept my resignation now. But I can't stay. After the election, I'll have to go elsewhere." He waited to see what her reaction would be. Sandi took a deep breath and let her fingers rim the coffee cup slowly.

"You want me to check at Georgetown for you?" she asked. Dennis broke into laughter.

"I love you," he said.

"Dennis, I mean it."

"I know. We'll see. Maybe I'll go back to teaching. Or I could work for Hendley International Industries."

"Dennis, I'm taking the Georgetown job in August," she said. "For at least one year. You don't have plans to leave town?"

"I won't leave town. And I don't have plans. I just can't work for Snelling. He's had me go along with him in two lies, keep quiet while he wires the Persian Gulf and sets his missiles on Riga. He has no need for a scientist. An analyst, maybe, but not a scientist. I'm a decoration for campaign show."

He sipped the last of his coffee and said, "It was a mistake. I thought it was what I wanted. You know, like at Christmas. You're dying for something, and when you see it in real life under the tree, it's smaller, takes batteries, or it wasn't what you thought it would be."

They turned in early. Dennis unburdened himself in the dark, talking about the conspiracy aboard Air Force One,

the dumping of the Vice President, and the comet odds
he had given to Snelling. For the first time in a long time,
he slept through the night.

IN THE MORNING Dennis felt refreshed, not even minding the slippery dusting of snow under his new radial tires.
He began his first day as a silent lame duck in conference
with tiresome representatives of the National Institutes
of Health. His attention flagged as seven well-meaning
professionals talked at length on the need for supplemen-
tal emergency funding to track killer bees about to descend on Texas and Louisiana. He toyed with the idea of
sending as many Department of Health fieldworkers
down there with bug spray, but decided he'd keep the decision to himself.

A call from his secretary advised him that she was holding Mrs. White on the line. He left to take the call and listened to a tearful woman tell him that her husband had
fallen into a coma. The doctors were not optimistic. Dennis phrased his condolences carefully. Then, hanging up,
he asked Heather about the propriety of sending flowers.
She said no.

White's condition closed another door. The man whose
office he now occupied, who couldn't handle Presidential Order 047, and who hated numbers, was slipping beyond reach. Gone, like David Horowitz. He returned to
his meeting in time to assure the health officials of his
support.

After lunch, Dennis tackled a drawerful of paper duties
that had been put aside while he was with the President.
A paper on Voyager 2 drafted for the National Science
Foundation sat atop a high pile on the work table next to
his desk. Underneath its bands of red and blue scratch-
outs lay another draft-in-progress, this one of a speech

destined for a National Press Club luncheon in April. And farther down in the pile, more projects, all with deadlines, all clamoring for his attention: meteorological reports for the Secretaries of Commerce and Agriculture, monitoring data on western earthquake patterns for the Army Corps of Engineers, a time-sensitive report on hazardous waste containment for the EPA. Under the table sat a quarterly budget awaiting his scrutiny and signature.

He fingered through two separate stacks of pink callback slips and hastily written notes from people whom he winced to recognize from their scrawled initials. Heather appeared at the door.

"Doctor, the technicians are here for the Alpha-One equipment."

"Fine," he quipped. "Think they'll take some of this paper with them?" But she had closed the door before he could see her reaction. He tried to get back to work, but the Alpha-One computer now being dismantled down the hall occupied his mind. He dropped his pen and went down to the conference room.

Two gray-suited men detached the wires between the untouched main console and its bright receiver box. They looped the multicolored cable into several marked boxes and shrouded the unused keyboard in its white protective hood. Standing in the doorway, he could smell the still-fresh plastic. Kitt Peak had been disconnected. And with it, all contact with the orbiting Alpha-One's Griboval camera. Astronomers have no time for cosmic jaywalkers, he remembered one colleague telling him as he begged off the tracking project. Palomar had said the same, and the Jet Propulsion Lab had refused to rearrange their schedule for a "wild-goose chase."

The technicians sealed the four boxes, and as he watched them being loaded onto dollies, Dennis recalled the President's willingness to cover the expenses. Expenses that would almost certainly be channeled now for other equipment aimed not at the heavens but at Riga. An exchange of ultimatums. Mutual threats. Silence. Disconnected giants at the brink of mutually assured destruction. MADness. They were right and he was wrong. Circular Error Probable of ten meters. A Russian ICBM aimed at New York City would detonate over Central Park, not on the outskirts of New Rochelle. CEP ten, rotation, and magnetic north was the formula for checkmate. The West could never match the advantage Einstein's physics allowed the East. Polar bias, defeated by CEP ten, makes a sleek bobsled downhill run for the East, uphill for the West. The ultimate missile accuracy was theirs. Anything the West could fire in retaliation would be a shot into the final darkness. And the science adviser, the odd man out, was the last to get the message that made Snelling so sure. Here he stood at the dismantling of a pet project that only he had believed in. A clown, a frantic court jester, with a soothsayer's warning to Caesar about an unseen comet.

The older workman bumped his arm, presenting a clipboard for his signature.

"Where's it go now?" he asked.

The technician took his cigar out of his mouth to answer.

"Pentagon warehouse number five," he said. "Alexandria. Where it came from." He tore off a copy of the form Dennis had signed and gave it to him. More paper to file.

The men left, passing Dr. Fortes in the hallway. She hailed Dennis.

"I have your numbers, Doctor," she said brightly. "I didn't know Seymour was into astrology."

"Astrology?"

"The number sequence corresponds only to celestial coordinates."

"What?"

"It's not a code." She handed him the printout and the attached explanation. "We checked it over several times. There's no mistake. These are coordinates for the constellation of the Charioteer."

Dennis blinked, dumbfounded at the final word: *Auriga*.

Chapter Thirteen

It made no difference to Dennis that the soft tap-tap-tap he heard on the overseas line meant that his call was being recorded, or that somewhere in the Pentagon's Oakton Communications Center a computer was printing out the name and number of Purple Mountain Observatory in Nanking. What mattered was the clear reception and the excitement in Dr. Cho Chan's voice.

"Dr. Covino. We have it in our sights now. Comet Tsuchinsan-Cato. It's been playing tricks with us for nights, but it is the Russian comet. That is certain."

"Auriga."

"Auriga. The Charioteer."

Dennis reached for a pad and pencil. "What do you have, Doctor?" he asked. In the background, he could hear loud voices and the familiar rustle of unfolding printouts. After a few seconds, Chan's high-pitched voice returned.

"We have a comet one to two point seven kilometers in diameter. At Right Ascension fifteen hours, thirty minutes. Declination seventeen degrees. West class."

"Yes." Dennis wrote the figures furiously.

"Fall sunward. Thirteenth magnitude, at decimal point seven seven eight Universal Time."

"The chart?" Dennis asked, taking down the last number.

"Epoch 1950. Mitor—excuse me. Your equivalent would be Gamma Star Chart sixty-three."

"And the speed?"

"Variable with considerable wobbling. Last reading shows seventy-nine thousand kilometers an hour."

"Fast," Dennis whistled.

"Very fast. But small."

"Are there other sightings?"

"Two here in China, and at least as many from Japan."

"They all say comet?"

"Yes, with one exception. Tokyo Observatory denies a comet until they confer with Sarantof in the Soviet Union. This is how we knew where to look."

Dennis dismissed the political implications of his associate's comment, but he made note of the name Sarantof.

"Calving?" he asked.

"No sign of splitting up. However, it seems quite unstable. Shaking. We are checking our mountings. It may have broken up on the other side of Jupiter. At least that's our explanation of the hour for the perturbations the Soviets detected."

"In August?"

"Yes," Chan replied. "Have you spotted it?"

"Not yet. But we have the coordinates."

"Very good."

Dennis jotted down some quick calculations as his free hand searched for the Sony calculator. He stored the numbers while his colleague continued.

"Tsuchinsan-Cato was rendered invisible by dust in the Crab Nebula until it spun out this side of Jupiter. That is our current theory, anyway. We have so many numbers."

Dennis shared the rising excitement, and at the same time, he felt a sudden dread.

"Is it accelerating?" he asked, counting on the remote chance the comet might speed up and toss itself out of the solar system.

"No. It is slowing," came the cautious reply. "If and when it calves, it will slow more."

"Do you have figures on perihelion? When will it get closest to the sun?"

"Rough estimate, in six weeks."

"April."

"Very rough estimate."

"A West class sungrazer," Dennis concluded with a sigh.

"Dr. Covino, Tsuchinsan-Cato is more than that. You will see. From our calculations what we have is an earth-grazer."

Dennis gripped the phone. He closed his eyes as Cho Chan continued. "In July, mid-July we estimate, this comet's outgoing path could intersect earth orbit. We await your confirmation on this, of course."

"Certainly," Dennis replied warily. "And the tail, Dr. Chan?"

"Only bursts of brightness so far. But a long and growing tail. We have not yet calculated its length. New sunspot activity should make it longer and brighter in—as the weeks go by."

"It will soon be visible from earth, then," Dennis said, "in the Northern Hemisphere."

"Yes. It should fill the sky, even in daylight, once it comes around from behind the sun."

"And then?"

"Outward bound, the tails should be spectacular if there's anything left in the coma. Naked-eye view by early July is almost a certainty. And we will be washed in its dust for some time. Magnificent sunsets, like Krakatoa."

The vision of the volcano's eerie artistry in the skies interrupted Dennis's calculations. As Chan spoke, he worked out the figures within a time frame to give himself an idea of the orbit.

"Any chance it's more than a show?" he asked at last.

"A show?"

"You mentioned an intersection with the earth's orbit. How close could it come?"

"Too early to calculate. We are far from establishing an accurate orbit." Chan hesitated. "Are you thinking of a fall?"

"Is it possible?"

"Mathematically, yes. But this—"

"I know," Dennis interrupted. "Two blind fireflies colliding in the area of a base—soccer field."

"I don't follow you, Doctor."

"I was thinking of Tunguska."

"Oh, yes."

The flat reply disturbed Dennis. In one corner of his pad, he etched the word *Cato*. "Well?" he asked.

"What do you want me to say, Dr. Covino? That Cato could collide with us?"

"Is a fall possible?" Dennis asked.

"It is unpredictable," Chan answered. "Both the comet and the chances. Yet Tunguska is a fact."

"It is more than a fact. It's a precedent."

"If you say so. But could this be it? I don't know. To tell the truth, I always fight the temptation to think the worst. A West class comet such as this one last passed maybe half a million years ago. We are in all likelihood the first of our race to see it. Surely there will be enough time to study."

"And time enough for warning?"

"Warning? Well, yes, of course. You are in the service of the President. I understand. You must be thinking of panic."

"We have cried wolf with all the comets in my lifetime, Doctor. If Cato is coming in close, people will have to be told."

"In China the Emperor used to be Keeper of the Calendar," Chan said, "and things we are discussing now were once classified top secret. Comets were secrets of state. Comet fever made the masses restless and foretold doom uncomfortable to the ruling class. Two thousand years ago, I would have lost my head for saying as much as I have." He chuckled. "Thankfully, we are approaching the twenty-first century."

"We should thank our lucky stars," Dennis quipped.

"Precisely. I would say a warning is at best premature. Sightings will rush in to Harvard and the International Astronomical Union within hours, I'm sure. But you need have no fear of panic, Doctor. Not after Halley's. In fact, you'll have a harder time telling people how bright and at the same time how distant Cato is than in convincing them it marks the end of the world."

"I'm sure you're right," Dennis granted. "Thank you, Dr. Chan. I will set our sights on Cato. And congratulations on your sighting."

"Thank you. But we must credit the Soviet astronomers. They've known of this comet for perhaps a year. For such a small size, this is a great feat. They have tracked it and named it long before we even knew where to look. They've named it Aurora."

"Aurora."

"Yes, for the dawn."

Cho Chan repeated the celestial coordinates, which Dennis verified, entering each equation into his calculator. He assured his colleague that he would secure an American sighting before week's end.

Dennis hung up, staring at the notepad whose symbolic jumble challenged deciphering. Tsuchinsan—"Purple Mountain;" Cato—"the Censor." Intentionally ironic? he wondered. The "Russian" comet, Aurora, visible, and therefore no longer Russian. Censored? A calculated discovery? Maybe the President was right: "more psychological than real." First the Hendley "plant," then the radio coordinates pointing straight to Auriga. Auriga. Were the Russians sending a message? Then why the secrecy? Don't they want boasting rights to a magnificent find? Or have their plans all along been more earthly?

He bit into the pencil eraser. A new comet. Confirmed. West class, on its first approach to the earth, perhaps, since man began to walk upright. An earthgrazer. Orbit not yet known. A lone traveler, older than the earth, born in the outer chaos, and as restless as the universe.

The phone rang once. As expected, Dr. Lyle was on the line from the Smithsonian Astrophysical Observatory, whose Central Bureau for Astronomical Telegrams had recorded four amateur sightings in less than forty-eight hours. Cato-Aurora's orbit would be known shortly, thanks to Einstein and a network of alerted astronomers reporting to the Cambridge clearinghouse. No problem, Lyle assured him, since the numbers they shared would bring the speck into telescopic view in a matter of days. Dennis glanced at the concentric circles he had drawn. The rough dots marking the sun and the earth stared back at him as the equation's third element, Aurora's orbit, appeared as a darkened question mark. "Could intersect earth's orbit in mid-July," he recalled Chan saying. July. Could.

He reached for the phone and ordered Heather to get him Dr. Palmer at Arizona's Kitt Peak. Over a line full of static, Palmer, after hearing Dennis out, apologized for not being able to help with tracking in Auriga. Once word had reached the observatory's director that the Alpha-One project had been scrapped, he had given orders to resume an ongoing project aimed at other stars. An Air Force general had booked the facility to search for interstellar radio pulses. With a resigned shrug, Dennis hung up to call Dr. Sanders at Palomar.

"Sorry to hear about your probe. What can we do for you?"

"Can you beam in on Auriga for us? For two or three uninterrupted nights?" Dennis asked. "I have coordinates on a new comet."

"New comet! I'm sorry, Doctor. We can't. Orders from the Pentagon and the JPL. We'll be nowhere near Auriga until July at least. I can't move a thing. We're locked in on Vega. Orders."

Silently cursing Sanders's detached tone, Dennis slammed the phone down. With two strikes against him, he asked Heather for Dr. Loren Gray at the U.S. Naval Observatory. Gray was a good friend and a frequent caller. His cultivated disregard for all things military held out some hope. Dennis read the Chinese coordinates to Gray's new assistant, Dr. Joan Kohler, who read each one back. She had a clear, sexy voice, but to Dennis, the sound of the observatory's massive computer banks in the background was even more attractive.

"We'll get on it," Dr. Kohler promised. "Dr. Gray and I can give you four days. Tops."

"I'll take it, and I'll be over."

That night, Dennis arrived by cab at the dark grounds of the nearby observatory. Out of habit, he checked the sky. Clear. Thirteenth magnitude, Chan had said. With luck, the clouds would stay away, and he might find something tonight. He entered the main lobby, showing his clearance badge to a woman whose voice he recognized even before she identified herself as Joan Kohler. The shapely young woman extended a slender hand in greeting. She wore rimless glasses with a tint of red that magnified her eyes without complimenting them. Straight blond hair fell down her bulky sweater's back, ending in a point just above the curve of her hips. As Dennis followed her down a long corridor, he noticed her jeans' round seat patch worn white. Her graceful gait reminded him of Sandi's, careless and supple, the sexy abandon of an attractive woman not used to being noticed.

Joan Kohler turned a corner and announced a stop at the deserted first-floor kitchenette. In the confining light, Dennis noted that faint fatigue lines had already claimed the corners of her otherwise pretty mouth.

"Coffee?" she asked.

"Yes. Thank you."

She pulled up her sleeves and began gathering the coffee fixings on a small counter. Her silence suggested overwork or else that she was not used to having company.

"Dr. Gray is upstairs?" Dennis asked.

"We can't get him down," she replied. "He spent all day with the charts and your coordinates." Her head bowed to the brewing coffee, she added, "This will be supper."

"Makes me feel a little guilty, but in the morning we could all be famous," Dennis said.

"I'm sure we'll find something." When the coffee was ready, she filled three cups and said, "This way."

Dennis followed her down another long corridor. With each echoing footstep, he realized how far his career had taken him from the cinder-block walls, the labs, the jargon, the advances measured now in months. It was at least a decade since he had walked inside an observatory and even more since he had jumped into the telescope saddle to view the stars. In another life, a facility such as the Naval Observatory would have been as comfortable, as homey as a dormitory room. No longer. Maybe it was his reticent escort, or the strange buzzing of the computers in each small room he passed, but it was not the same. While machines clicked away, piercing space way beyond human capacity, he was bursting with excitement over a new comet and celebrating with coffee served by a beautiful automaton.

They stopped underneath a blue light, where a tiny elevator lifted them to dome level. When the doors parted with a buffered snap, they entered an enormous dark room where the only visible shape loomed high above their heads. The telescope shaft thrust into the outer darkness to the clicking sound of programmed adjustments. Over the hum of several hidden fans, Dennis heard a hollow "hello" from a distant perch. With Dr. Kohler in the lead, he carefully mounted a circular stairway.

"Loren, it's Dr. Covino," she announced in a pilgrim's whisper. A gloved hand passed into Dennis's view. He shook it, peering up toward the eclipsed face of his colleague.

"Dennis, I'm in Auriga now. At Capella," Gray said. "Since I got your call we've been sweeping along the coordinates you gave us."

"Anything?" Kohler asked, passing a hot cup of coffee to each scientist.

"Yeah," Gray laughed. "Nebular dust. Thank you." He sipped the coffee, letting its rising steam warm his face. "I'm not used to this surgical scanning. Damn rough on the eyes. I don't know how amateurs have the patience to do this night after night."

"How's the viewing?" Dennis wanted to know.

"Couldn't be better. I have a light in view. Something that my charts say shouldn't be there." Gray, seated like a movie director on a boom, moved his notebook into the platform's red light. "Our computer read off those co-ordinates nicely," he said. "There's a new photographic plate being developed downstairs now. That'll tell us if the dot is moving."

Gray's profile caught the red light's glow, showing a straight nose and a full beard. He twisted his neck, shedding fatigue, and changed places with Dr. Kohler. Descending to the lower platform where Dennis waited, Gray took off the gloves, thrusting them into his oversize pockets.

"Plates are good quality so far," he said assuringly. "If there are still no smudges, we might see our comet. West class, you say."

"Yes. What do we have—so far?"

"A stiff neck and a bad case of fanny fatigue," Gray shrugged, a twinkle in his eyes.

"Loren, do we have a comet?"

"I think the chances are pretty good. But you'll have to be patient, Dennis. There's a lot out there tonight. If this new Schmidt camera is as clean as usual, we should have good pictures to go by."

"Tonight?"

Gray checked his watch in the half-light. "In half an hour maybe. How's that for service?"

The two men sat on the lower platform railing. Dennis gazed up three stories at the large silo of a telescope. Its nose poked through the roof slit, beamed on the stars of Auriga. A black rectangle hung taut like a diamond-studded belt taped over the dome opening. The room was silent save for the distant hum of the fans, hidden somewhere in the inner darkness above. Dennis grabbed a handful of cable that serpented the cold railing.

"Loren, I appreciate your quick cooperation."

"Don't mention it. It's been slow here. Don't mention that, either. We have a flexible schedule this month."

"Unlike Kitt Peak and Palomar," Dennis said, sipping his coffee.

"You mean you got nothing from those two?"

"Kitt Peak is back to cataloging infrared emitting sources for the Air Force. I was put on hold."

"For a comet sighting?"

"Because of a comet sighting," Dennis explained. "I've tied them up too long with an orbiting link-up camera."

"I heard." Gray nodded. He pulled at the back of his neck. "Well, no electrographic will be necessary for this puffball, if we can show that it's moved and that it is what you say it is. What's it called again?"

"Tsuchinsan-Cato."

"A mouthful. Chinese?"

"Purple Mountain," Dennis said. "Russians are calling it Aurora."

Gray repeated the name with approval, then crumpled his Styrofoam cup and tossed it into the blackness below. It hit with an echo that filled the room.

"Aurora," he said again. "Coma condensation could be as high as six."

"Bright."

"What I saw last night was bright. We've taken two or three shots already."

"Hey," Kohler shouted from above. "It's gone."

"Gone?" Dr. Gray jumped at the word, then ran up the stairs. Dennis followed him, feeling his way cautiously.

"Gone," Gray repeated. "Get another plate ready, Joan. I'll recenter."

She dropped from the chair and scurried down the stairs past Dennis. Gray, taking her place, punched a hand-size keyboard connected to the downstairs computer. The machine instantly chatted back fresh numbers. He touched another button, activating a loud warning buzzer. The telescope rumbled and tilted at his command, then halted. He put his gloves back on and focused the lens.

"That's it," he said. "I've got it back in focus."

Kohler returned with the plates and handed them to Gray. While the director installed the delicate squares into a lens tray, Kohler took a position below, then called out her okay. Gray, his eyes focused into the viewing piece, shouted back. "Go ahead, Joan."

Instantly, a clicking sound filled the dome room. From her station somewhere under the stairway's latticework, Kohler readied the next series of exposures.

"Go," Gray repeated. Another shot snapped, to the sound of an X-ray hum. Gray readjusted the micrometer setting.

"Again," he shouted. "Okay." With a glance down at Dennis, he added, "A thousand dollars says your lint ball has moved."

"Drift?" Dennis asked.

"I think I can see a tail. Come look."

Dennis gripped the railing, then bounded up to the perch. He lowered his eye onto the viewing piece, being careful not to touch it. Centered in the red cross-hairs, he could see a flickering, fuzzy ball of light. It gleamed weakly, one speck among thousands, a glint in a dusty soup of shimmering light. He gazed on what looked like a single, unfocused dewdrop in a cosmic spider web. So distant, so fragile. He drew back, awed by the view.

"See a tail?" Gray asked.

"No."

"The picture'll tell us. We know at least that it isn't an asteroid. It moved." Gray cupped the eyepiece and looked again. "Unless I miss my guess," he said, "this comet is a rip-roaring flash." Gray sat back, smiling at his colleague. He lit a cigarette. "Dennis, we've done a total of six hours of tracking for you. I'm sure it's your Cato," he puffed. "Micrometer readings show a small, hot, pre-perihelion comet. Just where you said it would be. If you need a quote, that's it."

"The other plates should be ready," Dr. Kohler said. "I'll develop these."

Dennis blew into his fists. "Boy, I forgot how cold it gets in here," he said.

"Not used to the night shift, huh?" Gray laughed. "And it's almost summer." His face turned serious. "You say the Chinese gave you the Auriga bearings?"

Dennis nodded. "By way of the Soviet Union."

"Soviet Union! Amateurs, I'll bet. God bless 'em. They deserve all the glory."

"I'll see that you get your credit," Dennis pledged.

"No thanks. If the Navy catches wind that I'm working with Russian numbers, they'll close me down. One backwater congressman can hold up a year's appropriations. To hell with them," Gray smiled. "This is my first new comet."

"Good work."

Loren Gray's tired shrug said thanks. Joan Kohler climbed the stairs.

"It's your comet, all right," she said. "Look."

She passed the men a silver-dollar-size disc and turned on a bright lamp at Gray's elbow. All three scientists squinted to focus on the tiny plate Dennis held in his hand.

"Blowup should show an incoming West class comet approaching the sun," she reported. "Right where you told us. Magnitude twelve. Faint type-one tail. Estimated speed, Mach sixty-five."

Dennis puffed his cheeks at the velocity.

"Bright and fast," he whistled.

"Whose is it?" Kohler asked.

"Chinese," he said. "Dr. Cho Chan. Nanking."

"Amateur?"

"Nobel professional," Dennis smiled. "Cato will be in next week's I.A.U. circular."

Gray nodded his head and clapped his hands.

"I'll shut down here, Joan. We can wait for the final plates downstairs. Then go home. Dennis, we'll send you the bill," he joked.

"Please do."

Gray stood up. "That's a thirty-thousand-dollar disc you're taking with you, including overtime. Be careful. There'll be at least two more."

The three descended the dark stairs to the observatory's ground-level lounge across from the developing room.

"A new star in the east," Dr. Kohler said. "I wonder how the shepherds will take it."

"That will depend on how we handle it. I'll prepare a statement we can all work from," Dennis said. "Best to explain rather than wait for questions. Some of them will be off-the-wall."

Kohler opened the door to the developing room and left the men in the corridor.

"Even though we can't claim Aurora as our own, we'll stay on it, Dennis," Gray said. "I'll call the I.A.U."

"Don't bother, Loren. I'll handle that. And I'll call you for updates too. When your switchboard lights up, you can direct the calls to my office."

Gray nodded his approval with the arrangement, then asked, "Between us, how did we get coordinates from China?"

"Executive privilege," Dennis replied. "Believe it or not, the Moscow Institute has known for at least eight months."

"Eight months! I didn't think anyone could keep a secret like this that long."

"We chose not to see it. We were looking for something else."

"I don't follow," Gray said.

"I'll explain later. First I've got to show these slides to the President."

"The President? What the hell's he going to do with a comet?"

Joan Kohler emerged from the developing room and handed Dennis the final photo discs. He placed them securely in his jacket.

"If we're lucky," he said, "he'll talk to the Soviet Premier before the sky lights up."

Chapter Fourteen

Three hours' sleep pushed Dennis from patient forbearance to a more assertive tack over the phone with the President's personal secretary.

"Mrs. Goresh, this is an emergency. I have to see the President this morning."

"Yes, Doctor. What is your security number?"

"My what?"

"Your security code number. Code XL."

"I have no number. Look, this is an emergency. I have information the President needs to know right away."

"Sir, I have orders. The President is in conference. He cannot be disturbed until noon without a code number. Only a clearance code can interrupt him."

"Shit," Dennis muttered. The Second Coming would be delayed unless Christ came with a number.

"May I take your message?" the secretary asked.

"Message? No."

"I'm sorry then. Procedures—"

"Is Ron Pryor there?"

"He is with the President."

"Can he be interrupted?"

"Dr. Covino—"

"I know. Orders."

"Yes, sir."

He dropped the phone and walked to the White House, cursing security codes with each step. He passed through the entrance gate routinely but stopped to show the guard his ID. Any attempt to bypass this system, he knew, would bring out three armed regiments within seconds. Orders. The electronic security machine immediately beeped and flashed its approval of his presence. Simon-Says security.

Dennis saluted the guard gruffly, then headed for Ron Pryor's office. Maybe the chief of staff's secretary would be more cooperative. To his surprise, Pryor's secretary was not at her post. As he entered the inner office, at the far end he noticed a crack of light. The door leading to the Oval Office was open a little, and when he approached, he heard the blaring of a television. It was David Henderson's voice. The President's conference consisted of the candidate, Pryor, and the videotaped presence of Snelling's opponent.

Pryor and Snelling, their backs to him, were watching selected campaign cuts on an oversize screen. The governor was announcing, "...crazy to enjoy good times with low inflation while everyone's at work making war machinery for Third World countries. This is as hazardous an occupation as that of supplying Indians with firewater two hundred years ago."

"What a relic," Snelling commented to Pryor. "The best damned system of self-government in history, and he wants to screw it up."

"He's got the Indians hopping mad over it."

"Good. Serves him right."

"...has put the nation back to work," Henderson boomed, "I would just remind you that unemployment was also low during World War Two. This administration has brought us a fragile prosperity, one that deceitfully offers bounty today and only promises tomorrow. The fact is, there will be no economy anywhere if the wrong button is pushed. When the boy who carried a rifle into battle fifty years ago has a grandson today on a nuclear submarine, you can tell how the stakes have changed. This sailor's grandfather killed armed Nazis one at a time, on foreign soil. He, in the safety of his submarine, can start the final war.''

"Cute." Snelling stamped his foot on the carpet. "Not a word about over four hundred safeguards. Thinks he's going to scare them into voting for him."

"Here's the latest cut on talks." Pryor pressed the fast-forward mode.

"...hell will freeze solid before the present stance leads to meaningful talks. And meanwhile we continue to slam doors while the Soviets enjoy acclaim as peacemakers—"

"Turn it off," Snelling ordered. "Peacemakers! Listen to that."

As Pryor snapped the remote button, Dennis pulled back from the door, unsure how to break in on the men. He listened to their muted conversation.

"...mostly cocktail-party stuff," Pryor was saying. "Polls say it isn't causing any danger."

"I can fight out front, not behind my back. Let's leave it there then, shall we?"

"Whatever you say, sir."

"I mean Jack Kennedy had girls going in and out of this place all night."

"That's right."

"Let him hit me for Lattimore. That's all. But on the mistress thing, silence." ·

"Okay."

"Just use the executive advantage. Stress in time of crisis, you know."

"Fine."

Dennis took one step forward and gripped the door edge. As he was about to open it, both men suddenly looked up in the direction of the Oval Office's main door. Wayne Ryan entered, waving a yellow paper that looked like a wire-service rip sheet.

"Mr. President," he said breathlessly, "we've got a problem. The Soviets have announced a new comet."

"A what?" Snelling and Pryor asked at the same time. Both got to their feet.

"A comet," Ryan repeated. "Aurora. An earthgrazer. Says it's going to keep us up nights."

Snelling grabbed the paper, which Pryor read aloud.

"'Soviet astronomers announced today discovery of a new comet. An earthgrazer called Aurora will light up large portions of the Northern Hemisphere this summer, according to Dr. Illyich Sarantof of Moscow's Institute of Science and Technologies. A close apparition is expected in mid-July, the scientist said. Premier Mirenkov has urged talks with all countries to help allay fears.'"

"This is it," the President said, moving to the desk. "We've got our response."

Pryor glanced at Wayne Ryan. "What's the source, Wayne?" he asked.

"Reuters. Good as gold."

"Simultaneous?"

"Worldwide."

"Shit!"

"Wayne, get me the Joint Chiefs," the President ordered.

"I'll verify the transmission," Pryor said, taking a step toward his office.

Dennis appeared in the doorway. "Don't bother, Ron," he said. "It's true."

Pryor stopped in his tracks.

"The comet is real, sir," Dennis said. "Confirmed at the Naval Observatory last night. There's no call for panic."

For a moment, both Pryor and the President seemed frozen in place.

"Make those calls, Wayne," Snelling commanded at last. Ryan left the room.

"How the hell—?" Pryor began.

"Back off, Ron," Snelling said, sitting down at his desk. He stared at Dennis. "So you've found your comet."

"Not mine, Mr. President."

"And no panic."

"That's right," Dennis replied.

The President pointed in the direction of his chief of staff. "Ron, call Lohmann. Tell him I want the Security Council in here first thing tomorrow morning."

After Pryor had gone, Snelling's fingers began to tap the desk blotter. His stare was now icy. "Are you saying they won't use a comet to cover a first strike?" he asked Dennis.

"I can't say that. I trust they won't."

"You trust?"

"It would never work."

"Speculation?"

"Sir, the only assumption I trust is that they know more about this than we do. They'll have to tell us more."

"Don't hold your breath."

"Sir, it's unprecedented."

"It's planned! Why else keep it a secret for nearly a year?" Snelling shook his head. "You don't know these people."

"But you do?"

"Open your eyes, Doctor. Instead of your mouth. We're advancing Red Alert exercises."

"Why?"

"Why? They've put antinuke armies into the street, and now they're calling out the freaks. It's a hoax to divert us."

Dennis moved closer to the President's desk. "They may be supermen, but they can't invent a comet," he said, almost pleading. "It isn't there because they say so anymore. My advice is to hold everything until we have a good idea how spectacular this comet could be."

"Like Halley's, I suppose."

"It is not like Halley's. Why don't you put down your sword?"

Snelling drew in a breath. His eyes enlarged. "Well, the science adviser is now the political adviser. Listen to me, Covino. You were wrong, then right, about this comet, but I can't go any further on your intuition. Not now. This is a trick. They're using it to stir up panic." The President clasped his hands together. "While we're all gazing up at this bright star, the Reds will take advantage. That's the plan."

"The plan?"

"They're set to fire a first strike. What better cover than a dose of comet fever?"

"A comet is not my idea of a secret weapon."

"Our reaction to it is. Newcombe outlined the scenario for me, and he's right. They warn about a comet, get us hopped up, then fire at will, blaming a light in the sky." The President's eyes glistened. "And we'll be ready." He tapped the pockets of his suit and reached for a handkerchief.

"Don't you think they're saying the same thing in Moscow?" Dennis said.

"That is not for you to say. We've been on hold for months. Now they've made their move." The President stood up, waving Dennis away.

"Sir, I—"

"That's enough. Get me everything you have on the comet for the Joint Chiefs of Staff tomorrow morning. That's all."

"Sir—"

"That's all," Snelling snapped. "And next time, use the front door." He turned his back.

Dennis walked out past a startled private secretary, damning the President's intransigence all the way back to his office. He slammed his office door closed, taking out his frustration on the word processor, where he banged out a press release for White House clearance. Pryor, he was certain, would edit it down to colder officialese: a new comet tracked, under control, updates forthcoming as appropriate. Cato-Aurora would claim its share of summer headlines. An inconvenience for the Snelling election team. Who would follow convention hoopla with a new light in the sky? How to upstage an earthgrazer on the front page when some comets hang around for months? Maybe Snelling has plans for this too. How about Armageddon to celebrate the Fourth of July? Easy, easy, he told himself. No panic.

Dennis ordered his press release copied and read verbatim over the phone. This might help calm the frantic, he hoped, but still his staff took a flurry of crank calls. More responsible queries were channeled to the Jet Propulsion Lab and to Kitt Peak. The phone wouldn't stop ringing.

He left the office early, snapping angrily at one too many staffers approaching him with another question. On the way home, his car radio announced the Reuters story with a brief question-and-answer interview with a Dr. Jackson. Suddenly the JPL was expert on comets. National Public Radio and a barrage of frantic calls to Pasadena had made believers of them. The report was low-key and direct, Jackson's responses delivered in an unhurried, authoritative tone. It was close to what I would have said had I consented to an interview, Dennis thought. He was glad now that he hadn't. He felt too close to the situation and too upset at a President who refused to listen.

He turned off Columbia Pike, shedding a bad day with each mile. He thought about the meeting with the Joint Chiefs of Staff. No alarm, just facts. Serve the President, answer their questions. Stay with the team, and pray it's the winning team.

He found Sandi on the couch watching the evening news. At her side on the table lay the telephone, its receiver prone beside it and buzzing.

"Good idea," Dennis commented.

"After fifteen calls I couldn't take it anymore," she said.

"Imagine if the number were listed."

"Richard Lohmann's been calling every ten minutes. I said you'd call back."

"I will." Dennis sat down beside her. The TV showed an artist's conception of a generic, sperm-shaped comet. The screen then flashed a black-and-white portrait of its discoverer, the stern Dr. Sarantof. The text of the report was a simple thirty-second rewrite of the wire-service account. Then on to the stock market quotations and a cat food commercial.

When Sandi got up to fix dinner, Dennis took *The Washington Post* from the table and scanned the front page. As expected, the International Astronomical Union had confirmed four comet sightings, and more were sure to follow, according to the Smithsonian Astrophysical Observatory in Cambridge. From England, the Grand Master of the Order of the Distant Cloud had called together his followers for a "Transformation Day" rite in the heart of the Yorkshire moors in July. The Master's Book of Revelations foretold a "sky event" for summer 1992.

"So it's begun," he said, tossing the paper onto the floor. "The crazies are already out."

"Day one," Sandi reminded him. "Shall I disconnect the phone?"

"After I make a call to Lohmann." He reached over, giving Sandi a kiss as he did. "I love you, by the way." She kissed him back.

"Prove it. Call Lohmann, then pull the jack."

Sandi got up and left the room while he pushed the National Security Adviser's coded home number. Instantly, Lohmann's gruff voice filled his ear.

"Dennis, I couldn't get you at the office. What's the idea of a recorded message, for chrissake?"

"We were swamped."

"You were? Listen, we have a meeting tomorrow."

"Yes. Nine o'clock."

"Eleven now."

"Why the change?"

"The boss is upset at Henderson."

"Henderson?"

"He's met with the Soviet ambassador. Behind Snelling's back. The President is ready to try him for treason on charges of a political end-around. The ambassador says Mirenkov has to talk with us."

"The comet?"

"That's why I've been calling."

"We need to talk with the Soviets," Dennis said.

"I agree with you. Snelling thinks the governor is after election points. I'm not so sure."

"Richard, we're in trouble as long as Snelling believes they're using a comet. It's crazy. I think he may be too."

To Dennis's surprise, Lohmann made no comment.

"So what do we do?" Lohmann asked at last.

It was a relief to hear an official offer of help. Dennis hesitated for a moment, then replied, "We have to make the President see the comet as separate from his Red Alert. And make him listen. I think he's ready to shut me out."

"Dennis, is Aurora any threat?"

"I need to put it down on paper for tomorrow. By itself the comet is nothing. Don't let the word *earthgrazer* scare you. But if Snelling uses it because he thinks the Soviets are going to, we're all in trouble."

"How can anyone use a comet?"

"The President is convinced the Soviets will try a first strike when Aurora gets close."

"God. No wonder he wants Henderson's head."

"He sees the whole thing as a plot."

"Tell me that's as crazy as it sounds."

"No," Dennis shot back. "I'll tell you about the comet. You're in charge of national security. And the first problem is panic."

"It's already started, my boy."

"Then the real problem is Snelling."

"Look, Dennis. Don't be upset if the boss doesn't listen to you. You were the boys he made an ass of when that fishing boat jammed the *Kennedy*. So don't let it get to you. We all get the same treatment, except Pryor and Newcombe. At least we're invited to tomorrow's meeting. Eleven."

"Eleven. Thanks. And get some sleep," Dennis advised. "We may not be able to shortly."

Chapter Fifteen

A somber string of uniformed men in dark shades of green and blue lined the corridor wall outside the Oval Office at eleven o'clock Wednesday morning. The assembled Joint Chiefs of Staff checked watches, shuffled dossiers from one hand to the other, and traded nervous small talk outside the closed door. Each man gripped his own copy of the Blue Manual, the book whose coded instructions outlined the recipe for nuclear strike.

Richard Lohmann's eyes darted from face to face as he tapped a Blue Manual against his leg. A fresh carnation in place, he was one of only three in civilian clothes.

Dennis was the last to arrive. Lohmann flashed a signal his way and drew him to a corner.

"I owe you an apology, Dennis. About the comet." His voice was soft, almost secretive. "I thought you were crazy."

Dennis waved off the remark. "Richard, don't apologize for something out of your control. Just help me convince the boss it's more than a hoax the Soviets invented."

"You have pictures, I trust. These guys only believe what they can see."

"Right here." Dennis tapped a large manila envelope.

"I'll do all I can," Lohmann said. "Newcombe's in there with him now."

Dennis looked around warily. "All this firepower?"

"That's just what it is, my boy."

The Oval Office door opened. Ron Pryor ushered in the crowd, directing each man to his assigned seat around a large table set up for the occasion. At the far end sat the President and the Secretary of Defense. Snelling greeted each arrival with a quick smile, then turned back to confer with Newcombe. When everyone had been seated, Snelling leaned into the table and addressed the assembly.

"Gentlemen, the Soviets have announced to the world a new comet. Dr. Covino has confirmed its existence." He bowed in Dennis's direction. "That is our given this morning. I will ask the doctor to brief us on what we can expect from the skies in the near future. Then I will ask your support in advancing our Red Alert exercises to active standby, as shown in your Blue Manual."

He pushed back from the table and placed his palms together under his chin.

"Secretary Newcombe and I agree that this comet occurrence will be used to divert our attention this summer, and that a first strike is pending. I am informed that Premier Mirenkov will be in touch with me within the week, no doubt with his own ultimatum. So we must prepare now for all contingencies. I ask you to be frank, to keep the questions pertinent, and to give me your cooperation."

Scanning the attentive faces to his left and right, the President turned to Dennis.

"Dr. Covino," he said, "will you tell us just what it is you discovered at the Naval Observatory."

Dennis took several photos from his envelope and distributed them along the table's ranks. "Mr. President, gentlemen, here is photographic evidence of the comet identified by Soviet astronomers as Aurora. These pictures were taken for me two days ago here in Washington.

Now while it might look to you like a magnified picture of a lint screen, I can assure you it is much more. Wild headlines aside, this comet is a one-of-a-kind event with its own dangers.'' The men looked up from the photos slowly as he continued. ''It has been sighted, confirmed at seven other observatories since the weekend, including Kitt Peak and at Palomar. What we have is a small but high-velocity comet in the West class. Very rare. Computer teams at the JPL are working on its orbit from data we are still compiling. From this one picture, we can tell Aurora is dying, and like anything in its last stages, that makes it unpredictable.''

General Brock struck his pipe against an ashtray to get attention. ''West class?'' he asked from the side of his mouth.

''Aurora, and its classmates, have very long orbits,'' Dennis explained. ''Over ten thousand years to complete a circuit. This comet may have last come in toward our sun that long ago. Maybe longer. I don't need to tell you then that we don't have this on record. For all practical purposes, we are the first to see it.''

The comment raised several eyebrows. The room was silent. All eyes were trained on the standing science adviser. He could now feel their attention as he continued.

''It's heading toward its closest approach to the sun at a speed of approximately Mach-65, close to eighty thousand kilometers an hour.'' Dennis paused at a second round of low murmurs. ''That's interstellar cruising speed, I should add. Aurora's size is two point four kilometers in diameter. Imagine, if you will, a snowball the size of a shopping center complete with parking lots. Also remember that these figures are constantly changing. What we know now will be fine-tuned as the weeks go by.

"As the comet falls to the sun, it picks up speed and it shrinks, shedding most of its energy into a dust tail. Aurora, we calculate from what we have so far, will disappear from view behind the sun in mid-April. Possibly, hopefully, never to be seen again. Now, because of where the earth will be in relation to the sun in four months' time, we are likely to see a flaming tail, visible to the naked eye within three months. Possibly in early June."

"You say possibly," the President said. "Explain that for us."

"A lot of variables enter here. One possibility is that Aurora will gain speed so fast that it will throw itself out of our galaxy by its own energy. It's small enough to do that. This means a bright tail, bright head only until the sun passes between us. The sun's rays will then make the comet invisible and soon forgotten. Like Halley's. That's the favorable possibility. Bright tail at night, maybe even during parts of the day, for perhaps as long as three weeks."

"I can hear the freaks predicting the end of the world," the Air Force Secretary said, twirling a diamond ring around his finger.

"Where have you been, Art?" Admiral Bulloch scoffed. "They're out in the streets already."

"What if the thing comes around the sun?" General Smalley asked. "What do we see then?"

"More tail filling the sky," Dennis answered.

"A light show," the general commented.

"Could be," Dennis agreed. "That tail might be millions of kilometers long by then. A lingering visit, with attendant meteor showers from debris if it passes close enough."

"How close will it pass?" asked General Brock, set to take notes. "How close to us?"

Dennis shifted in his chair.

"Too soon to say, General."

"Any safe guesses?" Brock asked, pencil poised.

"Halley's closest approach was sixty-five million kilometers. Aurora will be closer."

"How close?"

"I've heard estimates as low as nine million kilometers. But we're jumping ahead. We haven't even got an accurate orbit yet."

"Well, you know where it is," Brock began, "and you know where it's headed and at what speed. Why can't you calculate the orbit?"

Dennis fixed his eyes on the President. "We are awaiting more data," he said. "And there are more variables involved. It's so small we can't tell where it came from before we spotted it. It'll take more time." Dennis stopped, feeling suddenly ill at ease at the blank faces around the table. More than one pad was filled with doodles.

Lohmann raised his voice to ask the question Dennis hoped would come.

"Dennis, do the Russians know the comet's orbit?"

"They probably have a more accurate idea, yes. With at least a six-month lead on tracking," Dennis replied, looking eagerly for more questions in the same line. The Air Force general came to the rescue.

"Doctor," he said, "you've described a furious snowball. A runaway. I'd like to know where in hell we fit in on this planet of ours. Are we in the way of Aurora?"

All twelve faces turned toward the science adviser.

"In July," he said slowly, "the earth could be in the possible path of the outgoing comet."

"Sweet Jesus!" Bulloch exclaimed.

"Variables," snapped Brock.

"Something we call calving," Dennis said in a voice meant to regain attention. "Splitting up. Astronomers in China tell me this comet may have broken up beyond Jupiter. Aurora may be a fragment, which itself could split at any time."

"And then?" Smalley asked anxiously.

"Then it's a whole new computer run, gentlemen. We start from scratch with our numbers."

"Are you saying we could be hit? On earth?" cried Lohmann.

"If the comet calves, anything could happen. First we need to confirm the orbit."

The President leaned forward. "I might point out, gentlemen, that Dr. Covino assures me the chances of even a close encounter are millions to one. Isn't that right, Doctor?"

"Against, I hope," Newcombe joked to a silent audience.

"Can you break that down, Doctor?" Bulloch asked. "Odds like what?"

Snelling answered the question, "Like you sinking three consecutive holes-in-one, Marvin." The admiral grinned.

"Mr. President, those odds I gave you do not include calving," Dennis said pointedly.

"The possibility of calving," Snelling said.

"The possibility. Yes, sir."

The President drew back in his chair. "Well," he said, "now that we have an idea what might be out there, I'd like to cover some of the uses the Russians are likely to have for this visitor of theirs." He reached for a file on the table.

"Excuse me, Mr. President," Lohmann cut in. "I see another variable in all this. A disturbing discrepancy."

"What is that, Mr. Lohmann?" Snelling asked.

"Here we have a comet about which we seem to know everything but the orbit. Didn't Dr. Covino say the Soviets have the missing piece?"

"Probable, he said," Snelling quickly corrected.

"Well, don't we need to find out?" Lohmann asked the group. "I, for one, would appreciate knowing when we might know if a comet is or is not going to hit us. As a matter of national security, sir, we have a stirred-up, frightened public. Shouldn't we first address those fears before talking about Soviet motives?"

The President's fingers tapped the file as he glared at Lohmann like a judge trapped in a legal technicality.

"Dr. Lohmann," he said calmly, "my plans call for a televised address in the near future on this comet scare. But I'm sure you'll agree that we have other matters of national security to discuss in this forum." He lowered his voice to continue. "If I may return to our agenda. Ron Pryor has briefed you all on our November ultimatum's status. After three months of silence, the Kremlin has decided to announce the news of Aurora. I can't help but conclude that this is their response to the ultimatum and a part of their plan to activate missiles for a first-strike attempt. I have alerted all installations to stand by for further orders. Orders you men will be giving. In the meantime, a total of forty-six bases are ready and on call. Eight more will be status-set within twenty-four hours. Now that a Circular Error Probable of ten meters is the latest bright arrow in their quiver, we believe that at any time they are prepared to announce a counterultimatum and fire a first strike over the North Pole. I think we can all appreciate the sensitive timing here. Panic is to be avoided at all costs."

"Sir," Lohmann interrupted, "this returns us to my point. The public is upset just over the announcement. We haven't even acknowledged confirmation of this comet. I certainly hope we are not about to add a nuclear first strike to their present mood."

"I am talking about a Red Alert standby, Richard. Not about first strike."

"Not ours. No. But a response to the Soviets'."

"Precisely," Snelling said.

"Well, isn't first strike also in the realm of possibility?" Lohmann's voice sounded near the breaking point.

"We are planning preparedness in the event my hotline rings with an ultimatum we find unacceptable." Snelling's voice too seemed to crack.

Lohmann raised his head. "Mr. President," he said. "We are planning war."

Snelling turned toward Dean Newcombe.

"Richard," Newcombe said, "we are here to open the Red Alert Blue Manual. An authorized procedure in time of crisis." His words fell deliberately, each one measured by the patience afforded a troublesome pupil. Lohmann sat back in his chair. He shook his head, unconvinced.

"The first crisis we need to address is Aurora."

"I agree," Ron Pryor said. "The President will talk to the nation about it just as soon as we've established an accurate orbit."

"I hope sooner rather than later," Lohmann ventured. "If the military goes on Red Alert when a comet is passing, there'll be chaos." He turned to Dennis. "Dr. Covino, when will we know the comet's orbit?"

Dennis read the pleading in the security chief's eyes. All during the exchange, Lohmann had been on his side, and now when called upon to help an ally, he could only say, "I don't know."

"Before the thing is visible to the naked eye?"

"I can't promise that, Richard. I need—"

"Yes?"

"I need the numbers the Soviets have."

"It's their comet. Is that what you're saying?"

Dennis looked straight at him but did not reply.

Lohmann slumped in his chair. "We are faced with a one-of-a-kind space spectacular that the Russians control?"

"You've got it," Snelling nodded triumphantly. "We have no reason to believe the Soviet Union will share their information with us. We know what they're up to."

"Doctor, you can bet if there were any real danger from a comet, they would not use a wire service to panic the world," Pryor explained with an indulgent nod.

"Have we asked for their help?" Lohmann pleaded.

"Oh, for chrissake, Richard," Newcombe scoffed. "Wake up!"

"Dick, the last help we got from the Russians was their turning out the lights in Geneva four years ago," said the exasperated President. To the others he added, "We must act on the safe assumption that their discovery is a remarkable scientific feat. If and when we can find out otherwise, we can shift strategy. For now, we see this Aurora as another phenomenon useful to their purposes."

"Pardon, Mr. President," Dennis said. "It is not routine or planned to find a West class comet. Far from it."

"I stand corrected. We'll call it dumb luck, then."

"The comet is unpredictable even at a safe distance."

"How far away is it now?" Pryor asked for the record. Dennis checked his notes to answer.

"Two hundred and fifty million kilometers. This figure shrinks by two million every day."

"You see, Richard," Snelling smiled, "not quite a clear and present danger, is it? We think the Russians are plotting the time of brightest approach for a first strike."

"In that case, why did they announce?" Lohmann asked.

"Hope of panic," Snelling answered. "Gentlemen, I am ordering you to prepare your departments for Red Alert Code-Six standby on May first. I want firing status reports weekly up until then, all adjustments in personnel reported to the Secretary of Defense. And oyster-shell secrecy. I also want the names of anyone, including members of Congress, who give you any heat. This will be labeled an exercise. Routine preparedness. Target number one is Riga complex on the Baltic. Simultaneous target number two, the space port at Plesetsk—is that how you say it?"

Dean Newcombe nodded solemnly without looking up.

"May the first, we will gather at Mt. Weather for the SAC link-up. We'll go through the whole sequence."

Dennis blinked at the President's military jargon. Mt. Weather, he recalled, was the underground bunker reserved for the highest government officials during nuclear attack. It was never used for exercises. Dennis's glance met Lohmann's.

"Are there any questions at this time?" asked Pryor. Tossing a cursory look around the quiet table, he retrieved the papers.

"Good. Yes, Admiral," he said, acknowledging a raised arm.

"Has it occurred to anyone what a thing like this could do to our satellite network?" he asked.

"We're working on that," Pryor replied. "We expect some interference."

"Interference? Like the Riga jamming?"

"We'll know soon," Pryor pledged.

Dennis glared at the chief of staff, resenting the way he'd taken command. To his surprised satisfaction, Admiral Bulloch was on the pursuit, asking the sixty-four-thousand-dollar question.

"Is there any way to tell whether further interference comes from Aurora or from Riga?"

"That's an important point," Lohmann added.

"We've had no jamming since November," Snelling said.

Bulloch wasn't satisfied. "And if it starts up again," he said, "is it Riga or the comet?"

The President tilted his head toward Dennis. "Dr. Covino."

"There's no way to tell," Dennis replied.

The admiral squirmed in his chair, visibly shaken by the answer. His eyes scanned the room for an ally. Lohmann picked up the baton. "Sir, a lot can happen between now and May first," he said.

Snelling nodded at him. "That's right. And our ultimatum still stands," he replied.

"We fire in the event of interference," Lohmann said to the President, who stared blankly at the clarification.

"By then, we'll be sure of the comet," Snelling nodded. "By then we'll have our response from Mirenkov."

"By then we'll be at each other's throats," Lohmann countered.

Snelling made a condescending smile. "They will back down," he said. "You'll see."

Lohmann shrugged. "I'd give a million dollars for your kind of certainty."

Snelling turned to the Secretary of Defense. "Dean, tell him how he can save his money."

"Richard, Israeli intelligence says the Reds have launched two satellites in synchronous orbit over our West," Newcombe reported.

"Yes?" Lohmann demanded.

"They were Red Star Fourteens. Not designed to pick up cable TV in Wyoming."

The National Security Adviser lowered his eyes. His head dropped in defeat. Dennis felt the blow with the same impact. He and Lohmann had gone as far as they could go. Snelling had covered it all. He had bagged another trawler.

From the corner of his eye, Dennis saw the President stand up, blocking his view of the surging *Kennedy*. Then he heard the muted shuffle of polished shoes from under the table. As if on cue, the military chiefs rose one at a time, slid on their hats, and shook hands in a strangely silent farewell. The country's top brass filed out of the Oval Office, Richard Lohmann lost in their uniformed midst. Dennis caught the flash of his white carnation, a white flag swallowed up in a sea of green and blue.

"Dr. Covino," Pryor called. "May we see you?"

"Yes. Dennis." The President extended his hand. "Good job. Very clear."

Close up, he looked pale to Dennis, his eyes dull even in triumph.

"Sir, I have additional notes." Dennis tendered a thin report. "For a public statement."

"Just what I was about to ask for," Snelling said. He took the documents and handed them to Pryor, who filed them quickly in a bulging attaché case. "When the time comes, I want you to appear on TV with me."

"I'll get up some visuals," Dennis said dully.

"Good. And stand by for the hotline call. I want to see you the minute you've plotted this thing."

"Of course."

"I must know before Mirenkov's call." The President turned to Pryor. "Lohmann, for all his caution, is right about panic. We'll keep the press informed from here on it, from the White House." To Dennis he said, "Answer any questions you feel comfortable with, any questions on the comet, that is." He paused to catch his breath. "Everything else is top secret. You understand that?"

"Yes, sir."

"We'll set a date for our show," Snelling said, "Ron will be in touch with you on it."

The President turned to leave, Pryor at his side. At the doorway he stopped to add, "We have to counter some of the madness I've seen in the papers. I read there was a virgin sacrifice in Oklahoma in 1910 during the Halley pass. Imagine that." His eyes widened in amusement.

Pryor grinned broadly. "Incredible," he said. "Imagine finding a virgin in Oklahoma."

Chapter Sixteen

Confirmation of Aurora shifted the scientific community's gears. Overnight, expert attention turned from theoretical physics to the lighter recreation of comet watching. Not that there was anything the nonastronomer could see, but the impending close apparition kept well-known academic popularizers on the screen and eager to inform the masses. Just as in 1986, astronomers replaced surgeons on the TV news-show circuit, whose wide-eyed hosts were more thrilled than their expert guests. The new comet was an exciting anomaly, they all agreed, but cosmic distances, sunlight, and spring cloud-cover patterns in the Northern Hemisphere would dampen the spirits of those expecting a "shooting star." A comet is not a star, just a vagabond fragment from the Big Bang; a roving remnant of the first seconds of creation, a spinning ball, older than life on earth, that occasionally sprinkles the planet with spectacular meteor showers at sunset and before dawn. Aurora, like the previous decade's Kohoutek, was bound to spawn dry scientific debate, but "she" was sure to disappoint laymen expecting a fireworks show. Almost sure, the experts added with a gambler's smile.

At the Jet Propulsion Lab, at the Kitt Peak National Observatory at Yerkes in Wisconsin, at Mauna Kea, and at Palomar, telescopes turned away from deep space to focus on the tantalizing dustball moving from among the gaseous giants in toward the solid planets. Satellite ob-

servatories ticked back to earth stations reams of data on
the comet, while 1992-c spun in and out of the distant stars
as if playing hide-and-seek with astronomers. It became
another game to set the record for keeping the whirling
spot in sight. Word reached the President's science adviser that a Korean amateur had achieved the mark of
fourteen minutes, thirty-eight seconds. Dennis turned
down the staff's suggestion of offering a prize to the first
American to beat that record. At the same time, he declined another offer to be interviewed as an official media
spokesman. His colleagues teased him for it, claiming he
was suffering from "the Achilles Syndrome"—brooding
from jealousy for not having come upon Aurora first. He
broke the habit of lunching with coworkers, who remarked on his new habit of tapping impatiently during
staff meetings.

He was becoming distant, even withdrawn. He spent
more time with books than with people. His eyes would
wander when someone in the office spoke to him. Then
he would stare back blankly, as if distracted by other
matters. He came to resent intrusions for any reason while
he consulted another volume behind his closed door.
Sandi called it his own case of comet fever. Others who saw
him during the day were less understanding.

Aurora was new. West class. That bothered him for a
reason he couldn't understand. It was not like Encke's
comet, that tiny moonlet that sweeps around the sun every
three years. It was not like its more massive sisters, whose
paths had long been known. It was more like his own,
1971-e, except for the close approach. He studied the lit-
erature on Donati's comet and Coggia's; the semiannual
meteor showers from Alpha Aurigids; spectral analyses
from the comet Kohoutek in 1973; and the unending lists
of periodic and nonperiodic comets supplied by the

Smithsonian Astrophysical Observatory. He completed another ephemeris and stared at the celestial timetable's formulas, then made calls to Dr. Gray and to Cambridge to rework the numbers that now strained his eyes. At home, he reviewed mounds of his own notes on Covino 1971-e. Hour after hour, he pored over documents, making coffee at two in the morning, amassing data on everything he could find on comet research in the last two decades.

Aurora was different. There were no precedents, no duplicates. Comets were as distinct as human fingerprints, each with its own mark and its own destiny.

In the Executive Office Building, he studied daily photographs from the U.S. Naval Observatory and compared these with others from Hawaii and West Virginia. With each inspection, he noticed a different feature of the earthgrazer: a wispy tail; a dark, then brighter spot at the coma's rim; shifting concentrations of methane and ammonia—all part of a furious faint spot in the heavens, and headed in.

He shared his wonder on Aurora with Loren Gray three times a week. And by mid-March, these quick updates became as welcome as they were necessary.

"Resolution is very good, Loren."

"We're getting better at it," Gray said. "Did you see me on TV last night?"

"TV. No."

"The kids are all excited. It's funny, isn't it? You work your ass off for twenty years—every day. And fifteen seconds on TV makes you famous."

"Yeah. Loren, what changes do you have on coma density?"

"I'll get that for you."

"Do that, will you? Right away. And I need the latest figures on heliocentric distance too."

"What's the hurry?"

"The President'll need more updates before he talks with the Soviet Premier."

"You mean he's going to talk with the enemy?" Gray chuckled.

"Any day now."

"Comets do change things, don't they?"

"Density figures."

"And heliocentric distance. All right."

THERE WAS A NEW, quieter mood at the White House. The campaign road was temporarily grounded. Dennis suspected this was due to high-level preparations for the first hotline call in five years. But he also recalled the disturbing sight of the President and his lieutenant in conference, seated before a large viewing screen, and picking away at Henderson's rhetoric.

The campaign was all-important. The campaign and the November ultimatum moved the commander-in-chief. Everything else was interference, even an ill-timed comet. Aurora was an event to be controlled, nudged into place to justify the ultimatum and assure reelection. Part of the plan.

And maybe, just maybe, Loren Gray was right on target: "Comets do change things." True, if the President picked up the red phone, listened, and talked. Didn't he say he wants me to stand by when Mirenkov calls? And aren't the Soviet statements on the comet responsible and low-key? Good signs, he thought. Maybe comets move kings after all. Was that superstition or ancient wisdom? A new light in the sky had always shaken the masses, evoking portents and rumors of doom. At least now there was some warning. That might help. Still, he knew, predicted or not, a close-passing comet presented unprecedented problems. A very close pass would certainly bring panic to many quarters. But couldn't it also bring out the best in even the most advanced adversaries?

Other signs were not so good. Aurora wouldn't be visible to the casual viewer for months, yet already astrologers were screaming, crowding out more authoritative sources. In New York the Unicorn Society joined the Children of the Last Days and the Sisters of Armageddon for a Central Park media vigil. The phone lines to Lloyds of London were jammed, the Associated Press noted. And the Tokyo stock exchange had hired a cosmologist. Major department stores were running specials on telescopes, complete with home computer link-ups: "You can watch the comet from your own living room!" Sunglasses sales were up as well as bookings for a "Sunset Comet Cruise." K-Mart had ordered half a million T-shirts sporting the words, "Heads Or Tails?" A California suntan lotion manufacturer was offering a new product guaranteed to protect the skin from harmful "comet dust rays." At Dennis's recommendation, the Food and Drug Administration and the Federal Trade Commission were testing the suspect formula. The still-invisible Aurora was a hot market item.

Recalling Halley's-comet fever, Dennis accepted this mercantile madness as an inevitable nuisance. If only the papers wouldn't trivialize the apparition. Myth piled upon myth, as editors teased the public with stories of unexplained lights, irrational events linked throughout history with comet passings, and features on the Christmas star. Even *The New York Times*, looking more like its crosstown competitor, ran a week-long series on Velikovsky and his reckless theories.

As Dennis tried to keep to a regular schedule of conferring with colleagues, he cursed the insistent calls for clarification. He refused to release daily bulletins for the convenience of a press eager to sensationalize. Snelling wasn't the only one disturbed by interference.

He reserved his personal office line for fellow scientists. While he was awaiting a callback from Kitt Peak on March 23, his secretary buzzed that a Dr. Alexi Zoltov of the Moscow Institute of Science and Technologies was on line ten. The hair at the base of his skull tingled. His hand made the reflex move to the "ten" button, then he froze. A direct call from Moscow, from Sarantof's assistant. He hesitated long enough to sense Heather's impatience as she waited for his reply. Zoltov was calling with details on Aurora's orbit.

"Dr. Covino," she said.

He bit his lip, fighting the urge to press the button. He tightened his fist and tapped it on the desk. The orbit. The missing piece of the puzzle. A button away. But to take the call without clearance would be his last act as science adviser.

"Dr. Covino," Heather repeated.

The outgoing call made to Cho Chan was grounds for dismissal. Pressing the incoming button would blow the President sky high, and the fallout would send Dennis Covino back to the Rockies.

The orbit, he thought. Now, or later? Our numbers, or theirs?

"Heather, I can't take this call."

"Callback?" she asked.

"No. No callback."

He guided the leadened receiver into the cradle. His head was pounding.

Concentration was out of the question. The office simmered with tension for the rest of the day, and he was exhausted.

He left early and with no homework. The comet had changed enough things already. He would not let it drive Sandi away. He had been shutting her out, spending futile days chasing a comet and sleepless nights haunted by numbers. They weren't talking anymore. He tried to remember the last time they had shared a laugh. Aruba? Two months ago? Even their sex life had changed, their touches mechanical. Not tonight, he promised himself. He stopped to pick up an expensive Pouilly-Fuissé.

Why had he felt it necessary to spend so many hours brushing up on comets? he wondered. The President would be properly briefed for his television address. His duty was done. Now he needed Sandi.

For a change, he did the cooking, as in the Colorado days. Sandi served the wine.

"So you've solved the problems of the world," she teased.

Dennis's smile melted the thin layer of frost in her voice. "I'm home," he said. "I'm crazy, but I'm one hell of a chef."

It was good to hear her laugh. And the evening was better than a night out, he told her. It was a night together. With a kiss she agreed.

"I forgot my New Year's resolution," he confessed. "I'm sorry."

"Are you back to stay?" she asked, tilting her head, waiting for the right answer.

"Yes," he said. "I've done all I can for the President. He'll be in touch with Premier Mirenkov soon. Now I can sit back and answer questions."

After their first lovemaking in weeks, Dennis was still tense and restless. He got up for an aspirin. Back in bed, his eyes wouldn't close. At last he sat up and turned on the light. Sandi awoke and said, "I'll put on some coffee."

"No. I will," he said, but he made no move to get out of bed.

Sandi threw on a robe and headed for the kitchen.

At the door, she turned to ask, "Are you okay?"

He raised his arm as a signal he had heard.

"Yeah. I just can't sleep."

He felt the same way he recalled feeling the night before his second doctoral orals. A mixture of tension and dread. When he got to the kitchen table, they looked at each other without speaking. The coffee sputtered and dripped in the background.

"I obeyed orders," he said at last, as if to a third person. "I refused to take the call."

Sandi poured the coffee and sipped hers, watching him.

"I did what I was told," he continued. "My duty."

He put his head down, holding it in both hands.

"I'm a fool."

"Dennis—"

"Sandi, I don't even take my own advice. How can I expect the President to take it? I had the chance and blew it." The words fell out as in a confessional. "I denied a comet and won an advisership. Then, today, I refused advice that I need just to keep my job. I denied myself."

Sandi placed her hand on his.

"What call did you refuse to take?" she asked.

"A call from Moscow. With the comet's orbit. Without Russian help, Snelling has nothing to rely on. He's flying blind, right into what he thinks is a trick. And until I get the numbers they're using, I can't be sure it isn't."

He looked up into Sandi's eyes. "He's going to go ahead with Red Alert and blow us all up just to prove he was right all along. And I'm standing by with no opinion."

"What about the comet?"

"He's going to throw a warhead at it," he said.

"Won't the Russian call again?" Sandi asked.

"I as much as told him not to bother."

"Maybe he will anyway."

Dennis shook his head. "Maybe they're tired of trying to get through to us," he said. "The only way I found the comet was with that constellation code of White's, numbers he was given in Spain. They tried to tell us with numbers. Words didn't work, so they used numbers."

LOHMANN'S CALL AT THE OFFICE early the next morning confirmed Dennis's worst fears. Premier Mirenkov had called President Snelling on the hotline the day before. According to Pryor, Mirenkov's interpreter conveyed the Premier's insistence on immediate scientific exchanges on the comet, saying Aurora was going to hit sometime in July. When Snelling called it a hoax, Mirenkov called the President what the translator repeated as "bonehead." Then Snelling started shouting about the Gulf, about the Red Star satellites, about Riga. The Premier's only response was an ominous warning to prepare to evacuate.

"Evacuate!" Dennis couldn't believe what he was hearing. "A hit!"

The President tossed this aside, Lohmann said, and fumed about Trusedale. When Mirenkov refused to accept responsibility for the ambassador's death, the President slammed down the phone in a volley of obscenities.

"Cut him off?" Dennis blurted.

"Hung up, Pryor told me."

Dennis caught his breath. A hit. Was it possible? Nothing in what he had compiled even hinted at the possibility of a hit, a comet fall. He stood up and without hesitation called his secretary on the intercom. The order came rapidly.

"Heather, if it takes all day, get me Zoltov in Moscow."

Chapter Seventeen

From his office, Ron Pryor rang the Oval Office, telling the President that Covino had arrived. A long moment passed before Pryor gave the nod for Dennis to enter. When he opened the door, Snelling motioned for him to join him at the conference table.

"I've spoken to the Soviet Dr. Zoltov," Dennis said, getting right to the point.

"Should I be surprised by that?"

"We have no time for stupid comments," Dennis blurted. "He says Aurora will strike us in July."

"Does he?" Snelling's tone was offhand and maddeningly detached.

Dennis was careful to control his mounting anger. "Zoltov will call back today with numbers that he says will prove it. You were told to evacuate."

"A warning," Snelling said. "But they are dictators only in their own country."

"You hung up on him."

"I did."

"I need those numbers," Dennis said deliberately. "Zoltov is under orders to give them to me with your consent."

Snelling laughed nervously. "What about your famous odds?"

Dennis recoiled as if struck by a blow.

"The odds haven't changed," he said. "We've got a good track on it. The comet shows signs of calving, but no one here can say it will hit."

"Yet the Russians are sure." There was a defiant look on the President's face.

Dennis reached for a thick pad of paper on the table and hurriedly drew a diagram with several circles. "Here's the sun," he said. "Around it the earth, here. In July we will be here." His pencil struck the spot.

"Where's the comet?" Snelling leaned closer to the table.

"Out here." Dennis pointed. "All our simulations show Aurora flying out this way after coming around the sun. If it comes around at all."

"Still all those variables."

"Too many to count. Solar winds, orbital deflection, magnetism. It's like a ping-pong ball spinning in a groove."

"Hold it there," Snelling ordered, raising both hands. "How is it the Reds can be so sure of the orbit?"

"Tell me what the Premier said."

The President seemed hesitant for an instant, then breathed deeply and replied, "He told me 'zero probability for a miss.' That we should evacuate all coastlines and Hawaii."

Dennis nodded. "Tidal waves would follow a hit."

Snelling slid back in his chair. "'Evacuate,' he said. They may have that power in Mother Russia, but imagine me persuading Palm Springs bankers to anchor their yachts, pack up their deposit boxes, and trek into the Nevada desert. 'Trust me,' he said. 'Evacuate Hawaii.'" Snelling raised his voice. "How many people would obey an order to leave all their possessions behind? What are your odds there? And the looting. A perfect prescription for panic. That's what that Russian bastard is up to. Watching us scramble for cover. Launch a first strike, then plead innocence. Blame the comet. Capitulation through panic."

"I need those numbers," Dennis pleaded. Snelling went on as if he hadn't heard. "How close will it come," he asked, "according to what you have so far?"

"Estimate," Dennis winced. "Anywhere between four and sixteen million kilometers. Anything closer than eight will be very bright."

"And no damage?"

"Radio interference, satellite static. That's all."

"You're not sure of anything, are you?"

"I'm sure they're ahead of us."

Snelling drew in a deep breath, showing signs of impatience.

"Why hasn't the damn thing appeared?" he asked.

Dennis tapped his diagram. "It's behind the sun."

"You told me it will be bright. The skies full of it."

"Yes. On the way out. An incandescent tail."

"Can't you be more precise?"

"This one is rare and small. And we've never tracked it before. Sometimes it rotates, moving faster. Then it slows down. The spin may even change direction. It's all approximation. Already I've been getting conflicting theories."

Dennis searched for a helpful analogy.

"Look." He grabbed the pad. "We're on a boat at night in the fog. Port side, we see a light. You're the captain. Now, what is that light? Is it the QE II at four kilometers, or a pleasure boat at thirty meters? And as we're moving, is the light heading toward us or away from us?" He tossed the pencil down. "That's what you're asking me to answer."

"You've got it tracked. You know where it is."

"We estimate it will come close. The two orbits will intersect in four months."

"But it cannot hit," the President urged, eager for certainty at last.

"I'm not saying it will or it won't. I'm saying we can't tell."

"But the Soviets are sure."

"I can't see how," Dennis shook his head. "But their numbers will tell."

Snelling folded his arms. "It's a hoax, then," he concluded.

Dennis crumpled the diagram and gritted his teeth.

"Let's get those numbers. If we can see their math, we can tell for sure about the orbit."

"Why do they have numbers we don't have?"

"How the hell should I know?" Dennis shouted, desperate now. "They've got half a year's jump on us. The numbers will tell hit or hoax. If they're fooling you, goading you into a nuclear war, it'll show in the numbers."

There was caution in the President's reply, not the anger Dennis was expecting, but instead a guarded concession.

"Can they be trusted? The numbers, I mean."

"You gave me a code. It came out showing where the comet is." Dennis swallowed. "The constellation Auriga."

"What?" Snelling leaned forward, eyes wide in disbelief. "What did you say?"

"The code you gave me. It held the coordinates for spotting the comet. They told us where to look. You think we just came across it?"

Snelling looked away. "My God!" he cried.

He remained speechless for several seconds.

Finally, Dennis spoke, calmly now. "Mr. President, we are close to knowing once and for all if your fears about Riga are justified. Either you're right, or we have a worldwide crisis on our hands that can't be handled on our own. If it isn't a bluff, you'll be laughed out of office. All I know is that they flashed a signal that showed us a comet. They were right. Maybe they're right about a hit. As long as we pretend we don't care to know, they can do what they want. And they'll have you by the balls."

The President got up abruptly and, taking out his handkerchief, wiped his face; then he moved from the table to his desk. Dennis watched him and continued to speak. "I hope it *is* a damn comet hit. At least it'll be over and done with minimal loss of life. Your plans will kill us all and take the whole planet with us."

Snelling's arms were stretched wide on the desktop, his head bowed above one of the red telephones. For an instant, Dennis wondered whether he was about to share Seymour White's fate and be taken out of the office under guard.

When the President looked up, his face was drawn. In a deep voice he ordered: "Talk to your man."

He lifted the phone and recited a string of numbers and code letters. Then he handed the receiver to Dennis.

The President retreated to a wing chair near the fireplace, his hands alternately squeezing and releasing the thick fabric of the armrests, while for a full ten minutes the two scientists exchanged numbers with the ease of international correspondents. The numbers droned on, a tiring cantation repeated over and over with an occasional scientific term inserted. Dennis made sure he was writing down each figure in the correct sequence. There could be no mistakes here. No misunderstandings. Before ending the conversation, he asked Zoltov to repeat the entire series of numbers.

Dennis lowered the phone and stared at figures so close to his own that they looked familiar even in a jumble.

"We're ninety percent in line with their figures," he said wearily.

"Is that good or bad?"

"I can't tell yet. They claim Aurora's starting to split up. For the life of me, I can't see how they could know that."

"They're bluffing."

"No. It's not a report. It's a mathematical prediction. These numbers say it will impact earth." Dennis looked up to see a strange, distant look on the President's face.

"They're bluffing," Snelling repeated. "You'll see."

"Our computers will decide that."

"Get back to me as soon as possible."

"Of course."

"I need to know right away."

"You will." Dennis rose. He folded the paper and slipped it into his pocket. "You'd make a lousy scientist, you know that?"

"And I'm damn glad you're not the President."

"I'll run this tonight," Dennis said. "We should know tomorrow."

Snelling nodded. "Good. We have to be sure before we…" His voice trailed off as he looked down toward the empty fireplace.

"Before we evacuate," Dennis offered.

"Yes." Snelling looked up with a start. "Yes. Before we evacuate."

DENNIS TOOK THE PAGES of notation directly to the Naval Observatory's computer rooms. For seven hours and twice as many verifying runs, he and a roomful of short-tempered scientists threw around yards of printout formulae and insults. The observatory rocked with debate over the new numbers. The men fought to defend their own reputations, but the numbers on the blackboard could not be denied. It was not a bluff.

Fatigue broke up the mind-numbing session at two A.M. The ground-floor rooms looked like the site of a fraternity party. Coffee cups and cigar butts littered even the hallways. Dennis rubbed his eyes and, holding back another yawn, ordered a final verifying run. Sarantof's numbers were impressively accurate, his formulae complete and certain. The Russians' work led to the inescapable conclusion that Aurora would collide with the earth on or about July eleventh. Not close, but right on. The numbers showed everything except where it would land.

Can the numbers be trusted? Dennis asked himself. Can Sarantof be certain of calculations on solar wind velocity, coma dispersion, ionization levels, magnetic bounce, and atmospheric resistance—the basic values assigned to each stage of the comet's course? How can they know?

On paper, catastrophe was certain. No ifs, no perhaps, just data in a routine flight plan. But how can they know? Dennis repeated the question aloud to the now-empty room. Despite the hour, he telephoned his staff assistant.

"Tom, yeah. I know. We're both on overtime. Look, get out my Auriga file first thing in the morning. Before eight. That's right. I'll be at the White House first thing. And Tom, bring along my notes on Tunguska. Yeah. Tunguska."

The word echoed in the cold surroundings. Another Tunguska. He winced away a yawn, then tapped the first three digits of his home phone number before stopping. Three forty-five. No, I can't call Sandi, he thought. Not now. Why should she know before the President does? Why disturb her sleep again?

But he wanted to hear her voice, to tell her he was with her at least in mind. He moved his tongue around a mouth that burned from stale black coffee and dialed the digits. Suddenly he knew why he wanted Sandi. He had to share his fear that the President was losing control, that the door to hell was ajar, madness pushing against weakening hinges. What could Sandi do? What could he do but let her sleep? He hung up and dropped onto the cot that Loren Gray had ordered for him the night before.

AT EIGHT-THIRTY, Dennis reported back to the Oval Office. The President was at the window, looking out, hands clenched at the back of his pinstriped suit. Snelling tilted his head to one side, sensing he was no longer alone. His voice was deep and low, his question asked without turning:

"You're going to tell me it's true. Aurora will hit, won't it?"

"The numbers say so. Yes."

Snelling spun around on his heels.

"Then in Heaven's name, why did they have to tell us?"

Dennis looked into a pair of bloodshot eyes and a face the color of chalk. "The comet's been in their computers for months," he said. "Their figures check out. It's going to hit us in July."

"Millions to one, my adviser told me!"

Dennis stood his ground. "Zero now," he answered.

"That's a damned quick countdown, Doctor."

"It's also irrelevant. We are both sure it's coming. And they can probably tell us where, too."

"You believe their information is correct from the numbers you got?"

Dennis nodded. "We were off on two key calculations," he admitted.

"Off? I'll say you're off! And not for the first time, either. The same man who told me no one can be sure of a comet fall. Now you're sure. You were wrong about Bill Hendley, you were wrong about Alpha-One, you got your pants wet pissing into the wind in search of Horowitz." Snelling shook his fist. "You gave me odds, millions to one, against this thing happening. And now you're a convert. The sky is going to fall!"

"The numbers are accurate, Mr. President."

"Bullshit! Today's numbers, you mean. What in God's name am I supposed to do with advice that changes every week? Huh? Your track record sucks."

Dennis's eyes narrowed. He raised a hand. "Just a minute. Just a damn minute. No one—no one ordered a comet. I'm telling you what I know is true as of this minute. If that changes, if that upsets you, that's too bad. But it's no one's fault. Not mine. Not the Russians'. Do you hear me?" Dennis glared at Snelling. "For chrissake, you're the President. You're the one in charge. We may have a comet set to smash down on us, and you think someone is responsible, someone's out to offend you with facts."

"You are my adviser."

"And you've got my advice. Prepare for a comet fall."

"Evacuate?"

"Starting within hours, unless you have a plan to explain why you didn't."

"Evacuate? On a set of Russian numbers?" The words seemed stuck in Snelling's throat. "Suppose they're wrong."

"You mean let's play make-believe?" Dennis scoffed. "The numbers we've worked out show a direct hit. Not probability. Every variable covered. I don't know how they know, but the numbers are not a hoax."

"They've fed us what they want us to eat."

"Time is not on your side. I know you're not used to that, but that's where we are. How many second opinions do you want?"

Snelling scowled as he moved toward the desk. He sat, rubbing his temples with both hands. When he looked up, Dennis was standing squarely in front of him.

"Let's see whose pants stay dry now, Mr. President. I've told you an impact this size in water means tidal waves, seas maybe twenty meters high. A whole coastline underwater. A new ocean in as far as Bangor." Dennis paused, watching his words' desired effect wash over Snelling's face. "Let me tell you what land fall means."

"Tunguska?" Snelling guessed.

"No. That was eighty-four years ago," he replied. "The impact from an object the size and speed of Aurora hits with the force of a megaton. Hiroshima times eighty. All radio communications knocked out. No planes. No phones. Electronically, we go deaf if it hits anywhere near us. No signals to or from NORAD. A desert hit means a windstorm like in the Bible. Speeds in excess of six hundred kilometers an hour. Hurricane force times four. A blast wave, then a dustcloud. Mount St. Helens times seventy. Seventy, that's my figure." Dennis jabbed his chest and went on. "At the impact site, on land, combustibles ignite spontaneously. Everything from trees to flesh. The flames are spread by the windstorm. Spontaneous heat with strong X-rays. Prevailing winds take the top layer of earth up into the dustcloud, where it stays for years, blowing wherever the wind takes it, blocking out all sunlight in its path. Shall I go on?"

The President, staring blankly, did not answer.

"What I've described is a hit in central Australia or Canada. So far we're lucky. In a residential area, it'll look just like a nuclear explosion. A fireball in the sky. People within a radius of seventeen kilometers are burned instantly by the firestorm. Survivors have no hope of rescue. No one goes in. No one can come out; all buildings, all structures, collapsed and incinerated. Medical crews could arrive only in time to bury the remains. Schools, airports, factories collapse from the overpressure. But no one will be crushed to death or killed by flying glass; they'd be dead already. All oxygen would be sucked from the area. No air to breathe. All the oxygen feeds the fires; none left for humans. Shall I stop?"

Snelling appeared to be too dazed to speak. He opened and closed his eyes as if in pain.

Dennis plunged on with his prepared scenario.

"The overpressure develops into a mushroom cloud after three minutes, collapsing the lungs of those not already burned to death. No rescue, no transportation. Not even enough air to attempt an escape. Nowhere to run."

"A descent into hell."

"Annihilation."

"What you've described is a nuclear event."

"Exactly, except no radiation."

"No radiation?"

"Not from a ball of water and methane gas. That's all a comet is. The energy of mass. In a year or two, the desert would begin to recover. Wounds healed in a generation, like it never happened."

"And no radiation," Snelling repeated.

"None. Not from a comet."

"Then the only danger of a land hit is in a city."

"No. A thermal pulse—away from people—does the most immediate damage. The blast wave would be over in four or five minutes, and the fires would burn out soon after. There is another effect, though, that's longer lasting and unpredictable. It comes from what's called lofting, that cloud of floating dust. It may be harmless, or it may contain earth and cosmic elements suspended in the atmosphere for years. A hazy darkness would cover any part of the earth above the prevailing winds: a dark shadow cutting off the sun's rays wherever it went. If it hung in the stratosphere over our Midwest, say, there would be no growing season.''

"The greenhouse effect?''

"That's correct.''

"And this is what happened in Russia in 1908?''

"In the woods, yes. But back then, there was no satellite communication, no buildings, and no humans at the impact site.''

"And no nuclear bombs to confuse it with,'' Snelling said softly.

"Those who saw it from the village knew just what it was,'' Dennis replied. "The end of the world.''

"When will the thing be visible?''

"It's beyond perihelion. At its present speed, it should be at magnitude ten in about eight weeks.''

"Visible?''

"With binoculars the first week of May.''

Snelling began tapping his fingers on the blotter.

"Could we intercept it and blow it up in space?'' he asked.

"I've checked that with General Evans,'' Dennis said. "There's no time. He told me the Russians may have already tried it. They put something up right after Christmas. Anyway, Aurora moves so erratically, it would be impossible. Like spearfishing from a helicopter.''

"So," Snelling sighed, "we're locked into those numbers, and the comet's locked into our path."

"That's the view from here. Unless it changes course after calving."

"We evacuate, then." Snelling pushed away from the desk. "But where do we tell people to go?"

"To the hills," Dennis replied. "The higher the better."

"And Hawaii?"

"Total evacuation."

"That's not possible."

"We can only order. Compliance will have to be voluntary."

"I'll have to alert the Office of Emergency Preparedness. And we'll need the National Guard. There'll be looting. Oh, God." Snelling put his hand over his eyes.

"We have about two months before the sky lights up. Before people get frantic."

"Two months," Snelling scoffed. "When the Russians made their announcement, people got frantic. Nothing to see, and they went crazy."

"As it gets brighter, in May and June, we'll be able to pinpoint where it will fall."

At that, the President seemed to make a conscious effort to get a hold of himself. He stood up. "Dennis," he said firmly, "let's get that televised address ready before they announce anything else. We'll use pictures, no numbers."

"I'm all set."

"We must avoid panic. That's the important thing. Contain panic. Keep in touch with Lohmann and Marantof."

"Sarantof," Dennis corrected. Then the order struck him. The sworn enemy of the Soviet Union, the creator of Executive Order 047, was telling him to confer with a Russian.

"Mr. President, I'll give you as much certainty as science can offer."

Snelling smiled dully. "Yes."

Dennis shook the President's cold hand. As he turned to leave, he saw Snelling move slowly toward the window, then stop, withdraw his hands from his pockets, and reach for the red phone.

"Code four," he said.

Dennis recognized the exchange right away. And the number sent a chill through him. After agreeing to a security evacuation for an incoming comet, the President was calling the Secretary of Defense.

Chapter Eighteen

Pink buds at the Lincoln Memorial exploded from winter sleep into a breezy April sunlight. And with spring came a change in public temperament from wintry frenzy to sunny stability. News of the still-invisible comet was relegated to the back pages now, pushed out by accounts of a minor scandal in the Treasury Department, a revolution brewing in Ecuador. New-car sales were up twenty-four percent, and the coming of the baseball season brought optimism north with the first robins.

The presidential campaign hit a lull despite former Vice President Raymond Lattimore's surprise endorsement of Governor David Henderson. This sudden news brought few smiles to the sagging Henderson effort, now in Florida, where the young candidate struggled to woo the gray vote. Henderson focused his remarks on the dangers of nuclear war, lamenting the lost SALT talks of the seventies. But to an audience still holding Harry Truman in high esteem, his words fell on deaf ears. As perilous as the bomb was, Sunshine State voters remembered Hiroshima as the blow that forced the Japanese to surrender. The elders enjoyed the Coloradan's company, but at every stop they showed that patriotism in time of military alert had won their hearts.

Meanwhile, the incumbent appeared in public only to thank voters in each of the primary states. The new Vice Presidential candidate, Steven Woodward, swept through New England, Ohio, and Arkansas, expressing his personal appreciation and the President's best wishes with a wave of his Stetson. He and Ron Pryor carried most of the campaign burden, allowing the President "time to relax," the papers said.

Snelling conferred with his Secretary of Defense and the Joint Chiefs of Staff on matters far removed from fund raisers and delegate counts. While New Hampshire voters got the ball rolling for him in mid-April, he was poring over Israeli intelligence reports detailing the final phase of "Power Pack One." From the eastern Mediterranean and the Persian Gulf, American fleets on maneuvers beamed an uninterrupted flow of data to military hideaways in the Virginia hills. Three Trident submarines cruised the Gulf of Bothnia and the Baltic Sea, silently awaiting further instructions.

The day after his Ohio electoral landslide, the President monitored a preparedness drill at SAC from the underground bunker at Mt. Weather. Defense Secretary Newcombe informed him the May Day deadline would be met. Red Alert—the countdown status for nuclear firing—was in place ahead of schedule.

Dennis searched the papers in vain for any mention of evacuation preparations. Aurora, out of sight, seemed to be out of mind to everyone but him. He convinced himself that the President was saving the evacuation statement for the television address. Just the same, each time Dr. Zoltov called from Moscow, the issue was not the comet, but the evacuation. Soviet scientists, he learned, were pressing the Politburo for a May first public disclosure on "Earth Impact." Dennis conveyed the news to the White House, and within two days he received a memo setting April 25 as the date for the official announcement. Dennis was ready.

He went over the numbers for what seemed like the thousandth time. The data he shared weekly with Zoltov told it all. The world's first predicted comet fall was twelve weeks away. No more guessing, no more speculation. Aurora was gaining nearly two kilometers with each rotation of the earth; one point three-eight-zero Astronomical Units from point of impact somewhere on the water planet.

In the newly redecorated East Room, the President adjusted his eyes to the glaring television lights. He turned on command, accepting the touch-up dust that immediately softened the lines on his face. Three lamps converged on the desk, engulfing it in surgery-room brightness. He moistened his lips, checked the microphone volume, and arranged the papers before him. He squinted at the teleprompter; then, looking over to his science adviser in a darkened set to his left, he made a quick thumbs-up sign. A red light blinked on. A voice from the darkness cued: "The President of the United States."

"My fellow Americans," Snelling began, "some critics are quick to point out that the White House has been silent since the unprecedented news alerting us to a comet called Aurora. I address you tonight to allay some legitimate fears and to put to rest criticism of a presidential blackout on a matter of the highest national security." He looked down at the text.

"I can assure you this comet is under study. In some quarters, 'round-the-clock study. At the same time, I hasten to add that fear will not be allowed to creep into our preparations for any eventuality, nor will hysterical talk about a comet collision.

"First, some facts: American scientists and Pentagon officials are in agreement with Dr. Sarantof in Moscow.

Both the Moscow Institute of Science and Technologies and our own astronomers can confirm that a new comet is in the heavens, millions of kilometers away, beyond the sun. We concur with the sightings elsewhere showing a small comet presently hidden from view on the far side of the sun. Now, scientists classify this comet as an earth-grazer. Many such objects approach earth each year, yet these appear so small and fall in places so remote that they are of little interest. However, this will not be the case with Aurora.

"I have chosen to address you this evening with facts and in the hope that what I tell you will help to avoid panic. Once we know what to expect, we can all face the future without fear." He coughed, glancing down again at his text.

"The comet will be visible in about one month. Then a spectacular tail will brighten the sky during the first days of July. At this time, Aurora will be at a distance of some ninety million kilometers, thirty percent more distant than Halley's was at its closest approach six years ago. The outgoing comet will pass through earth orbit in mid-July. Our calculations show a high probability that the comet will hit somewhere on the earth, most likely in the ocean, far from land." The President turned smoothly to face the red light of the camera to his left.

"While in the past we have been alerted to falling Soviet spacecraft debris, both the size and the spectacle of a falling comet make this event quite a different matter.

"I have asked my respected science adviser, Dr. Dennis Covino, to help me explain what we can expect in the next few months. Before introducing him, however, let me clearly state that I am prepared to call for unprecedented cooperation in the days to come. I will ask—ask us all to put aside both business-as-usual and unwarranted fears.

We face possible worldwide danger from the uncharted comet, a danger rivaled only by the chaos of panic. We must not panic. Rather, we must become informed and remain informed each day. With this objective in mind, today I have ordered activation of the Emergency Broadcast System. Starting in twenty-four hours, you will be alerted to precautions prepared by the Office of Preparedness via radio and television.

"Let there be no mistake. On the highest-level peacetime security advice, I will call for evacuation of all property along all our shorelines. The National Guard will protect against the probability of looting. Our military might is on standby alert around the globe to keep us updated on comet trackings and on preparations elsewhere." He paused. "Civil Defense officials will shortly outline orderly evacuation routes in every region. Businesses, banks, schools, and government offices will remain open. Broadcasts will announce where to go and what to do once you get there. In addition, I will announce penalties for failure to cooperate in settling evacuees.

"While we remain on alert for the worst, we must neither delay nor give ourselves over to crippling 'comet fever.' The stakes are high; the odds of a catastrophic hit are mercifully low. But as long as there is any chance of a hit near land, I have the constitutional responsibility to protect the country I serve as commander-in-chief.

"The precautions I am calling for are unprecedented in peacetime. Our emergency-status programs were designed for a different crisis. These measures will place us on warlike alert when there is no war. The danger is literally 'out of this world,' and we need fear no threat other than that posed by this comet intruder. I repeat. The danger is potential.

"Be assured. When Aurora appears, we are in control. We know what to expect and what to do. All of us. With your cooperation, we will weather this storm from the stars and perhaps even grow closer for its passing."

The President shuffled the papers before him, drew a measured breath, and then leaned forward into the central camera's eye.

"Dr. Covino knows more about comets than anyone else in the world. He has briefed me, the National Security Council, and the Joint Chiefs of Staff. His work, and the untiring efforts of his colleagues, has impressed me with its seriousness and clarity. I call upon him now to tell us what the dangers are and what we can do to overcome them. Dr. Covino."

The cameras swept to the President's right, illuminating Dennis's composed figure. With rehearsed stiffness and a steady hand gripping the black pointer, Dennis explained the impending fall's mechanics. He moved three colored balls along wires to show the changing relative positions of the earth, the sun, and the comet. Speaking slowly, as if to high school students, he simplified the physics of the fall, making certain to avoid too many numbers, too many scientific terms. He balanced his presentation carefully between indisputable principles and Sir Isaac Newton's advice to simplify. There would be no time, he knew, to argue with specialized colleagues over what he was now telling the American public.

He showed clear diagrams of a comet splitting up and of the charred remains of satellite debris fallen from orbit, adding the caution that predicting where the comet would fall and in how many pieces was as risky as forecasting next month's weather. Slides prepared at his office showed the effects of a tidal wave in Java. He pointed out detailed photographs of bright, close comets with a heavy sprinkling of analogies: "like a snowball"; "as bright as the full moon on a clear night"; "a kitelike tail trailing like vapor tracks left by a high-flying jet."

"Simple probability tells us a water hit is the most likely event," he said. "In deep ocean, the effects will be minimal, bothering only cruise ships and inconveniencing air traffic for a short time. However, we enjoy over twenty thousand kilometers of coastline. A hit closer to land, say in the Gulf of Mexico, would put in immediate danger lives and property from here to there."

His pointer traced a small arc over the Gulf Coast on a prepared map. "This fact makes temporary evacuation vital." Dennis moved away from the map, brushing aside the microphone cable. Three cameras followed his steps to a spot before a black-and-white photo showing the broken trees of Tunguska.

"As far as a land fall is concerned," he said calmly, "we know from our school days that seventy percent of Mother Earth's surface is water. Of the remaining land mass, only one two-thousandths contains urban density. You can see, then, that the chances for a direct hit near any given city are very slim. In fact, the odds are one in fifteen thousand against."

His eyes shifted away from camera contact as he moved closer to the picture behind him.

"This photo was taken in 1929, twenty-one years after impact, near the village of Tunguska in the Soviet Union," he explained. "This forest was flattened and wildlife was burned instantly here after impact by cosmic debris in 1908. Since this fall, eighty-four years ago, of part of Encke's comet, our records confirm over three hundred like events. Comet debris, meteorites, and apollo objects enter our atmosphere regularly with little or no fanfare. However, a comet the size of Aurora is a rarity. Its path is erratic. Its speed changes, and until we can measure its approach velocity in the upper atmosphere, we cannot tell where, or how, it will land. The chances exist that it might even break up on entry, falling into pieces that no one will notice.

"If its head, or coma, remains intact, the hit will be powerful, a wallop that will raise a lot of water. I join the President in urging you to keep informed and updated via the media. Every day now our data will change. Even if what you hear sounds contradictory as the days go by, follow the directions, evacuate, and secure coastal property. Above all, maintain alertness to bulletins until the danger has passed."

Dennis turned in the direction of the President, seated at the brightly lit desk.

"Thank you, Dr. Covino," Snelling said. "My fellow Americans, the danger is remote, but real. The time is short, and the task before us is enormous. We can be thankful our electronic age allows us to stay in constant touch. The first President to use this amazing technology over fifty years ago told another brave generation of Americans, 'The only thing we have to fear is fear itself.' I echo those words tonight, confident that once again our people will show their calm strength in a time of crisis. Thank you and good night."

When the studio lights faded, the President wiped his face, removing moisture and makeup at the same time. He rose slowly to shake his approaching adviser's hand.

"Good job, Dennis," he said limply.

"Not too many numbers?"

"No. Just right."

Something in the President's reply lacked the confidence the cameras had shown, making his "just right" sound not so much like a compliment as the whispered

hope of a desperate man. Snelling was no longer in charge.
The people at home would take over now, and either follow their leader's direction or scatter in panic; they'd believe the only threat was the comet, or else they'd wonder,
as Dennis did, how Red Alert could possibly help matters. Dennis tried hard to believe the President. If their
address was playing well in American homes and beyond, everything could be "just right."

THE TELEVISED ANNOUNCEMENT HIT the public like a
hammer. Within days, phone lines were jammed from
coast to coast; Hawaii was all but cut off from the main-
land. Civil Defense offices beeped a recorded message
advising callers who were able to get through to turn to
radio and television EBS bulletins. Meanwhile, Civil Defense authorities huddled in Washington to take direction on recommended local actions. After two weeks they
dispersed, orders in hand, to pass along advisories and
distribute maps to the public at banks and gas stations.
The free pamphlets, fresh off the presses, described how
families should pack their belongings, secure what had to
stay behind, and drive to the designated "safe area" on
the map. The illustrations showed a typical family of four
on what could be a carefree vacation in the wilderness,
singing around a campfire. After an initial run on the
pamphlets, they began to pile up in unopened boxes. The
toll-free number on each cover was unreachable after the
first week.

Calls to the White House were automatically routed to
the Defense Department Office of Public Security's eight
hastily built phone banks located in an unfinished wing
of the Veteran's Administration building.

Congressional leaders, pleading for an audience with
someone at the White House, screamed frustration at the

recorded message they got in reply. Back home, their own phones rang unanswered.

On April 27, AT&T announced disconnections for those not paying bills in advance. After two weeks, collections finally caught up with the company's overtime payroll account, and their billing system broke down. New-phone-installation orders dropped further down the waiting list as emergency lines took priority. Two sprawling warehouses, one on each coast, housed reclaimed phone equipment under tight security. Nonessential calls were cut off in midconversation to the recorded apology of an authoritative voice. Television screens flashed the ten-second message, "Limit your calls. Pay in advance. And cut back on credit-card use. We will continue to serve all our customers as we have faithfully for generations." The AT&T chairman called Washington several times on his private line for assurance that commercial satellites would not be affected by any scheduled orbital missions. After five attempts, he gave up and worked on the positive assumption.

Under the threat of FCC sanctions, network television granted time slots for EBS advisories. Industry protests could not hold back the tide of, first four, then six bulletins a day. All major networks turned back repeated demands from the Henderson camp to open up equal air time for the candidate. A federal magistrate in New York dismissed the legal plea on national security grounds. In May, the governor cut his losses upon hearing that the appeals process would take over a year and consume precious funds better spent on August's national convention in Boston.

Both CBS and PBS quickly mounted new series dedicated to disaster survival. The popular shows demonstrated evacuation tips on how to secure the house, how to schedule departure, when to leave, where to go, how to get there. ABC's offering was more clinical: a doctor showed how to survive the outdoor rigors and how to provide safe water and sanitation in close quarters with and without infants. The show's ratings soared as high as the profits claimed by its sponsor, a mail-order house specializing in home survival kits starting at twelve hundred dollars.

Television preachers and prophets played to overflow studio and home crowds. In ringing tones, they read from the Bible and warned of the last days with the admonition to contribute now for the relief of the unfortunate displaced by the impending act of God. They led the faithful in hope-filled hymns, while the camera swept past teary-eyed faces of all ages. A vicarious brotherhood of misery comforted each other with verses selected for the occasion. The Reverend Dr. Russ Campfield filled his studio with the most popular: "Not by water, the fire next time." The cameras panned to swooning worshippers, rescued within seconds by the hymn-singing, uniformed assistants. Campfield told interviewers proudly that this "celestial cleansing" was good for the country, a long-awaited harrowing of the faithful. Pressed further, the Reverend confessed that contributions were up four hundred percent.

Real estate prices from Florida to California flattened. The market for homes with an ocean view fell the day after the President's television appearance. What property was for sale attracted fewer and fewer takers as the weeks went by. Some developers moved in quickly to buy up undesirable lots bordering on rivers. Even they could not keep up with offers to sell at basement prices. Summer homes were the first to leave private hands and enrich the holdings of local land barons.

Cash received for the sale of property detoured banks, going instead for the purchase of practical, durable goods. Electrical-appliance sales faltered the first week as consumers lined up for their manual counterparts. Gas-powered generators and portable fuel-powered heaters sold at premium.

Movie houses enjoyed a sudden boom. Low-grade comedies played to full houses, and more theaters responded by staying open twenty-four hours.

To the dismay of overworked police departments everywhere, traffic, especially at night, was up, and rush hour became a sunrise-to-sunset aggravation. Absenteeism from work and school increased markedly, with thousands staying home, complaining of hard-to-describe symptoms ranging from insomnia to depression. Medical centers were dispensing drugs that suppliers couldn't produce fast enough.

Pharmacists in Los Angeles frantically wired Midwest distributors with new orders to restock their depleted shelves. Even aspirin was hard to come by, and sleeping pills and tranquilizers were now black-market items, available on the street for fifty dollars a bottle.

Luxury car sales fell immediately, but trucks and used off-road vehicles kept it a sellers' market. Stolen car reports showed a sudden switch from sporty BMWs to Toyota minivans and motorcycles.

The travel industry reeled in confusion as travelers canceled vacation plans altogether or else changed course away from ocean resorts. Since broadcast bulletins advised heading for the hills, soon resorts from the Catskills to the Rockies displayed "No Vacancy" signs. Regional bulletins listed the names of places where there were still accommodations. Each day, the list shrank.

Within three weeks, Sears was cleared out of tents, portable lanterns, camping gear, and bottled gas. Many families could no longer afford the price of what little mountaineering gear remained in stock. Rainchecks were thrown back into salespersons' faces, followed by blows and a growing number of arrests.

Sugar supplies were limited, and canned goods were now the hottest items on the growing black market. Gasoline dealers on interstate highways gave top priority to truckers and fought off threats from motorists waving plastic rather than paper money. In North Carolina, a motorist and a station owner shot each other to death while cash customers waited in line.

On April 28, the President ordered the FAA to issue an advisory to all airlines that flights scheduled from that date on were subject to official clearance. The same order was delivered to all embassies for incoming flights. Although pilots grumbled over new orders to monitor levels of radio interference, nevertheless cooperation was immediate, and not a single foreign carrier filed a protest.

The only group to gain direct access to the President was the panicked National Alliance of Insurance Underwriters. Snelling had promised to address the group at their June convention in Philadelphia. Instead, both parties settled for a brief Rose Garden reception. While the harried Secretary of the Treasury tried to allay the fears of bankers assembled in New York, President Snelling told the insurers that nothing had changed, that they continued to share evenly in the risk of a comet fall.

"With luck," he commented, "you marine reinsurers might have to pay for a few ships. If we're not so lucky, you'll all hear from us through the federal flood insurance unit. Both ways, you're covered." He closed with the same message he had delivered on television: "Keep your families calm. Keep informed. We are on top of this crisis.''

With a bow, he left the crowd of over a hundred to take
a call from the governor of Puerto Rico, who demanded
the same attention to evacuation for his island that the
governor of Hawaii enjoyed. The President's reply
screamed from the next day's headlines: "He's fifty-first
on my list."

That afternoon, Secretary of the Treasury Meeker relayed to Ron Pryor the news that businessmen and bankers were set to break ranks with the President over credit.
"Cash Only" signs now appeared in filling stations and
department stores all over the country.

California bankers were leading the charge to recall all
credit cards, as depositors increased the demand for cash.
New York banks agreed to hold out for one more week
before invalidating the nation's three largest international charge cards.

"No panic yet," Meeker's memo to the White House
read. "But I'd call it the huddle before the first play of the
game. Once the comet appears, we could have a second
crash." Pryor wrote back, "That will not happen."

The Chicago grain market closed early that same afternoon to "readjust." The next morning, the New York
Stock Exchange followed their lead.

It was Richard Lohmann who reported that many store
chains were planning to close down for a month. Despite
his best efforts and the help of the Federal Reserve Board,
the major retail chains had decided to lay off workers and
regroup, opening sometime in July. Even their desire for
presummer profits could not stand up to the onslaught of
comet fever. Fights were breaking out between storekeepers and irate customers.

Marinas were swamped with demands to relocate everything from yachts to twelve-foot outboards. The Coast Guard needed more manpower to cope with the increasing frenzy caused by fuel hoarding and theft.

Ron Pryor advised the President to gather the governors of all the states for a briefing on evacuation. Those from coastal states accepted the invitation eagerly, while inland governors balked, calling for more National Guard assistance along the interstate network. The meeting was scrubbed.

The President spent April 29 behind closed doors talking with FBI head Malcolm Tibbits. Looting had reached epidemic proportions, and the chief reported that carriers were losing two dozen shipments a day on the highway. In addition, liquor shipments and liquor stores were becoming so hard hit that escort teams and vigilante squads were dispensing instant sidewalk justice even in the wealthiest suburbs. San Francisco and Miami were sold out of ammunition and guns. The FBI was stretched to the limit. Tibbits requested and received backup help in fifteen major cities.

And just in time. Police departments from Los Angeles to New York City were helplessly trapped between keeping roads open and disarming bands of looters. Law and order was quickly escaping their grasp.

That afternoon, Snelling nationalized the states' guards, whose orders were to speed up evacuation, using national parks first, then private property. Looters were to be shot on sight. Under cover of the mobilized National Guard, the First Bank of California announced that it was closing until further notice. That word came within hours of the Secretary of the Treasury's order for federal takeover of all banks—until further notice. As the President had promised, the banks would remain open. Now, fully equipped soldiers stood at every door.

Before sunset on the final day of April, all National Guard armories were reinforced, and the military was officially called to full Red Alert status.

At dawn on the second day of May 1992, the President excused himself from a meeting of hospital administrators to take a call from his science adviser. The message was short and definite.

"She's headed in, sir," Dennis said.

"In?"

"Visible tonight at sunset. The bright nights begin."

Chapter Nineteen

By May first, the Department of Education had already recommended early school closings, and the Department of Health and Human Services was working overtime training and assigning emergency medical squads to every hospital in the country. Official Washington seemed to be on war alert status, with everyone frantically busy carrying out hastily conceived orders and pausing only to catch up on the latest television advisory bulletins. In between rapid updates on interstate tie-ups and food shipments, the networks were inserting taped reports of wild campus comet parties, of overfill crowds in France attending free lectures at the Observatoire Nationale, of the Bishop of Rio de Janeiro remarking that both Mass attendance and confessions were up to post-Carnival levels.

The week after his television appearance, Dennis had begun conferring with scientists from the Chesapeake Foundation, a dozen experts on sea channels and ocean depths. Together they charted over six hundred areas most prone to coastal flooding damage, from Miami to Juneau. Their list filled thirty printout sheets, and when it was completed, it came back from Richard Lohmann's office with the notation that evacuation compliance in the areas cited was approaching only forty percent. Millions were staying home, hoarding food, and watching television, stunned into inaction.

Taking advantage of Senator Browning's departure from home, Sandi quit work early Wednesday to make a trial run to their rented cabin at Round Hill in the Blue Ridge Mountains. It took three hours one way, following tractor trailers and packed station wagons. Her report to Dennis was no more hopeful than Lohmann's: no telephone and no running water. Bottled water was available for the right price, and she would make another midweek trip to stock up. Dennis agreed that that was a good idea, then returned to an argument with Pentagon scientists over television blackouts on any satellite photos of the comet.

DEPARTMENT OF SCIENCE

MEMORANDUM   May 7, 1992

TO: President James F. Snelling
FROM: Dr. Dennis Covino, Director
ROUTING CODE: C Z 118
STATUS: 09

Mr. President:

I learn from Richard Lohmann that most evacuation warnings go unheeded. This is no surprise, since there is little discernible sky change. The more families successfully resettled by the end of this month, the better. Once Aurora/Venus-bright appears, studies here show a shock effect that will keep most people in place. SEE ENCLOSED.

In this regard, I recommend consistent public reference to the 1982 fall of the Soviet Salyut satellite. While this event is not a strict parallel to our present dilemma, I believe it will serve as an easily perceived precedent. We have no idea where Aurora will land, or in how many pieces. This at least puts us in the same boat as summer 1982.

We may hope that last night's pathetic attempt by the networks to be first to show the comet will prove too expensive to continue. Irresponsible journalism. As you ordered, no satellite pictures have been or will be released in this country. I point out that this order will be meaningless as the weeks go by, and backyard photographers are able to get shots just as good.

No appreciable change in Aurora's status. We expect the first phase: Aurora/Venus-bright June 8. Advisories should include this. SEE ATTACHED VISUALS.

Dennis Covino, Director
ENCLS/3

THE WHITE HOUSE
OFFICE OF THE CHIEF-OF-STAFF
RONALD M. PRYOR

MEMORANDUM   9 May 1992

TO: Dr. Dennis Covino
FROM: Ron
ROUTING CODE: M Z 811
STATUS: 09

Dennis— We agree with your recommendation on using the 1982 precedent in future statements. Why was there no panic then? Lohmann is correct. Polls show a 50-50 split on heeding evacuation advisories. There is a stubborn streak of rugged individualism we now consider impenetrable. Future advisories will therefore target the most frantic 50 percent, dropping plans for forced evacuation in some areas. It's the Mount St. Helens Syndrome. Major resistance in New York and Los Angeles, as expected. We are pre-

paring all national and state parks in high elevations
for temporary settlements with projected cutoff set for
June 30.

People magazine's comet spread was a big help!

Neumyer has been appointed new information officer. Your code number for him enclosed. Address
all subsequent memos to me using ROUTING CODE *M
Z* 118. We've developed a leak in *C Z*.

Ron
ENCLS/1

Leak or no leak in C Z, Dennis quickly discovered the
reason why his memos weren't reaching the President.
Snelling was on vacation. His doctors had insisted that
more stress could cause him to snap, according to Lohmann. So while millions scrambled to the hills for shelter
and just as many stayed home to read about it, the
President calmly sailed his yacht, *Zephyr*, toward the
rocky respite of Penobscot Bay.

Maybe it made no difference to families gripped by
personal panic that their leader was enjoying a week off.
Who cares how the President is faring when park rangers
have just dropped a "capacity" sign in front of your car
and told you to try another one five hundred miles away?
There was no time to waste on an absent President when
the night sky brightened with what looked like a new
planet jumping from orbit.

DEPARTMENT OF SCIENCE

MEMORANDUM   May 14, 1992

TO: Ron Pryor
FROM: Dennis

ROUTING CODE: M Z 118
STATUS: 09

Ron,

Last night's wobble was an optical *illusion* caused by atmospheric conditions in most of the country. Aurora is *not* gyrating, *nor* is it splitting up, as widely reported. *No* change here. Please advise Neumyer to check with the Naval Observatory before accepting other "opinions." If he is to be the one official voice, let it be accurate; any retractions can only cause further damage to credibility.

Computer simulations confirm strong interference in satellites A, B, H, *and* Y. Read-outs will be erratic in these installations until transmissions cease in at most two weeks. No time here to monitor others in synchronous orbit. Cause: ionization bombardment ripples from comet, *not* from sunspots. A, B, H, and Y will *not* fall from orbit.

Dennis
ENCLS/0

The week the President returned from Maine, a Comsat-17 satellite shook from orbit, scattering starburst debris across the Arabian Sea and triggering riots along India's west coast. By the weekend, American evacuation compliance had reached sixty percent. But millions still were digging in to protect their property and chase off strangers at the point of a gun. In towns along the Gulf Coast, squatters and residents shot it out between National Guard ranks, who were then pulled out to quell panic and control looting in Mobile Bay, where the

Attorney General's cabin cruiser was moored under twenty-four-hour guard.

THE WHITE HOUSE
OFFICE OF THE CHIEF OF STAFF
RONALD M. PRYOR

MEMORANDUM 2 June 1992

TO: Dr. Dennis Covino
FROM: Ron
ROUTING CODE: M Z 811
STATUS: 09

Dennis—Preparations are complete for Aurora/Venus-bright. Our thanks. Amateur photos fill the papers and the screen. Can't be helped. FCC blackout requires congressional action not possible in time remaining. There is no quorum on the Hill. Everyone's back home filling sandbags for the papers.

The President asks you to reverify read-outs on silo integrity. Can all MX bins withstand one megaton jolt, and at what safe distances?

Ron
ENCLS/0

DEPARTMENT OF SCIENCE

MEMORANDUM June 12, 1992

TO: Ron
FROM: Dennis
ROUTING CODE: M Z 118
STATUS: 09

Ron,

Silo integrity assured to 94 percent certainty. This

confirms Air Force report 03–766 of 7/9/88. It is a mistake to assume land fall in continental U.S. Any nuclear leakage from impact of *minimal* concern. Ocean fall still safest bet. Land fall brings "safe dust"—*no* radiation at or near impact site, only heat.

Also, *no* explanation yet on "on-off" in SkyLab cells. Aurora/Venus-bright is here to stay until impact, estimated for July 14. Dust tail one million kilometers, growing. Comet heading in. Magnetosphere alterations detected at J.P.L. Interference will increase through post-fall.

Dennis
ENCLS/0

THE WHITE HOUSE
OFFICE OF THE CHIEF OF STAFF
RONALD M. PRYOR

MEMORANDUM   15 June 1992

TO: Dennis
FROM: Ron
ROUTING CODE: M Z 811
STATUS: 09

Dennis—

The President wants evacuation inspection of Tampa, Florida. This is a model program and needs encouragement elsewhere. Please free your schedule fifth of next month to accompany him on trip. I know you need to be at observatory, but he wants it. Recommendations awaiting re: *Evacuation* of coastal cities on enclosed list. Strong resistance in Starred Cities.

Sunrise spectacular. If you are able to sleep, tell us how.

Ron
ENCLS/4

Dennis commuted between his office and the Naval Observatory, keeping in daily contact now with Pasadena's Jet Propulsion Laboratory. He verified each night's apparition and left evacuation worries to Lohmann and the others. Sixty-five percent compliance would have to do, he decided. Within two weeks, all parks would be overcrowded with refugees anyway.

Sandi had finished preparing the mountain cabin. All that remained was to determine the impact site to see if their evacuation would be necessary.

Dennis spent two days assuring local authorities that damage risk to nuclear power plants was minimal, then made it back to Falls Church to catch up on sleep.

DEPARTMENT OF SCIENCE

MEMORANDUM   June 20, 1992

TO: Ron
FROM: Dennis
ROUTING CODE: M Z 118
STATUS: 09

Ron,

No sleep. Coordinates stable despite loss of *one* tracking satellite. Aurora is 46 million kilometers distance. Speed range: *Mach 82–85*.

Next week any cloudy nights will bring eerie light.

Tell the President Camp David is safest retreat. Maine is out of the question. Strangle anyone who

advises otherwise. Barnyard panic assured with fear-
less leader seen near Penobscot Bay now.

I'll be glad to get away July 5 for 24 hours.

Dennis
ENCLS/0

THE WHITE HOUSE
OFFICE OF THE CHIEF OF STAFF
RONALD M. PRYOR

MEMORANDUM   23 June 1992

TO: Dennis
FROM: Ron
ROUTING CODE: M Z 811
STATUS: 09

Dennis—

You are authorized to appear on ABC's *Nightime* show
for Landry interview pending my approval of questions. I'll meet you at studio Wednesday 10:30 A.M.

Ron
ENCLS/0

"Channel eight?" Sandi called to Dennis from the living room.

"Is that ABC?"

"I think so." She snapped on the set. As he came in
from the kitchen, the colors were arranging themselves
to show thirty-five million viewers Dr. Dennis Covino's
image. Dennis remembered the taping session, with Ron
Pryor in the next studio's glass cage pacing like a feverish
stage mother; how the earphone scratched; and how per-

spiration flowed down the sleeves of his new brown suit under the heat of the studio lights.

The screen now flashed his name as commentator Merv Landry asked the first question.

"We are doing all we can," Dennis said, touching the ear that held the speaker connecting him with the New York studio, "which for the present means watching, measuring changes."

"What changes are you seeing, Doctor?" Landry asked rapidly.

"The comet is settling into its postperihelion orbital groove," he explained. "We are tracking it the same way we monitor deep space satellites, with the help of telescopes here and in orbit. To answer your question, Aurora is burning up quickly. Perihelion, when it passed closest to the sun, tore a good deal of it apart."

"Is there any truth to the rumor that the comet will burn itself up completely before it gets near us?"

"Unfortunately not. The incineration rate will decline as she falls away from the sun. That's happening now, in fact. Aurora is too large to burn up completely. What is burning is visible as the tail we saw last night."

"How far away is what we saw last night?"

"Thirty-eight million kilometers. Tonight's apparition will be around thirty-six."

"Million kilometers?"

"That's our current estimate. Yes."

"Will it be brighter each day?"

"Not brighter. The naked eye will see no change for a week or ten days."

"When it does appear brighter, how bright will it get?"

"It will appear as bright as the sun on a hazy day in two weeks or so."

"In July?"

"Yes. When Aurora is as close to us as the moon is, it will be only five hours from impact."

"The speed is incredible," Landry said. For a moment he seemed to have lost his place. Dennis picked up on the comment.

"The speed is only a third of the earth's velocity around the sun."

"That sounds like little comfort."

"It's no comfort. Impact is a mathematical combination of these two speeds. Like a baseball struck by a swinging bat."

"And the force of impact?"

"Close to one megaton, depending on its mass at that time."

"Is there any way you can tell where it could hit?"

"Not yet, I'm afraid. However, the earth is a large target, with over three hundred million square kilometers of surface. As I mentioned when I was with the President on television, that surface is mostly water. There's where we enjoy some comfort. We're hoping for a midocean impact, a large body of water that can absorb most of the shock."

"And a smaller body?"

"Hudson Bay or the Gulf of Mexico would present tremendous problems from a tidal wave," Dennis said. "So our greatest comfort—water—also presents the greatest risk. Our Great Lakes or the Mediterranean are really no more than large bowls. An impact of this magnitude could virtually empty Lake Erie, for example. I mention that only as an example, not a prediction."

"No predictions?"

"Absolutely not," Dennis smiled. "I don't like giving odds."

"And I'd rather not ask."

The camera moved in to show Dennis in closeup. Beads of sweat glimmered from his forehead. Dennis could still recall the heat.

"Doctor, what will we do once impact site has been determined?" Landry's voice was less urgent, his words more measured.

"By then we hope that site will be empty, of course. If it is not, we will secure it by whatever means are needed. And help secure it for other countries."

"So the greatest danger is from a tidal wave."

"Yes. That's why the President has ordered evacuation of coastal areas."

"Are you satisfied with evacuation efforts so far?"

"There is no way to force evacuation on such an enormous scale. I can only hope everyone will cooperate with the help offered. Even the President and all the troops cannot move everyone. And this is not a hurricane with a narrow path. It's a knockout punch. So our duty is to warn and to help." Dennis wiped his forehead. "Without sounding like an alarmist, by the Fourth of July I'd be as far away from large water as I could be."

"Will it reach the point of every man for himself?"

"I hear that in some places it already is approaching that. I don't know what to say. After impact, we will do all we can to restore order."

"And in the meantime, what do you recommend?"

"Stay as calm as possible. And cooperate with civil authorities, as we did in '82 when the Soviet satellite fell in Canada."

"In that event there was commotion but no panic," Landry recalled. "What makes this fall different?"

"The satellite fall involved a much smaller object and a dead weight. A comet won't drop so much as accept gravitational pull, adding to its own velocity."

"Speeding up?"

"Yes. Speeding it up."

"Dr. Covino, has there been active cooperation with other countries?"

"Very good cooperation. Without exception, we've been able to share important data with observatories everywhere."

"Including in the Soviet Union?"

Watching, Dennis squirmed on the couch, recalling the question that had worried Pryor.

"Especially in the Soviet Union," came the answer. "As you know, they were the first to confirm Aurora. Since March they have led the way in tracking and in updating astronomers on Aurora's course."

"We've heard stories that the White House is less appreciative than you appear to be about their cooperation."

"Is that a question?"

Landry rallied with a smile. "Is the White House as pleased as you are about Soviet help?"

The camera shot back to Dennis.

"I am pleased. I can answer only for myself."

"Has the President been in contact with the Soviet Union?"

"Not to my knowledge."

Sandi turned suddenly to face him.

"Dennis. You lied."

"Sandi, I heard from Lohmann that the President hung up on them. Not direct knowledge."

"You told me he talked to Mirenkov." Her face tightened. "You told us a lie."

Dennis snapped off the remote button. "Pryor wouldn't accept any other answer," he said. "It was that or no interview."

"A staged interview."

"It's the last one I'll do."

"Until Pryor orders another one."

"That's not fair."

"Oh?"

"People need information."

"People need the truth," she shot back. "Why are you covering for him? Is it such a damn sin to admit that the Russians know more than we do?"

He stood before her, feeling the sting of each accusatory dart that her eyes shot his way.

"What advice are you giving him? Keep the passengers calm while we count the lifeboats?" Her voice broke.

"Sandi, you should be the last to panic. Stop it!"

She crossed her arms roughly, throwing up a barrier. "What are you helping the President hide?"

It was foolish to try denying it. Dennis met her stare. "He's on nuclear standby," he said calmly. "He's ready to fire."

"And you're helping him!"

"It's under control."

"Under control? We both know better. Don't lie to me. Look at the sky. Look in the streets. Tranquilizer bulletins. Jesus!" She grabbed a soft pillow and punched it with both hands.

"There is no immediate danger," Dennis said.

She looked up at him.

"Liar!" she spat. "Browning's in hiding back in Colorado. The city's deserted. I hang around answering obscene calls. Nothing's open but churches."

"There's no reason for panic."

"Why? Is your ivory tower sandbagged?"

Her voice cracked, and she burst into tears. Dennis reached for her. He could feel her shaking all over as he tried to hold her.

"Sandi." She sobbed in his arms. "I lied. It wasn't for the first time. Listen to me. You're right. The comet is no danger. Snelling is."

He brushed back the hair from her face and as he did he saw a girl young enough to be his daughter crushed by the burden of lonely nights and his own neglect.

"I'm buying some time," he said softly. "Every day that passes makes it safer. Believe me. No more lies."

His closeness seemed to calm her. He felt the trembling subside. As she shut her eyes, he held her harder, as if to coax understanding.

"I'm scared," she sniffed into his handkerchief. He took her hand and led her to the front hallway. "Where are we going?"

"I want to show you something," he said, opening the door. They stepped out onto the damp grass of the Falls Church lawn, and he led her beyond the twin oak trees whose dark leaves rustled in a gentle wind. He stopped halfway down the flagstone walk and pointed up into the clear June night. A cloudless sky shimmered behind an ivory sliver of a moon, below which Aurora's tail cut the blackness like a gleaming arrow dropped from the moon's bright quiver.

The comet's jewellike head pointed downward to the horizon as if falling to shed its wispy veil. Mounted in flight against a measureless ebony void, it froze, a bright necklace in the heavens' display window.

Above the murmuring sound of far-off gazers' voices, Dennis spoke to the sky. "In two weeks it'll all be over. We'll clean up the site, and only scientists will be interested. Magnificent, isn't it?"

"It doesn't seem any closer," she said in a soft voice.

"Both it and we are moving," he said. "Aligning ourselves for rendezvous."

"Rendezvous. You never called it that on TV."

"No, I didn't."

"And where she stops, nobody knows."

He took her hand. "We'll be safe. You'll see." He looked at her. "Remember the sky in Aruba? How it looked so close, we tried to touch it. And the sunsets? So deep and far away? Aurora is both, close and far away. It's both, and we have nothing to fear."

"Shall I make a wish?" Sandi asked, looking up and blinking back more tears.

Dennis hugged her. "Go ahead. It's already come true."

Sandi smiled as if she understood, then, turning, they went inside arm in arm.

THAT NIGHT THE SAME CELESTIAL SHOW played to rave audiences on rooftops all over the Northern Hemisphere. At one Manhattan party, two inebriated revelers fell to their deaths from fifteen stories. In London, the warm weather kept crowds out until after midnight, when the comet slid under the horizon, and pubs refilled till dawn. In San Francisco, National Guardsmen supplemented local patrols on the Golden Gate Bridge. Despite their vigilance, seven desperate souls had dropped into the strong current since the comet first appeared. Police records everywhere showed a marked difference in emergency calls between clear and cloudy nights. Forces were beefed up as soon as the weather forecast called for clear skies.

In the country, people gathered and sang around campfires, telling stories to children unable to sleep. The parks were still at night, after the day's chores of collecting wood and water and keeping intruders at a safe distance. Armed park rangers patrolled until dawn, rounding up the drunks and listening for sounds other than the cry of sobbing children.

Aurora was brightest at dawn and just after sunset. As the night hours moved on, its brilliance melted into the backdrop of stars, save for the gossamer tail that trailed like a silver feather. Daylight sightings mounted as June slipped into July. Others echoed Sandi's question about why Aurora never seemed to get closer. Except for a brightness that seemed constant, the comet appeared like a nocturnal visitor, hardly moving, coming to the same space in the sky at the same hour each day. The press explained that Aurora was indeed moving, getting larger. The new comet was so small, and its orbit so "off-plane" with the much larger earth, that only slight changes could be expected until the second week of July—Impact Week.

The New York *Daily News* bolstered circulation with a contest offering a week's vacation in Bermuda for the closest guess as to where the comet would land. The *Times* asked in a snippish editorial if their competitor had planned a consolation location in case Bermuda proved to be ground zero.

Astrologers pushed their way onto the front pages with more exciting, more exotic theories, as the daily reports from scientists became as dry and routine as the television bulletins. According to a noted local expert from Pennsylvania, the comet had stopped, caught between the earth's gravity and the moon's. It was stuck; a new, stationary Star of Bethlehem, announcing the birth of another, unidentified king. From Kansas came the opinion that Aurora was slowly melting. Its milky tail would circle the world as a warning that the end was near. California groups spread the word that the comet was a heavenly messenger sent on orders from a race responding at last to Voyager 2's earthly code. A renowned Belgian astronomer concluded that Aurora was really a fragment of the lost asteroid Hermes and would soon self-destruct over Copenhagen. An Ohio doctor endorsed a baglike mask that would keep out cosmic flu germs and prevent a second Black Death. People with real and imaginary maladies filled emergency clinics staffed by medical students, who were set on edge by the lack of medicine and the frequent calls for disaster drills that were never real. Each day, the drill horns sounded to smaller staffs, depleted by defections to first-aid stations in the national parks.

By the Fourth of July, the sky was lit up brightly, the comet an eerie second moon, formless and dusty. The same week, radio and television reception became impossible, with static and scrambling lasting hours now rather than minutes. Emergency Broadcast System bulletins were curtailed, the texts printed in newspapers. Word of mouth replaced electronic messages, and rumors of all kinds spread further panic.

Candidate David Henderson dropped scheduled engagements in New England to help evacuation efforts along the Connecticut coast, where he joined student volunteers in resettling New Haven families along Long Island Sound. Newsphotos showed a sad-faced man in shirt sleeves bending to hand another McDonald's carton to a mother of five. The gloomy picture looked like it had been taken during a relief operation thirty years before in some remote part of Central America.

Along both coasts and in cities and small towns rimming the Great Lakes, the same standard layout appeared on the local morning paper's front page: GRAND HAVEN YACHT CLUB AIRLIFTED TO GRAND RAPIDS, ISLE

ROYALE BRACES FOR BIG SPLASH, NEW ORLEANS BE-
TWEEN LAKE AND A WET PLACE, MIDSHIPMEN BRACE
FOR WAR OF THE ELEMENTS, MARINA DEL REY LOOKS
INLAND. Always a picture, and underneath, the day's
predictable advisories listing what stores would be open
till nightfall, what goods were still for sale, the best hours
for TV and radio reception, emergency phone numbers,
and recycled reminders on food storage and sanitation.
While the newspapers ran record-high numbers off the
presses, the lack of advertising shrank even the largest to
only six pages filled with advisory updates from Washington, missing persons bulletins, spiritual messages, and
an official daily diagram of Aurora, now equally bright at
sunrise and sunset.

Dennis began the habit of checking the Aurora Watch
in the *Post* every morning before he left the office for the
Naval Observatory. A silly habit, he knew, but one that
helped start the day with some semblance of routine.
Seeing the paper afforded him the illusion of comfort,
even though he was more interested now in the numbers.
He kept his own record of radio transmission hours,
which, like tidal charts, shifted twice daily. He charted a
clear pattern of fewer and fewer static-free hours. The
numbers closed in day by day, like a closing door letting
in thinner strips of light. He arrived at the Executive Office Building late and exhausted yet eager to record the
July first readings. If they showed him the small frame he
expected, if interference from Aurora's charged presence
continued to follow form, his worries would be over. No
more lies, no more cover, and no more nagging doubts
every time he told Sandi, "It's under control."

Chapter Twenty

Dennis looked out toward Rock Creek and up into a sky of swirling clouds. Pale greens and oranges, sunset opaque, churned above, while below the full trees lining the grounds gave no hint of wind. Security men patrolled on a nearby ridge. He could see them walking against the sky but with the difficult clarity of dusk. He checked his watch. His eyes read afternoon in the strange light. The watch read ten-twenty. He approached the security entrance of the Naval Observatory to show his badge and his face to another uniformed stranger. After three weeks of showing badge number three, they still checked. It annoyed him, yet with three bomb threats a week, he understood the precaution. Freaks as well as scientists haunted the observatory, night and day. The director was smart to insist on extra security, even at the cost of turning the building into a military outpost.

Once inside the door, Dennis was bombarded by familiar terms spoken in many languages. "Speed, direction, mass, coma density, tail configuration"—how similar they all sounded, couched in international numbers, whether they were coming in from Spain, Germany, or Canada. Astronomers from Kitt Peak to Yerkes Observatory in Wisconsin were following the bright speck each day, keeping the phone lines open as they exchanged numerical data with Washington. The numbers were what counted most, and the numbers were coming in now with more accuracy.

He passed a phone bank and moved over curled wire that snaked against a far wall. More twisted cable wound its way around corners, connecting the phones with another room downstairs. A woman he didn't recognize handed him a file she said was from Bellevue Naval Research Lab. Opening the file, he read the bad news that fifteen continental tidal zones could not support impact without devastating flooding. Long Island could disappear in two weeks. Ditto Detroit, Chicago, and Baja California. The port of Houston and the entire West Coast topped the list of Assured Inundation Zones that went on longer than he cared to read. Twenty-six million people, only half of whom had headed inland, were "at risk."

He caught the wave of a white-coated assistant, who signaled him with a raised telephone.

Professor Murikaio of the University of Hawaii was on the line. The scientist expressed his apology, saying evacuation red tape had delayed his departure. The island of Hawaii was deserted, as well as all the others, except for Oahu, where hourly air shuttles took most evacuees to China Lake Naval Weapons Center in California and the recalcitrant to Haleakala National Park on Maui.

"So you'll be late for our party," Dennis commented.

"Not too long. Any signs of calving?" Murikaio wanted to know. "Your hemisphere has the monopoly this time."

"Strong wobble. No calving," Dennis replied, aware that he was sounding as lifeless as the official bulletins Sandi said she no longer heeded. Murikaio asked about distance. Dennis flipped a page on the morning's readout.

"Within the hour. Twenty-eight point oh-five million kilometers. Bearing steady."

"Close," Murikaio commented. "Gaining or losing velocity?"

"Losing, fast."

"Speed?"

"Seventy-seven thousand kilometers an hour."

"Right on schedule."

"We estimate intersection July fourteenth. Ten days."

"And the Soviets concur?"

"Give or take an hour or two."

"Then what?"

"Just be sure you're off-island," Dennis said.

"I promise you that."

The line crackled with static when Dennis asked, "What's the weather where you are?"

"A Chamber of Commerce sunrise. Why?"

"We're getting atmospheric luminescence here."

"Strong?"

"I just noticed it this morning."

"It's beautiful here, Doctor. Another day. You're the ones getting the show."

"Yeah," Dennis said. "Well, happy Fourth of July. I'll see you when you get here. Aloha."

"Aloha."

Dr. Nathan Sims from the Goddard Space Center bumped Dennis's elbow with a clipboardful of bad news. Vela 6 was no longer transmitting from orbit. The twenty-two-year-old satellite, designed to detect nuclear detonations from 120,000 kilometers above the earth, had fallen silent. Without any warning, the spinning polyhedron was now floating beyond signals. To add a sting to the blow, Sims also reported that a primary dish on Intelsat 4 had expired during the night. Both television and telephone transmissions to and from ATS-6 dimmed to a flicker. Dennis ordered verification on both interruptions and an update on all orbiting craft. The ordinarily glib Sims shrugged exhaustion through a wreath of pipe smoke, then disappeared between Dennis's station and a crowd of observatory workers hunched over humming computer decks.

"Line six, Dr. Covino," a voice shouted from behind. "Pulkovo Observatory."

The name of the Soviet observatory sent a hush through the crowd. Dennis pushed the phone deck's button, waving off a call from the JPL. He heard the deep, deliberate tones of a speaker struggling with English.

"Dr. Covino... This is Alexi Zoltov... at Pulkovo."

"Yes. I hear you."

"I call to match new data with you."

"Go ahead." Dennis cupped an ear.

For weeks, he had routinely recorded tracking reports from the Soviet Union. This was the third Soviet observatory to call since the President's hotline conversation with Premier Mirenkov. He matched each report carefully, looking in vain for the slightest hint of inconsistency.

Taking down the numbers dictated by Zoltov, he suspected the poor connection was due to third-party taping of all conversations. He called for a second reading, and again each entry coincided almost exactly with his own running figures. Speed, size, coma density, distance—all checked out to within a few hundred meters. Another perfect match. He was about to sign off when the Soviet scientist interjected a statement that jolted him like an electric shock.

"Dr. Covino, we have verified other figures on impact site," he thought he heard Zoltov say.

"What? Repeat please."

Zoltov repeated the assertion, this time with more insistence and exaggerated diction. Pencil set, Dennis prepared to take down new numbers. The line hummed static.

"Dr. Zoltov."

"Yes, Doctor . . . we have discounted the possibility of further calving."

"Go ahead."

"We plot impact site at . . . latitude thirty-four degrees. Longitude . . . one hundred and four . . . July fifteenth. Thirty-four. One hundred and four. Northern Hemisphere. The fifteenth. Llano Estacado . . . American Southwest."

Dennis shook his head. "It is not possible to plot impact site at this time. Please explain."

"I cannot explain. I have been ordered to tell you . . . our impact coordinates only," Zoltov said. "These have been confirmed at several computers here."

"How can you say this?"

"Earth rotation is a constant," Zoltov answered in the same detached, distant tone. "The comet's speed is now projectable, the orbit—"

"But the atmosphere. Gravity. You—"

"Mass readings give us all we need . . . here. Thirty-four. One hundred and four. At speed thirty-six kilometers per second." The voice faded.

"Doctor—"

"I am ordered to convey this information, and no more. Evacuation must . . ." The line clicked dead.

Dennis dropped the phone into its cradle and looked up in a daze. Oblivious to the scientists scurrying around him, he grabbed the sheets and stood up. How was it possible to calculate a hit site with accuracy? Not possible, he repeated to himself. It must be a trick. A hoax. At such a distance, no one could tell where Aurora would hit. "No one," he said aloud, pounding his fist hard on the desk. "Impossible," he shouted.

He headed for the main telemetry room, where there was a large wall map, and checked Zoltov's numbers. Thirty-four. One hundred and four. Northern Hemisphere. Eastern New Mexico—West Texas. Llano Estacado. He stared at the map, sweeping an open hand over its dry surface. Without turning, he called for display enhancement of the area—a flat expanse of desert between the Pecos River and the Cap Rock Escarpment. Within minutes, he was studying a computer grid showing topographical features of the Llano Estacado. Poring over the map like a surgeon examining an X-ray, he saw a broad sandy sweep of land, criss-crossed by new highways and timeless hills. At its perimeters stood Lubbock, Texas, and Roswell, New Mexico. Inclusive populations: 325,000, evacuated to forty-five percent. In the square grid, he noticed four red triangles marking the locations of Air Force bases. No target could be more open, more vulnerable. A prime hit site. Was the President right after all? Was Zoltov's call a "plant," a message to clear the area before a first strike? They can't know. Just the same, he ordered an assistant to call the National Security Office for forced evacuation of Lubbock and Roswell. Then he pushed past hurried colleagues to Dr. Gray's office.

"Loren," he shouted to the director, who was talking on the phone.

"It isn't enough that you take over this observatory," Gray sputtered. "You're commandeering my office now."

"Loren, I need your help. Get off the phone. I need a computer run on impact."

Gray sat up, muttered an apology into the phone, and hung up. "Impact! From sixty million kilometers? You've got balls of brass, Covino. What are you raving about?"

"Impact," Dennis repeated. "The Russians have given us a fix on impact site."

"You're crazy. Fourteen-hour days are catching up with you, Dennis. Take a deep breath and think about what you're asking. There's no way to calculate a hit site at this distance. Get a hold on yourself."

"Loren, Zoltov from Pulkovo told me they have a fix on impact. Somewhere in eastern New Mexico."

"You need a drink. Your own fix," Gray said, moving toward a side cabinet. Keeping one eye on Dennis, the director felt for two glasses and a bottle of Bell's.

"Here. New Mexico, you say."

"All he gave me were coordinates," Dennis said. "He was ordered to say no more. The transmission scratched off."

"Tracking and Data Relay Satellite is on half power."

"I know." Dennis gulped the Scotch.

Gray studied his friend's face for a second.

"I meant what I said, sport," he said. "You're working too hard. You've got coordinates on where the comet will hit. You understand what that means?"

"Either I'm nuts," Dennis said, "or they're planning a first strike."

"An announced first strike?"

"It's crazy, but ground zero is an Air Force base. Cannon."

"How can they say they know the target of a self-propelled falling object a hundred and fifty times farther away than the moon?"

"You tell me," Dennis said.

"Did you record the call?" At Dennis's nod, he said, "Let's listen to the tape." Gray emptied his glass. "But afterward, for a friend, get some sleep before you say anything on the outside. Agreed?"

Gray waited several seconds for Dennis's nodding agreement. Both men walked to the telecommunications room upstairs, where they listened to the recorded call from the Soviet Union. When the tape ended, Gray stood up.

"I heard it, but I don't believe it," he said. "Dennis, I'll vouch for your sanity, but I don't buy it."

"The Air Force can plot where a space capsule will land within meters," Dennis said. "And before takeoff."

"Yes. From six hundred meters up," Gray allowed. "We're talking here about ten thousand times that. And something we don't control. You're reaching."

"I may be."

"Keep in mind, with Aurora knocking out our satellites, theirs must be going off too. They can't know."

"You think Zoltov's lying?" Dennis asked.

"I say he can't know. Scientists over there are government employees. You heard him say orders. He's under orders."

"Then why tell me?"

Gray scratched his head, then said, "Go home and get some rest."

More out of defeat than compliance, Dennis took his colleague's advice.

HE HEARD THE PHONE RING at nine-thirty. The hands of his watch waved into focus. Remembering where he was and that Sandi was staying with her friend Lisa, he staggered from the couch, stretched the stiffness from both legs, and went to the kitchen. His eyes blinked at the brightness as he lifted the receiver.

"Dennis. Richard."

"Richard," he groaned.

"Where the hell have you been?" the National Security Adviser scolded. "The President's been calling for you. Have you been sleeping?"

Dennis glanced out through the door curtains and squinted at the strong light that lanced his half-closed eyes.

"Richard, is it morning?"

"It's nine-thirty."

He wiped his face, suddenly remembering the date. July fifth.

"Tampa," he said.

"Forget Tampa. We're at Mt. Weather. I've sent a car for you. The President is getting Mirenkov on the line. He needs you."

"Mirenkov?"

"We're on nuclear alert. The sequence has started."

"Listen, Richard. I have an impact site."

"New Mexico. We know."

"No one can fire."

"Get over here."

Dennis threw the phone down, the word *sequence* ringing in his ear. Wide awake now, he rushed upstairs to shower and shave.

As the hot water pellets struck his neck, still stiff from the sofa, he sorted out Lohmann's call. Mt. Weather, the

underground Safe City. The War Room. Snelling was
starting the sequence. He could see the silver-haired
leader in short sleeves slumped over a dimly lit console,
nervously eyeing hundreds of buttons and flashing lights
that the commanders pointed out to him. He could see
fluorescent wall scopes filling the room with orange and
red as their silicon chips obediently dotted maps on any
one of several plotting screens. Dean Newcombe, headphones crowning his bald head, would be signaling orders and listening to NORAD commanders under
another mountain two thousand miles away. The Joint
Chiefs—was there room for them all?—would huddle in
groups, each man hooked to a console, muttering numbers to far-flung field subordinates while they waved to
circling aides, who were taking mental notes on each programmed command, privately giving thanks for being at
arm's length in time of crisis.

He saw a restless Richard Lohmann, shuttling silently
between the commander-in-chief and the generals, the
always-present white carnation in place and the eyes
twitching to adjust to the constantly changing glow of the
War Room. A hum would fill the carpeted room with that
closed-in sound that computer terminals make when digesting data or just purring in neutral, awaiting further
instructions. And the black box, the President's own
command center. He had seen it once out of the corner of
his eye, nestled against the Oval Office desk, always an
appendage away from the commander-in-chief wherever
he went, even to the bathroom.

Dennis dressed hurriedly, struck by how vividly he
could imagine a place he had only heard about. Mt.
Weather. The Response Room. The Button Room. It
leaped into his mind like some dark, shadowed room of a

house that he may have once occupied. When the shadow lifted, he saw in focus the cushioned armchairs below-ground, the double phones strapped to each viewing station, where everything had a backup, the rows of bright read-out numbers marching at ceiling level like stock exchange quotes, the telescopic cross-hairs adjusting finer to Target Zone One—Riga.

He shook off the strange sense of having peered into a dark room prepared for a wake; electronic display lights for candles, dull huddled shapes for flowers and, half-hidden by a looming figure with back to him, a closed gleaming coffin.

As he adjusted his tie in the mirror, he laughed at himself for the concession to vanity. Was he dressing for a wake? Downstairs, he snapped on the FM receiver. Twisting the cold silver knob, he switched from FM to AM and ran the red needle from left to right three times just to be sure. If his charts were correct, there would be no wake. At the sound of static, he smiled with renewed confidence. He checked the same effect on the portable Sony in the kitchen. More static.

He dialed Sandi's number at Senator Browning's office. The phone produced a strange, hollow sound that echoed with each ring.

"Sandi, I've been ordered to Mt. Weather."

"Mt. Weather." Her voice fell.

"Not to worry," he quickly added. "Don't think the worst. I'll be home for supper. Hot dogs and beans?"

"Mt. Weather," Sandi repeated.

"It's all right. Trust me. I love you."

"Dennis, have you seen the sky?"

"No."

"A Walt Disney production."

"I'll check the sky," he said. "You turn on the radio."

She drew a confused breath. "It's all static."

Dennis grinned. "The music of the spheres," he said. "See you for supper."

A copper-colored Lincoln glided into the driveway, its amber lights flashing urgency. The Army driver remained inside motionless, mouthing words into a black CB microphone. At least Army channels are still open, Dennis thought. He waved from the kitchen door. The driver saluted and continued talking into his fist.

Dennis grabbed his raincoat and tossed a calculator into his briefcase. He flipped through the case to make certain he had his charts, then headed outside. On the steps he froze. An eerie glow shimmered over everything. The limousine's motor puffed pale exhaust into a yellowy haze that had settled onto the yard like a sunset in a coal mining town. He looked up at the trees. Green foliage had become dark gray patches against the overcast sky. If sky it was. A murky light surrounding the house moved in shadows, at first dull, then brighter. The world seemed to swim around him as he went down the steps, groping for the handrail the way a blind man reaches out for familiar landmarks.

Aurora's light was sharing the sky with a sun hidden somewhere in clouds that now churned and piled as if angered by some new force. The air was damp and warm, with forecasts of more showers, reminding Dennis of the frightening hours before a hurricane.

He got in beside the driver, who smiled lightly, his moustache glimmering in the new light. Neither man spoke above the occasional squawk of the CB. On the road they passed rows of boarded-up stores, most displaying handmade CASH ONLY signs. A deserted post office lot was filled with jeeps and vans parked with undeliverable mail. Beyond it, a 7-11 store stood lit up and as lonely as that Hopper painting he remembered seeing years before in Chicago.

The highway leading to Interstate 66, rimmed by a shopping mall past its prime, several closed gas stations, and an abandoned brick fire station, reminded him of pictures in a family album taken during the war years. Only essential personnel remained on duty in Washington: police, some government workers, and congressional staff, like Sandi, to give the impression that someone was still in charge, and firemen pressed into Civil Defense service to man emergency shelters.

The only traffic they encountered came at a rotary outside Tupper's Ridge, where dark Army trucks were moving in a convoy, headed for the Chesapeake or farther south. Vans weaved in close, then headed off in all directions, past motorists camped out along the roadside following the Department of Transportation's directive to "get where you're going and stay put." Evacuation, all there would be of it, was complete. But the only one that counted now was in the Llano Estacado two thousand miles away.

At the rotary's edge stood a Methodist church, where the faithful were gathering to seek shelter from the threatening sky. Lights—candles?—flickered through the church's frosted windows. It was every man for himself, Dennis decided. Time for prayers and hymns.

The sky was now greenish yellow, its texture like an opaque sheet that urged them westward into the Appalachian hills. It seemed to wave them on, veiling and occasionally showing a hint of the sun. It was close to eleven o'clock, but the view north showed a ghostly imitation of sunset. There was no blue in sight, only vertical streaks of color, pastels, flowing back and forth as if swaying to an unheard beat. Sandi was right on target, Dennis thought. A Walt Disney sky. *Fantasia* without the sound-track.

He had read all the reports, recalled all the forecasts from Georgetown to Perth. He knew what was coming, what was happening around the earth, yet nothing could have prepared him, an expert, for what he was seeing. The brave new world of satellites and instant communications had been stripped away, making the planet a Siberian village. And the villagers of the new Tunguska, what could he have said that would have made this spectacle easier for them to accept? It was a curse he carried: to know, to explain, then to watch a prophecy unleashed. Never in his lifetime had isolation come so suddenly. No electronic communication, intermittent telephone transmission, unpredictable backup on all frequencies. It brought to mind accounts of the air battle for Britain—the shelters, the sirens, the sky.

He thought about his public statements, how he had given in to Pryor and withheld any mention of the sky colors. "Panic is one thing," Pryor had told him. "Mass trauma would be an overload." For once, Pryor was right. Dennis felt no regret at having kept all the details from them. Better selective disclosures than an end-of-the-world prediction.

His driver spoke at last.

"I've never seen anything like it," he said in awe. "Northern lights, maybe. What's it called?"

"Aurora," Dennis said.

"Aurora. Yeah."

Off the highway, they headed up a hill beyond a silver pond. To their right, no more than a dozen spotted cows grazed in slow motion under a light drizzle. Another, smaller group lay on a nearby slope chewing their cud, oblivious to a liquid sky and to several vent stacks they had long since learned held neither food nor anything of interest. The stacks, rising out of the Virginia meadow like so many tree stumps, filtered air from the building below a carpeted roof of thick spring grass. Burrowed beneath the broad meadow, and sprawling for acres in all directions, hummed the top-secret emergency command center of Mt. Weather.

Designed a generation earlier as the Presidential fallout shelter, the subterranean post was a self-contained "secure city" from which the executive branch could function during and after a nuclear attack. Once a year, with no notice, the President reported to the "meadow" to await the ordered arrival of his Cabinet, the Joint Chiefs of Staff, and the four men next in the line of presidential succession. From this central command post, the President would lead the drill leading up to and following a first strike.

The Lincoln descended the entrance tunnel and stopped at a security barrier, where a Marine guard studied their faces and badges. When the driver pronounced the day's code word, "snowstorm," the guard waved them on without a word. Dennis got out at a guard house and showed his badge again to a clone of the first Marine. His unsmiling escort led him down a sloping corridor to the circular command room and opened the door with a key hanging from his neck. Dennis entered alone to the click of the door relocking behind him.

A haggard Richard Lohmann came forward from a side room. His suit was rumpled, the white carnation missing. His grip as they shook hands was weak, and the lines on his face gave evidence of a lack of sleep. Like some bowed guardian of the underworld, Lohmann led the way past an array of lookalike windowless beige rooms and black signs designating function only by numbers. They walked silently along a curved corridor high above the dim operations room below. Smoky glass beyond a railing separated them from a roomful of dark-uniformed men who moved calmly from console screen to computer deck. Lohmann stopped at a door marked C–180 and ushered him into a plush cafeteria.

Dennis sipped black coffee across from the National Security Adviser, whose hand shook as he loosened his tie.

"How long have you been down here?" Dennis asked.

Lohmann added a cloud of cream to his tea, then said, "Twenty hours. Snelling brought us all here when Air Force One couldn't take off for Tampa."

"Grounded?"

"Everything's grounded." Lohmann's voice lacked its natural ring. Twenty hours with no sleep. Dennis felt a sudden twinge of guilt at being relatively refreshed, newly arrived from the land aboveground.

"Is New Mexico evacuated?" he asked.

"It's being done. Last we heard. Communication is breaking up. That's why Snelling called for you." Lohmann turned away, his tea untouched. "He's got one hand on the hotline, the other on the strike button."

Dennis shook his head. "Richard, the firing sequence won't work."

"What do you mean?"

"Aurora's knocking out all signals. We're covered in ionized particles."

"Well, Snelling wants you to fix it."

"Fix it? Nothing will stop a hit. The signals will be out for at least two weeks."

"You tell him."

"Let's go." Dennis moved to get up.

"Finish your coffee." Lohmann reached for the adviser's arm. "There's something you should know first. Snelling is falling to pieces. He's ranting about punishing the Russians. I had to leave when he started cursing the Rockwell technicians. The man's raving."

"Richard, I—"

"He's put Mirenkov on hold until the translator gets here. We had a State Department translator on a phone link-up, but the signal was so scrambled he couldn't hear through the static. So they're bringing him down here."

"My God."

"It's as bad as it sounds. He's been yelling about Trusedale, the *Kennedy*, Korean flight 007. He wants to punish them."

"What do you want me to do?"

Lohmann reached deep for a last reserve of humor. "I don't suppose you brought a straitjacket with you," he said. "Dennis, if he can't fire, just save him from making more of a fool of himself. The Rockwell boys are sneaking out one by one. A quiet exorcism would do."

Dennis didn't smile.

A staircase led to the main console room. Inside, on a tiered platform, stood Ron Pryor, Dean Newcombe, and the President, backs to the room, like celebrants at a high mass. Facing the trio flickered a bright orange map grid that showed the shadow of a passing operations commander.

Snelling was the first to turn. Stress had etched deeper lines across his forehead, and the lighted screen fringed his silver hair in gold. He gazed down at Dennis with eyes enlarged by the wild play of luminescence. As he spoke, Pryor and Newcombe, also haloed against the lights, turned slowly.

"Dennis, what's this I hear you've been sleeping, huh?" The President's voice sounded jumpy, high pitched, from too little rest.

"I was at home," Dennis replied.

"You didn't see that sky last night? Like wartime."

"Mr. President, the sky is filled with cosmic dust, particles knocking out all signals."

"Tell me about comet dust. We're having trouble getting Mirenkov."

"Cosmic," Dennis corrected. "You won't be getting anyone soon."

"How about a truce, Doctor," Snelling snapped. He pointed to the blinking electronics around him. "We've got redundancy on top of redundancy here, so no more predictions. Okay?"

"No prediction. This isn't like nuclear scrambling. It's cosmic."

"Fail-safe," Snelling boasted, throwing a crazy grin at Newcombe.

"Has anyone told you differently?" Dennis said. "Don't turn away. Tell me."

"Doctor, one man gives orders in this room. Do you understand? Fail-safe, I said."

"Dammit! So was the *Kennedy*!"

Dennis stared up at three sets of glazed eyes. He paused as his words echoed back to him, sweeping up in their wake the attention of the military men at their screens.

"Is the hotline fail-safe, too?" he shouted for all to hear. "You said you were having trouble."

"Static," Pryor said.

"The hotline is fail-safe, sir," Newcombe whispered to Snelling.

"Not this time," Dennis shouted.

Snelling raised a hand. "Gentlemen, gentlemen, let's settle in here. All right? Mirenkov will be back on the line any minute. He can make us evacuate a state, but let's not give him the satisfaction of hearing us bicker. All right?"

"They've already told us New Mexico," Dennis said. "What more does he have to say?"

Snelling drew a breath. "He's got to show us he's obeyed our ultimatum first," he answered. "Then we'll talk about New Mexico."

"I can't confirm a New Mexico hit," Dennis said. "No one can."

"There. You see. First strike. That's their plan all along." Snelling stiffened as he turned his back again.

"Sir, they've been right about everything else."

"They're bluffing."

"Then why did they announce it?" Dennis screamed. "Tell me. What's the operative theory on that, Ron?"

"To minimize loss of life," the aide replied.

"And the objective? To be fired on?"

"They think we won't," Newcombe said.

"I know we can't," Dennis exploded. "Nothing here is fail-safe from the comet. Nothing. You told me you had static on the hotline. That'll get worse. I've charted it. It'll go dead. You're ready to talk to them. Why not listen to me?''

"They've targeted New Mexico. White Sands, Holloman," Snelling said, his back still turned.

"I don't know that," Dennis said, "and neither do you."

"Doctor, take a seat. Please." Newcombe's voice, directed at the screen, echoed icily.

Dennis moved to the platform's first step.

"Nobody can fire," he insisted. "New Mexico is not their target. It may be the comet's, but it is not preselected. All this electronics is buffered from nuclear interference, not from cosmic. Are you listening to me?'' Dennis was shouting and, without really realizing it, had moved another step higher, closer to the silent trio. Newcombe half turned.

"You don't belong here," he said. "Step down and wait for the hotline call."

Dennis dropped back down the steps, feeling a stiffness at the back of his neck. Before he could drop into the seat next to Lohmann, he saw the general's shadow descend on the President with a message: "The Premier is back on the line, Mr. President."

"We're ready," Snelling said in a low voice. Then louder, "We're ready."

Dennis jumped up to shout, "If you threaten to fire a strike, he'll laugh in your face."

"The translator is here," the general said, as if Dennis wasn't there. "In C-200."

Snelling picked up a white phone at his desk. At the same time, Pryor and Newcombe reached for theirs, and Lohmann picked up a wall phone from behind his chair and handed it to Dennis. The line was scratchy, but Dennis could hear the initial security exchange clearly in both languages.

"Mr. Premier," Snelling said. "We are on nuclear alert. Confirmation of any damage to U.S. territory will launch a retaliatory strike."

Chapter Twenty-one

Before the translator had finished speaking, Dennis dropped his phone and dashed up the platform stairs. He grabbed the twin phone at Snelling's elbow to hear the Premier's response.

"Mr. President, Aurora is coming down. Very soon. Dr. Zoltov has told as much to your science adviser. The comet will strike your desert within ten days."

"You cannot know this for certain."

"It is confirmed. Have you not confirmed the same?"

"We have not."

"You must not take this event as a first strike. We will fire if you do."

Dennis covered the President's phone with his hand. "That's a bluff," he said. "They can't fire either."

Snelling pulled the phone away from his grasp to say, "We believe your plan is to fire in any case. And we are ready."

After a pause the Soviet leader replied, "This is not true. Not true. The only danger is a comet fall. Do not be deceived. I trust you have evacuated the site."

"I can say nothing about that."

"Surely the skies tell you time is short."

"We both know gravity will tear Aurora to pieces. It will scatter debris all over the world just like one of your falling satellites. There will be no single impact site. Anywhere. No way to tell."

"You are wrong."

"How do you know?" Snelling shouted.

The Premier's voice remained calm. "We are not scientists. But our scientists can tell."

"*Your* scientists."

"We have shared our information. It is for you now to believe. The comet is headed for your country."

"Mr. Premier, can you hear me? Do not tell me what to believe."

As soon as the translator had finished the Russian version, Dennis heard a shuffling sound through the phone, a distant scratching, as if the Premier were about to hang up. No one spoke. Snelling glanced his way, then looked beyond at a perspiring Dean Newcombe, who clutched his own phone. Were the Russians going to return the President's gesture and hang up? The long pause brought a twitch to the corner of the President's mouth. He spoke again.

"Premier Mirenkov. I have my science adviser on this line. Is there someone there who can speak to him?"

"Dr. Zoltov is here. Yes. Let them speak."

Snelling leaned toward his adviser. "Talk to this guy," he said. "See what proof they have for a New Mexico hit. We've still got people there. Go ahead."

The President slumped back into his chair. He tucked the phone under his chin and rubbed a cheek against its cold plastic, the way a child coaxes comfort from a blanket. Dennis, watching him, had the sinking feeling that Snelling was tuned in to some unheard frequency, his own private channel of distress, groping for help in a situation slipping beyond his control.

Dennis wondered what to say to Zoltov. Aurora would impact somewhere within ten days. Evacuation, even in

New Mexico, would take four at most. The world was braced for a terrible hit, but the real danger was no comet. It was the President's meaningless impulse to punish. And that menace filled the underground War Room.

"Dr. Zoltov," he said at last.

"Yes. Dr. Covino. I have given you impact coordinates. These are absolutely accurate."

"They mean nothing to us, sir. Your equations include data you could not have." The line cracked loudly of static. "You have placed numbers where there should only be guesses, estimates. Disintegration rates—"

"Our mathematics is confirmed here," Zoltov interrupted. "And aboard Soyuz 17." Static now filled the room.

"Soyuz 17?"

"Aurora has been tracked from orbit for three months. We have calculated solar wind parameters, coma rotation, tail density, and strike angle."

"And earth rotation?"

"To a factor of point five-six." Through louder and now irritating static, the Soviet scientist went on in an almost boastful tone. "We have coordinated earth-based studies with spacecraft data to arrive at all our numbers. There will be no changes in the numbers I gave you at this close range."

Dennis cupped the phone. "Mr. President, can you shut this off for a minute?"

Snelling sat up and pushed a red button.

"What is it?"

"I know nothing of a Soyuz-17 mission. Is it true?"

"How the hell should I know. Dean." Snelling glared at the Secretary of Defense, who snapped defensively, "What difference does it make?"

"What difference?" Dennis shouted. "Zoltov's numbers back up what we have from earth data. We're working with less than half a puzzle. All the numbers are theirs. What he says about impact in New Mexico could be true." After a pause he asked: "Do I accept it?"

Snelling tapped the edge of his console with four fingers, his pale face streaked in greens and oranges from the station's screen. Suddenly he lunged forward to open the line.

"Premier Mirenkov. This is President Snelling. We have no knowledge of Soyuz 17. Why are you telling us this now?"

"I can give you only the mission's scientific data. No more."

"So we must believe you?"

"Or go to war. That is correct."

"On your numbers? Your say-so?"

The crackle of static now overpowered the voices.

"This is a trick," Snelling blurted, his eyes aflame. "How does Riga fit in? Tell me." He pounded a fist on the deck. No reply followed. "What about Riga?"

"There is nothing I can tell you...tell you about...Riga. Riga is . . . not involved."

"Bullshit! Bullshit it isn't," the President screamed into the speaker. "Secret mission, my ass! You have created a hoax. To cover a first strike. We have planned accordingly. We have no alternative but to fire."

Snelling drew back, out of breath. He looked over to Secretary Newcombe, who just shook his head. Snelling drew himself to the edge of his chair to catch the Premier's faint words now drowning in interference: "In good faith . . . we have . . . warned you. If the impact area

is secure...secured, there will be safe...dust. Safe dust...
No radiation. We...are...losing..."

"We will fire," Snelling blared into the speaker. "We
will fire." The words echoed in Russian. "Did you hear
me? We will fire."

"The line is dead," Pryor said.

"They've hung up," Snelling insisted.

"No. It's interference," Dennis said. "The atmosphere is charged with particles from the comet. The line
is dead. Telcom satellite is knocked out."

The President bolted upward.

"To hell with the comet! They tell us what they want
us to know, then they switch off. Cowards! Dean, Condition Red. Prepare to authenticate Emergency War Orders. 'Riga is not involved.' Bullshit! They've got us
where they want us. Evacuation in good faith. Sit by a
hard silo. Pearl Harbor."

Newcombe didn't move. He stared ahead, transfixed
by the flashing lights only inches away. Dennis left the
President's side, moving quickly to Ron Pryor.

"General Valchis," Snelling called to the far side of the
room. "Punch up Alpha Green. Up, everybody up." As
he put on a headset-microphone harness, he said, "Dean,
hang in. The time's come. Come on, all good men. You're
in? No sitting now. Push."

In the distance Dennis caught sight of a figure coming
to life at a console. He looked at the stunned chief of staff,
his eyes searching frantically for help.

"Ron, he's falling apart," he whispered. "Is his doctor
here?"

Pryor nodded as if in a trance.

Suddenly a loud click came from the overhead speaker,
then a new voice: "Eagle Nest One. Go ahead."

"General Broussard, this is the President. Your condition is red. Stand by for authentication sequence. Repeat. We are red."

"Affirmation, sir."

"Emergency War Orders. No test. Stand by for numbers."

"We copy, sir. Red and ready."

The President turned to his advisers and, eyes gleaming triumphantly, said, "Fail-safe." He turned back to the console. "General Broussard is supreme commander at SAC," he announced. "Not a bad connection, huh?"

"Ron, get the doctor," Dennis said urgently.

Pryor didn't move.

"Get him." Dennis called to Newcombe. "Mr. Secretary, will you tell him nothing's happening?"

Newcombe looked past Dennis to Ron Pryor. Both men looked lost, unsure how to make the next move in a game out of control. The President, lost in his own world of vengeance, squinted down at General Valchis. He wet his lips and smoothed down hair the headphones had tussled—a helmeted Don Quixote awaiting fearsome windmills.

"If neither of you will get the doctor," Dennis said angrily, "tell me where he is. I'll get him."

Moved to action at last, Pryor and Newcombe both left the room. Dennis came down from the platform too and fell into the chair next to Richard Lohmann.

"Without the comet we'd have nuclear war," Lohmann said.

"They're all play buttons now," Dennis said.

"Do you think the Russians have tried to fire, too?"

"After a call from a madman, would you?"

"This is the Meadow," Snelling was saying into the microphone. "General, your condition is red." He was reading from an open looseleaf manual. "Activate Emergency War Order zero nine zero five two two five one."

The overhead speaker boomed instantly: "We have zero nine zero five two two five one. Set."

"Keep this channel open," the President ordered.

"Repeat, sir."

"I said keep this channel open."

"Channel open."

"I want confirmation of firing."

"Repeat, sir."

"My God! I said no test. Fire. Is the sequence sent?"

"Sequence: zero nine zero five two two five one."

Snelling threw his head back and looked up to the ceiling speaker.

"Sequence sent," the SAC Commander said. "Standing by for confirmation." The overhead voice was strong, confident. The order to fire the first warheads was transmitted from Colorado to the distant launch sites. All that remained was confirmation. The voice came back. "Meadow. Meadow. Sequence sent. No confirmation. Stand by."

General Valchis came up to the President's level. He shot a glance toward the two seated advisers, then up to the President.

"Sir, there is no response at the firing site," he said.

"General," Dennis called out, "this is not Soviet jamming. You can try all five frequencies."

"Send on channel two," Snelling ordered into the microphone.

"Nothing will work," Dennis said to the harried general.

"Shut up," Snelling shouted.

The overhead speaker snapped back to life. "Channel two sent. No response."

"Dammit, General, this is not a drill. Go," Snelling yelled. "Valchis. At your post. Dean? Dean."

Standing by Lohmann and Dennis, General Valchis saw what he couldn't have noticed from below. He watched the President mumbling at the speaker and thrusting his hands in his pockets.

"Sir, the order to fire is sent," the speaker announced. "Nothing's coming back here. Both channels are out."

"You've got backup on top of backup," Snelling said. "Get through."

"Repeat, please."

"Get through! I want confirmation of my firing order."

"No confirmation, sir. Alpha and Beta silent."

"NavStar. I want NavStar. Fire and confirm. NavStar."

"NavStar?" General Valchis repeated. At the mention of a program still two years from completion, the general withdrew to a side console and switched on a microphone that defeated the overhead speaker. His voice boomed.

"Confirmed," he said. "Firing confirmed."

Immediately the President sank into his chair. "Thank God," he said. "It's over. We're up. Good job. Dean, we did it. Dean?"

Just then, Ron Pryor entered with the President's physician, who mounted the steps alone and crouched at chairside to speak softly to the President. Snelling nodded weakly at what he was hearing. Pryor walked over to where Lohmann and Dennis were seated.

"Dean's gone back to the White House with the Cabinet," he said. "The Secretary of State will take over."

Dennis nodded. "Ron, I recommend General Valchis for cleanup operations in New Mexico."

"Okay."

The general, still visibly shaken, acknowledged the appointment, then lowered his head.

"You'll help with cleanup too?" Ron Pryor asked.

Dennis waited until the physician and the President had silently crossed the room before he answered, "Yes, but now I'm going home."

His driver took him to Lisa's Arlington apartment, where he picked up Sandi, and he took her home to Falls Church. In the driveway he dismissed the driver with orders to pick him up again in three days. Sandi, clutching a red overnight case, waited for him at the door.

"Everything's all right," he said. "This comet prevented a nuclear war. If the President had waited a few more weeks, there'd be no interference to stop a firing order. In August he would have gotten off his shot." He led her inside. The lights flickered on at half power, barely matching the light outside. They went up to bed.

THE NEXT MORNING he made breakfast, and they talked about what the next few days would be like. He was glad to hear her say that it would be an adventure.

"No phone. No TV," he said. "You don't remember the '67 northeast blackout, do you?"

"I was two."

"We're blanketed in this stuff for at least two weeks."

"Then it will be back to normal?"

"Almost normal," he said, taking her hand. "When Aurora falls, its cloud will change the weather. How, we won't know till it hits. But it'll make El Niño changes seem like a local inconvenience. The whole food chain could be disrupted. And we'll see less of the sun.''

DENNIS LEFT BY CAR two days later for the long trip to New Mexico. All aircraft were grounded, his driver told him, their instruments made useless by particle bombardment. The driver had no idea of the change in government. All he talked about was the sky, the sleepless nights, and the rations he and his displaced family ate by lantern light. The kids were overtired, his wife frantic with fear. He was glad to get away, knowing nothing would change for weeks. He complained of no TV, no news on anything, and tried to get Dennis to fill him in on what it would be like after Impact Day. Dennis made vague replies and tried to sleep through a midnight glow over the valleys of Tennessee.

As the Lincoln connected with a nearly deserted U.S. 40 in Oklahoma city, they joined a drab military convoy heading west. This would be part of the cleanup crew, Dennis guessed. And they would have their hands full shortly, keeping the crowds away from ground zero once the comet hit.

On the ghostly outskirts of Amarillo, the sky became appreciably brighter and stayed that way, disguising sunset. Night and day were now the same.

Two days later, at one P.M. local time, forty kilometers south of Elida, New Mexico, the desert sun suddenly shared the sky with a bright twin. Moments after, a shimmering fireball appeared on all horizons, overtaking the sunlight. The newer sun paled the landscape, wilting cactus and brush pines. Birds fell silently in the tightening air, the wind dying as they dropped. White sand stopped its timeless drifting, then froze in place as in a kiln. The atmosphere shook as if drawn into the new sun.

Then a flash of blinding white engulfed the landscape, turning the desert into an X-ray of its elements. A shattering sound shook the desert floor, sending tremors out in all directions. The baked earth cracked. Boulders shook crazily, then rifled skyward, shattering into fist-size rockets. Sand swirled and quickly shot upwards. Tons of rock and sand rose with the force of several twin tornados. The wind shook hills and mountains, gusting upward in a mad chaotic dance. Gathering force by the second, the windstorm drew everything to itself—a whirling witches' sabbath of destruction. Aurora was down.

Funnellike, a growing pillar of debris rose higher and higher into a pale brown sky. The desert darkened in the afternoon light, the rusty sun screened by the rushing winds.

Plants and brush ignited, sending flaming torches in a mad course across the sizzling ground. From the desert floor, a glow mounted into a central dusty white cloud. A biblical pillar of fire spread vertically. As the wind-fed cloud reached the colder upper atmosphere, its top leveled to form a mushroom shape, visible from Cannon Air Force Base a hundred kilometers to the north.

Dennis felt the tremors and watched the cloud take shape from the base's control tower. He glanced away now and then, allowing himself the thrill of seeing the console's only light flicker dimly above the words SAFE DUST.

Within minutes at the impact site, the winds abated. Airborne debris began to fall to the scorched earth. Tumbling rocks and flaming fragments hit the surface furiously in a hellish imitation of a rainstorm. The desert darkened further, the air now filled with dust that brought with it instant twilight. Lightning flashed into the distant control room and sent further tremors through the cinder blocks. Boulders and chunks of mountain rolled and fell, following the command of the slowly returning gravity. The mushroom cloud remained motionless and mounting above the rubble. The ground stopped trembling as a deepening darkness spread out from the impact center.

The sun, a dark amber disk, showed as through a photographer's light filter. Polluted air hung over the area, and barely visible heat waves swam in all directions. Dennis's eyes drew away from the sight to catch the reflection of a bright red light above the words SAFE DUST. Aurora was down. The earth vibrated in microvolts and would hum for hundreds of years. And the dust was safe.

Outside, the mushroom cloud stirred, awaiting the returning wind's direction.

FRED DICKEY

BURIAL IN MOSCOW

Khrushchev lives!

This astonishing discovery sets an embittered CIA agent on the perilous trail of this ghost resurrected from the Soviet past—and traps him in a deadly web of espionage and intrigue!

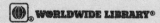